THE BLIND FISHERMAN

MESSAGE FROM CHINUA ACHEBE:

Africa is a huge continent with a diversity of cultures and languages. Africa is not simple – often people want to simplify it, generalise it, stereotype its people, but Africa is very complex. The world is just starting to get to know Africa. The last five hundred years of European contact with Africa produced a body of literature that presented Africa in a very bad light and now the time has come for Africans to tell their own stories.

The Penguin African Writers Series will bring a new energy to the publication of African literature. Penguin Books (South Africa) is committed to publishing both established and new voices from all over the African continent to ensure African stories reach a wider global audience.

This is really what I personally want to see – writers from all over Africa contributing to a definition of themselves, writing ourselves and our stories into history. One of the greatest things literature does is allow us to imagine; to identify with situations and people who live in completely different circumstances, in countries all over the world. Through this series, the creative exploration of those issues and experiences that are unique to the African consciousness will be given a platform, not only throughout Africa, but also to the world beyond its shores.

Storytelling is a creative component of human experience and in order to share our experiences with the world, we as Africans need to recognise the importance of our own stories. By starting the series on the solid foundations laid by the renowned Heinemann African Writers Series, I am honoured to join Penguin in inviting young and upcoming writers to accept the challenge passed down by celebrated African authors of earlier decades and to continue to explore, confront and question the realities of life in Africa through their work; challenging Africa's people to lift her to her rightful place among the nations of the world.

Chinua Achebe

CONTENTS

Voices Made Night

Every Man is a Race

VOICES MADE NIGHT

THE FIRE

The old woman was seated on the mat, waiting motionless for her man to return from the bush. Her legs suffered a double weariness: from the time-worn byways, and from the times trodden.

Her worldly goods were spread out on the ground: bowls, baskets, a pestle. Around her was emptiness, even the wind was alone.

The old man approached slowly, as was his custom. He had shepherded his sadness before him ever since his youngest sons had left on the road to no return.

'My husband is shrinking,' she thought. *'He is a shadow.'*

A shadow, yes indeed. But only of his soul, for he scarcely had any body left. The old man came nearer and draped his leanness on the neighbouring mat. He raised his head and, without looking at the woman, said:

'I'm thinking.'

'What is it you are thinking, husband?'

'If you die, how shall I, alone, sick and without strength, how shall I bury you?'

He passed his skinny fingers over the straw mat on which he was sitting, and went on:

'We are poor, all we have is nothingness. Nor do we have

anybody else. I think it better that we start digging your grave now.'

The woman, touched, smiled:

'How good you are, my husband! I was lucky to have you as the man of my life.'

The old man fell silent, lost in thought. Only later did he open his mouth:

'I'm going to see if I can find a spade.'

'Where are you going to get a spade?'

'I'm going to see if they have one at the store'

'Are you going all the way to the store? It is a long way.'

'I shall be back this side of night.'

All the silence remained hushed so that she might listen for her husband's return. When he came back, ragged tatters of dust were retaining the last rays of sun.

'Well then, husband?'

'It cost a lot of money,' and he held up the spade the better to show it to her. *'Tomorrow morning I'll start work on your grave.'*

And they lay down on their separate mats. Softly, she interrupted his drift into sleep:

'But, husband ...'

'What?'

'I'm not even ill.'

'You must be. You are so old.'

'Maybe,' she agreed. And they fell asleep.

The next morning he looked at her intensely.

'I'm measuring your size. After all, you're bigger than I thought.'

'Nonsense, I'm small.'

She went to the woodpile, and pulled out some faggots.

'The wood's almost finished, husband. I'll go to the bush to get some more.'

'Go, woman. I shall stay here and dig your grave.'

She was already moving away when an invisible hand seemed

to tug at her *capulana* and, pausing, but still with her back to him, she said:

'*Listen, husband. Let me ask one thing ...*'

'*What is it you want?*'

'*Don't dig too deep. I want to be near the top, just below the ground, so that I'll almost be able to touch life a little.*'

'*Very well. I shan't put much earth on top of you.*'

For two weeks the old man busied himself with the hole. The nearer he got to completing it, the longer he took. Then suddenly the rains came. The grave filled with water. It looked like a brazen little puddle. The old man cursed the clouds, and the heavens which had brought them.

'*Don't talk silliness, you'll be punished for it,*' she warned. More days of rain and the walls of the tomb began to cave in. The old man walked over and surveyed the damage. There and then he decided to go on. Soaked under a river of rain, the old man clambered in and out, his groans ever louder, the amount of soil he carried, ever less.

'*Come on in out of the rain, husband. You can't keep on like this.*'

'*Stop fussing, woman,*' ordered the old man. From time to time, he would pause to see how grey the sky was. He was trying to see who still had more work to do, himself or the rain.

On the following day, the old man was woken up by his own bones, which were pulling him further into his aching body.

'*I'm in pain, woman. I can't get up.*'

His wife turned to him and wiped the sweat from his face.

'*You're full of fever. It's because of the soaking you got.*'

'*No it isn't, woman. It's because I slept near the fire.*'

'*What fire?*'

His reply was a groan. The old woman got alarmed: what was this fire the man had seen if they hadn't even lit one?

She got up to take him his bowl of mealie porridge. When she turned round he was already up, looking for his spade. He grabbed it and crept out of the house. At every other step, he would pause to gather strength.

'Husband, don't go out like that. Eat first.'

He made some drunken gesture of dismissal. The old woman persisted:

'You don't know your left from your right. Rest a little.'

He was already inside the hole and getting ready to start work again. The fever punished him for his obstinacy; giddiness caused the sides of his world to dance before his eyes. Suddenly, he cried out in despair:

'Woman, help me!'

He fell like a severed branch, a cloud rent asunder. The old woman ran over to help him.

'You're very sick.'

Pulling him by the arms she brought him to the mat. He lay there taking deep breaths. All his life force was concentrated there, distributed among those ribs which rose and fell. In this lonely desert, you slide into death as quietly as a bird folding its wings. It does not come with a violent flash, such as happens in places where life glitters.

'Woman,' he said in a voice that left no trace, *'I can't leave you like this.'*

'What is it you are thinking now?'

'I can't leave that grave without a use. I must kill you.'

'That is true, husband. You worked so hard to dig that hole. It is a pity that it should remain empty.'

'Yes, I'm going to have to kill you; but not today for I have no body for it.'

She helped him to get up and made him a cup of tea.

'Drink it, man. Drink to get better, for tomorrow you will need your strength.'

The old man fell asleep, and the woman sat down in the doorway. In the shadow of her repose she watched the sun, king of light, gradually drain. She thought about the day and laughed to herself about its contradictions: she, whose birth had never been registered, now knew the date of her death. When the moon began to light up the trees in the wood, she leant back and fell asleep. She dreamed of times far away from there: her children were present, the dead ones and those still alive, the *machamba* was full of crops, her eyes slid over the green of it all. There was the old man in the middle, with his tie on, telling stories, lies for the most part. They were all there, her children and grandchildren. Life itself was there, unrolling, pregnant with promise. In that happy assembly, all believed in the truths of their elders, for they were always right, and no mother opened up her flesh to death. The noises of morning began to summon her out of herself, while she tried hard not to abandon her slumber. She begged night to stay so that her dream might linger, she begged this with the same devotion as when she had beseeched life not to take her children away.

She felt in the shadows for her husband's arm to give her strength in that moment of anguish. When she touched her companion's body with her hand, she saw that it was cold, so cold that it was as if, this time, he had fallen asleep far from that fire that no one had ever lit.

THE TALKING RAVEN'S LAST WARNING

It happened right there, in the middle of the square, full of people queueing at the store. Zuzé Paraza, a retired painter, spat out bits of his two-a-penny cigarette. Then he coughed, shaking the gauntness of his body to its bones. Suddenly, so those who witnessed the event say, he vomited a live raven. The bird emerged whole from his belly. It had been so long inside him that it already knew how to talk. All covered in spittle, at first it didn't look like a bird. People gathered round Zuzé, peeping at the creature fallen from his cough. It shook itself free of its mucus covering, raised its beak, and to everyone's astonishment, uttered some words. With conviction, despite the bad pronunciation. Those present asked:

'He's speaking is he, the fellow?'

Some laughed. But the voice of the women interrupted them:

'Don't laugh.'

Zuzé Paraza warned:

'This is no ordinary bird. You'd better respect it.'

'Hey, Zuzé. Translate what he's saying for us. You must be able to understand the raven's dialect.'

'Of course I do. But not now. I don't want to translate now.'

And feeling himself the centre of attention, he added: *'This raven knows many secrets.'*

Then, placing the bird on his left shoulder, he withdrew, leaving behind him a babble of comments. So that was why the painter had those coughing fits. There was a stretch of sky inside him. Or maybe it was the bird's feathers tickling his gullet. There were more questions than answers.

'Can a man give birth through his lungs?'

'Give birth to a bird? Not unless the old boy went around courting the she-ravens up there in the trees.'

'It's the soul of his dead wife that crossed over into the widower, you'll see.'

On the following day, Zuzé confirmed the latter version. The raven had come from the furthest frontier of life, nestled in his inside, and chosen a public moment for its apparition.

Others might take this opportunity to obtain information about their dear departed, the circumstances and whereabouts of their ancestors. Through the intermediary of the raven, they would be given answers to their questions. Requests came flocking in immediately. Zuzé no longer had a room, it was an office. He no longer talked to people but conducted a surgery. He gave special concessions, kept a long waiting list of appointments, and then made his clients wait. Payment was made according to a tariff: deceased within the current year, fifty escudos; communication with the deceased from the previous year, one hundred and fifty; those deceased outside the stated period, two hundred and fifty.

And this is where Dona Candida comes into the story, a mulatto woman of capacious virtue, a woman without enemies. Recently widowed, she was already an ex-widow. She married quickly second time round, to make up for the excesses of her abstinence. When she remarried, she chose Sulemane Amade, an Indian trader in the village. No time had gone by since her first husband, Evaristo Muchanga, had died.

But Candida could not keep herself to herself. Her body still yearned to be aroused, she was still of an age to be a mother. The truth is that in the interim she was never much of a widow. She was lonely by accident, not conviction. Her woman's needs never subsided.

'*I got married. And so what? Do I need to explain?*'

And with these words, Dona Candida began to tell of her complaint to Zuzé Paraza. When he knew he was being sought after, the fortune teller even brought forward the date of the consultation. He had never been visited by a mulatto woman. Zuzé's services had never been called upon from such a lofty quarter.

'*I'm not just anyone, Senhor Paraza. How could such a thing happen to me?*'

The buxom lady explained her troubles: her second marriage was proceeding without any mishaps. That is, until her new husband, Sulemane, began to suffer mysterious fits. They occurred at night, just when they were getting ready to make love. She would remove her bra; Sulemane's great bulk would turn towards her. It was then that the spell would have its effect: grunts instead of words, foam on the lips, eyes asquint.

'*Sulemane,*' she confessed, '*my own Sulemane jumps out of bed and then, still dressed, crawls on all fours, sniffs, rubs his belly on the floor and ends up snuffling the carpet. After that he's sweating so much that I have to give him water, and he knocks back one great big bottle. He doesn't return to his senses straightaway. He takes time to recover. He stutters, only hears on his right side, and goes to sleep with his eyes open. All night through those cross-eyes pretending they can see, it's horrible. Please, Senhor Zuzé, please help me. I'm going through such a hard time, and I'm even having my doubts about God. This is Evaristo's work, it's his curse. We were happy, Sulemane and I. Now the two of us are three. My God, why didn't I wait? Why doesn't he leave me alone?*'

Zuzé Paraza began to think while all the time stroking the raven. He had his suspicions: Evaristo was a black man, a native of the area. Dona Candida had probably not carried out all the rituals which would have freed her from her dead husband. He was wrong, she had.

'All the rituals?'

'Of course, Senhor Paraza.'

'But how? If you are brown in your skin and nearly white in your soul?'

'He was black, you know. It was his family who asked, and I obeyed.'

Paraza was intrigued, and still appeared to have his doubts.

'Did you kill a goat?'

'Yes, I did.'

'Did the animal bleat while you were singing?'

'It did.'

'And what else, Dona Candida?'

'I went to the river to wash his death off me. The widows took me and bathed too. Then they took a piece of glass and cut me here, in the groin. They told me it was there that my husband was sleeping. Poor things, if they only knew where Evaristo was sleeping ...'

'And did you bleed well?'

'Yes, all the blood came out. The widows saw it. From the blood they said that I had come to an agreement with him. I didn't deny it. I thought it better not to.'

Zuzé Paraza made a show of being deep in thought. Then, he let the raven go. The creature fluttered about and alighted on Candida's ample shoulder. She flinched, her flesh creeping with ticklishness. She eyed the animal suspiciously. Seen from that position, the raven was as ugly as can be. If you want to admire the beauty of a bird, never look at its feet. The claws of a bird preserve its scaly past, a legacy of creepy-crawling reptiles.

The raven turned this way and that on the mulatto woman's

smooth, round perch.

'Pardon me, Senhor Zuzé: he's not going to shit on me, is he?'

'Don't talk, Dona Candida. The creature needs to concentrate.'

Finally, the bird made its pronouncement. Zuzé listened with his eyes closed, engaged in the effort of translation.

'What was it he said?'

'It wasn't the bird that spoke. It was Evaristo.'

'Evaristo?' she exclaimed doubtfully. *'With a voice like that?'*

'Don't forget, he spoke through a beak.'

The fat woman became serious as she regained her confidence in him.

'Senhor Zuzé, now that you're on the line to him, ask him to ...'

Changing her mind suddenly, Dona Candida ditched her medium, and began herself to shout at the raven perched on her shoulder:

'Evaristo, leave me in peace. Please leave me alone, and let me get on with my life quietly.'

The bird, upset by all the shouting, jumped from its perch. Paraza imposed some order:

'Dona Candida, it's no good getting flustered. You see? The bird got scared.'

His exhausted client began to sob.

'Did you listen to the dead man's request, Dona Candida?'

She shook her head. All she had heard was the raven, the same as all the other ravens that can be seen flitting around among the coconut palms.

'The deceased, Dona Candida, is asking for a suitcase full of clothes, the ones he used to wear.'

'But I haven't got his clothes any more. Didn't I tell you I carried out those rituals of yours? I ripped his clothes up, tore holes in them when he died. That's what they told me to do. They said I should make holes, that his clothes could let his

last breath out. Yes, I know: if it happened now, I wouldn't cut anything up. I'd make use of everything. But at that time Senhor Paraza ...'

'This is very annoying, Dona Candida. The dead man really wants them. You just can't imagine the cold that the dead feel out there.'

The mulatto woman stood there motionless, and imagined Evaristo shivering with cold, without a stitch of clothing to cover him. For all his wickedness, he didn't deserve such vengeance. She decided what to do: she would steal Sulemane's clothes and deliver them all in a concealed package.

'Sulemane mustn't know of this. And by God, if he comes to suspect anything!'

'You can relax, Dona Candida. Nobody will know except for me and the raven.'

And as she was about to leave, the fat woman pondered:

'How is it that Evaristo, with all that jealousy he took with him to the next world, how is it that he can agree to put on the new husband's clothes?'

'He will. Clothes are clothes. Cold is more powerful than jealousy.'

'Are you sure, Senhor Paraza?'

'That's my experience of the matter. The dead feel the cold because they are exposed to the wind and rain. That's why they envy the warmth of the living. You'll see, Dona Candida, these clothes will appease Evaristo and his desire for revenge.'

And the fat mulatto woman confessed her fear, which was neither totally of the dead, nor of the living:

'My fear now is of Sulemane. He will kill me, and you as well.'

Zuzé Paraza got to his feet confidently. He placed his hand on his client's arm and reassured her:

'I've been thinking to myself, Dona Candida, and I've found the answer. You will discover the robbery and tell your husband.*

There you are! It was some thief or other, there are so many round here.'

A week later, a suitcase arrived packed full of clothes. Trousers, shirts, underpants, ties, everything. A bonanza. Zuzé began by trying on the brown suit. It was large, cut to a trader's girth, a man used to being waited on, a man who ate well, whereas he, a painter, tended towards a slighter build. He was so skinny that neither bugs nor fleas chose him.

He rummaged around in the suitcase for a tie to match. There were more than ten, together with longjohns, and socks without holes. Sulemane must have been left without a pair of pants to his name. His clothes' cupboard must now be a nothing cupboard.

Dressed in the product of his deceit and inventiveness, Zuzé Paraza took out a bottle of *xicadju.* He knocked back more than ten glasses of the cashew liquor by way of celebration. It was then that the alcohol began to play tricks with his acuteness as well. A voice from deep inside kept telling him:

'These clothes are my own, no one gave them to me, and they came from nowhere. They're mine!'

And so, convinced he was the owner of such fineries, he decided to go out and parade them. He stopped at the store, showed off his vanities, his jacket and tie. Voices around him were full of envy:

'Those clothes aren't his. I'm sure I've seen them on someone else.'

Racking their brains, those present finally arrived at the true owner: the clothes were Sulemane Amade's. Yes, of course, they were his. How had that bastard Zuzé got hold of them, that switchboard operator of the spirit world? The fellow had stolen them. That keeper of ravens had broken into Sulemane's house. And off they went to tell the Indian.

Unaware of such manoeuvres, Zuzé went on exhibiting his stolen goods. The raven observed him, cawing from above, while Zuzé, swaying and unswaying, played the role of chorus.

At this point, Sulemane arrived near the store, huffing and puffing with rage. He walked up to the painter and seized him by the scruff of the neck. Zuzé began to swing about in his oversize suit.

'How did you get hold of that suit, you thief?'

The painter tried to explain but was unable. The raven hopped around him, looking for a chance to perch on his limp head. When the Indian let up, Zuzé mumbled:

'Sulemane, don't kill me. I didn't steal these clothes. They were given to me.'

The Indian had not abandoned violence. He had merely changed his tactics: from throttling to kicking. Zuzé leapt about as if competing with the raven.

'Who gave you my clothes you great crook?'

'Stop kicking me! I'll explain.'

Zuzé Paraza took advantage of a brief ceasefire, and came straight to the point.

'It was your wife, Sulemane. It was Dona Candida who gave me these clothes.'

'Candida gave them to you? That's a lie, you son-of-a-bitch.'

Blows, kicks, punches rained down on him while the bystanders cheered.

'Tell the truth, Paraza. Don't shame me with stories about my wife.'

But the old painter couldn't answer, for he was too busy trying to avoid the hiding he was getting. One of the punches flying in the direction of Paraza's nose hit the bird instead. Knocked flat, the raven spun round on the ground in its death throes, its wing broken. Everyone paused to watch the bird in its agony. Then, one or two anxious voices could be heard.

'Sulemane, if you've killed the raven, then you'll be unlucky in your life.'

'Unlucky! Don't talk shit! Who is it that believes a raven can

talk with spirits?'

Zuzé, his nose bleeding heavily, answered solemnly:

'If you don't believe it, then it's up to you. But I tell you that raven you knocked about is going to bring a curse on you.'

Zuzé Paraza's reminder was ill advised. The Indian set to work with his fists again. Two punches found their target, three missed. Zuzé's resistance grew even feebler. The alcohol in his bloodstream hampered his ability to dodge. Finally, a straight left caught Zuzé off balance and sent him crashing to the floor on top of the raven. Covered in dust, Zuzé Paraza pulled the dead bird from under him. Then, raising the magic raven, he brandished it in front of the Indian.

'You've killed the bird, Sulemane! You're done for. You'll see what's going to happen to you! You're going to crawl around on all fours like a pig!'

Then, the unbelievable happened. Sulemane began to quiver, to grunt and snort, and foam at the mouth. Falling to his knees, he dragged his belly along the ground, and rolled in the sand. The terrified onlookers took to their heels: Zuzé's curse had come true. Sulemane twitched convulsively like a chicken when it has had its head cut off. Finally, he stopped, weary of the demons which had shaken him. Zuzé knew that the next thing he would feel would be thirst. Seeing his opportunity, he commanded:

'You are going to feel thirsty you great porcupine! You're going to cry out for water!'

There was proof of Zuzé's power: Sulemane begging for water on bended knee, beseeching them to kill the thirst that was killing him.

The news went through the village like a lightning flash. So it was true, after all, about this fellow Zuzé. He really did have a sorcerer's power. The following day, everyone got up early. They ran to Zuzé Paraza's house. Everybody wanted to see the painter, all wanted to ask him a favour, to bless them with good fortune.

When they arrived, they found the house empty. Zuzé Paraza had left. They scanned the horizon for some sign of the soothsayer, but their gaze perished in the distant grass where the crickets are quiet. They searched the abandoned house. The old man had taken all his things. All that remained was a cage hanging from the ceiling. It rocked gently to and fro, a widowed guest of the surrounding silence. With fear gradually mounting within them, the visitors went out to the back. It was there, in the yard, that they saw evidence of the curse: a dead bird, as yet unburied. Over that still scene, a breeze began to blow, which little by little detached the talking raven's scrawny feathers from its carcass and cast them into the air.

Believing this omen, the inhabitants began to abandon the village. Some left in groups, others alone, and for many days they drifted aimlessly like the feathers that the wind slowly scattered in the distance.

The day Mabata-bata exploded

Suddenly, the ox exploded. It burst without so much as a moo. In the surrounding grass a rain of chunks and slices fell, as if the fruit and leaves of the ox. Its flesh turned into red butterflies. Its bones were scattered coins. Its horns were caught in some branches, swinging to and fro, imitating life in the invisibility of the wind.

Azarias, the little cowherd, could not contain his astonishment. Only a moment before, he had been admiring the great speckled ox, Mabata-bata. The creature grazed more slowly than laziness itself. It was the largest in the herd, ruler of the horned fraternity, and it was being kept aside as a bride price for its owner, Uncle Raul. Azarias had been working for him ever since he had been left an orphan. He would get up when it was still dark so that the cattle might graze the early morning mist.

He surveyed the disaster: the ox pulverised, like an echo of silence, a shadow of nothingness.

'*It must have been a lightning flash,*' he thought.

But it couldn't have been lightning. The sky was clear, blue without the slightest smudge. Where could the bolt have come from? Or was it the earth which had flashed?

He questioned the horizon beyond the trees. Perhaps

the *ndlati,* the bird of lightning, was still circling the skies. He turned his gaze towards the mountain in front of him. It was there that the *ndlati* dwelt, there where all the rivers are one, born from the same desire to be water. The *ndlati* lives concealed in its four colours and only takes to the air when the clouds bellow and the sky grates. Then it is that the *ndlati* rises into the heavens on the wings of its madness. High in the air, it dons its clothes of flame, and casts its burning flight upon the creatures of the earth. Sometimes it throws itself to the ground, making a hole. It remains in the cavity and urinates there.

Once upon a time it was necessary to resort to the skills of the old medicine man to dig out that nest and retrieve its acid deposits. Maybe Mabata-bata had trodden on some malign vestige of the *ndlati.* But who would believe it? Not his uncle. He would want to see the dead ox, at least be shown some proof of the accident. He had already seen thunderstruck cattle: they became burnt out carcasses, a pattern of ashes reminiscent of a body. Fire chews slowly, it doesn't swallow in one go, which is what had happened here.

He looked about him: the rest of the cattle had scattered into the bush in fright. Fear slid from the little cowherd's eyes.

'Don't come back without an ox, Azarias. That's all I say: you'd better not come back.'

His uncle's threat blustered in his ears. That anxiety consumed the air he breathed. What could he do? Thoughts rushed at him like shadows but found no way out of the problem. There was only one solution: to run away, to travel the roads where he knew nothing more. To flee is to die from a place and, with his torn trousers, an old bag over his shoulder, what would he leave behind to regret? Mistreatment, running after cattle. Other people's children were allowed to go to school. Not he, for he was nobody's son. Work tore him early from his bed and returned him to sleep when there was no longer any trace of childhood left in him. He only played with animals: swimming the river clinging to the tail of Mabata-bata, making bets when the stronger animals fought each other. At home, his uncle told his fortune:

'This one, judging by the way he lives mixed up with livestock, will surely marry a cow.'

And everyone laughed, without a care for his tiny soul, his mistreated dreams. This was why he looked back at the fields he was going to leave behind without any regrets. He considered the contents of his bag: a catapult, some *djambalau* fruit, a rusty penknife. So little cannot inspire any remorse. He set off in the direction of the river. He felt he was not running away: he was merely starting out along his road. When he arrived at the river he crossed the frontier of water. On the other bank, he stopped without even knowing what he was waiting for.

As evening fell, Grandmother Carolina was waiting for Raul at the door of the house. When he arrived, she let fly with her anxieties:

'So late, and Azarias hasn't come back with the cattle.'

'What? That brat is going to get a good hiding when he gets back.'

'Isn't it that something has happened, Raul? I'm scared, these bandits ...'

'Some fun and games have happened; that's what.'

They sat on the mat and had dinner. They talked about the matter of the bride price, the wedding preparations. Suddenly, there was a knock at the door. Raul got up, casting Grandmother Carolina a questioning glance. He opened the door: they were soldiers, three of them.

'Good evening, do you want something?'

'Good evening. We've come to inform you of an incident: a mine exploded this afternoon. An ox trod on it. Now, that ox belonged here.'

Another soldier added: *'We want to know where its minder is.'*

'The minder's the one we're waiting for,' Raul answered. And shouted: 'These bloody bandits!'

'When he arrives, we want to talk to him, to find out how it was that it happened. Nobody should go out towards the mountain. The bandits have been laying mines over there.'

They left. Raul remained, hovering round his questions. Where's that son-of-a-bitch Azarias gone? And was the rest of the herd scattered out there goodness knows where?

'Grandmother, I can't stay here like this. I've got to go and see where that good-for-nothing has got to. It must be that he's let the herd scatter maybe. I must round up the cattle while it's still early.'

'You can't, Raul. Look at what the soldiers said. It's dangerous.'

But he disregarded her and went off into the night. Does the bush have a suburb? It does: it was where Azarias had taken the animals. Raul, tearing himself on the thorns, could not deny the boy's skill. Nobody could match him in his knowledge of the land. He calculated the little cowherd would have chosen to take refuge in the valley.

He reached the river and climbed the big rocks. At the top of his voice, he issued his command:

'Azarias, come back, Azarias!'

Only the river answered, disentombing its gushing voice. Nothingness all around. But he sensed his nephew's hidden presence.

'Show yourself, don't be scared. I shan't hit you, I promise.'

He promised lies. He wasn't going to hit him: he was going to thrash him to death, when he had finished rounding up the cattle. For the time being he decided to sit down, a statue of darkness. His eyes, now used to the half-light, disembarked on the other bank. Suddenly, he heard footsteps in the bush. He stood on his guard.

'Azarias?'

It wasn't him. Carolina's voice reached Raul's ears.

'It's me, Raul.'

Curse that old hag, what did she want? To interfere, that's all. She might tread on a mine and blow herself up and, worse still, him too.

'Go back home, Grandmother!'

'Azarias will refuse to hear you when you call. He'll listen to me though.'

And she put her assuredness into effect by calling the cowherd. From behind the shadows, a silhouette appeared.

'Is that you Azarias? Come with me, let's go home.'

'I don't want to. I'm going to run away.'

Raul began to creep down the rock, cat-like, ready to pounce and seize his nephew by the throat.

'Where are you going to run away to, child?'

'I've nowhere to go, Grandmother.'

'That fellow's going to come back even if I have to cudgel him back in little pieces,' Raul's guileful voice cut in quickly.

'Be quiet, Raul. In your life you don't know the meaning of wretchedness.' And turning to the cowherd: *'Come my child, I'll look after you. It wasn't your fault that the ox died. Come and help your uncle to herd the animals.'*

'There's no need. The cattle are here, alongside me.'

Raul stood up, unsure. His heart began to do a drum dance inside his chest.

'What's that! The cattle are there?'

'Yes, that's right.'

The silence became twisted and tangled. Azarias' uncle was not sure of his nephew's truth.

'Nephew, did you really do it? Did you round up the cattle?'

The grandmother smiled, thinking of how the quarrels of the two of them would now end. She promised him a reward and asked the boy to choose.

'Your uncle is very pleased. Choose. He will respect your

request.'

Raul thought it better to agree to everything at that moment. Later, he would correct the boy's illusions, and his sense of duty as a cowherd would return.

'Tell us your wish then.'

'Uncle, next year can I go to school?'

He had guessed this would be it. There was no way he would consent to this. By allowing him to go to school he would lose a minder for his oxen. But the occasion required bluff and he spoke with his back to his thoughts:

'Yes, you can go.'

'Really, Uncle?'

'How many mouths do you think I have?'

'I can continue to help with the cattle. School is only in the afternoon.'

'That's right. But we'll talk about all that later. Come on out of there.'

The little cowherd emerged from the shadow and ran along the sand to where the river offered him passage. Suddenly, there was an explosion and a flash which seemed to turn night into the middle of its day. The little cowherd swallowed all that red, the shriek of crackling fire. Amid the flecks of night he saw the *ndlati,* bird of lightning swoop down. He tried to shout:

'Who are you coming to get, ndlati?'

But he spoke not a word. It wasn't the river that drowned his words: he was a fruit drained of sounds, pains and colours. Round about, everything began to close in, even the river sacrificed its water's life, and the world engulfed its floor in white smoke.

'Are you going to land on Grandmother, poor thing, so kind? Or have you chosen my uncle, after all repentant and full of promises like the true father who died on me?'

And before the bird of fire could decide, Azarias ran and embraced it in the passage of its flame.

THE BIRDS OF GOD

Begging your pardon, I don't know anything more like a pilgrim than the river. The waves pass by on a journey which has no end. For how long has it been water's job to do that? Alone in his old dugout, Ernesto Timba measured his life. At the age of twelve he had entered the school of pulling fish from the water. Ever in the waft of the current, his shadow had reflected the laws of the river dweller for the last thirty years. And what was it all for? Drought had exhausted the earth, the seeds were not fulfilling their promise. When he returned from fishing, he had nothing to defend himself with from his wife and children, who impaled him with their eyes. Eyes like those of a dog, he was loath to admit, but the truth is that hunger makes men like animals.

While he contemplated his suffering, Timba made his craft glide slowly along. Under the *mafurreira* tree, there on the bank where the river narrows, he brought the boat to rest so that he might drive away his sad thoughts. He allowed his paddle to nibble the water and the dugout clung to the stillness. But he could not stop his thoughts:

'What life have I lived? Water, water, just nothing else.'

As it rocked to and fro, the dugout caused his anguish to multiply.

'One day they'll fish me out of the water, swallowed up by the river.'

He foresaw his wife and children watching him being pulled from the mud, and it was as if the roots of the water were being torn up.

Overhead, the *mafurreira* retained the sun's fierce dispatch. But Timba wasn't listening to the tree, his eyes were peeping into his soul. And it was as if they were blind, for pain is a dust which drains light away. Still higher above, morning called and he caught the smell of the intense blue.

'If only I belonged to the sea,' he sighed.

And he felt the burden of thirty years of tiredness upon his life. He remembered the words of his father, uttered to teach him courage:

'See the hunter there, what he does? He prepares his spear the moment he sees the gazelle. But the fisherman can't see the fish inside the river. The fisherman believes in something he can't see.'

That was the lesson of the bound-to-be of life and he now recalled those wise words. It was getting late and hunger told him it was time to go home. He began to move his arm while casting a last glance upwards, beyond the clouds. It was then that a huge bird passed over the sky. It was like a king, pleased with its own majesty. The creature, high on the wing, held his eyes and an uncanny anxiety took root within him. He thought:

'If that bird were to fall on my canoe now!'

He uttered these words aloud. Hardly had he finished speaking than the bird shook its huge wings and quickly flew in a downward spiral towards the boat. It fell as if expelled from life. Timba picked up the damaged bird and holding it in his hands, saw that the blood had not yet unbuttoned its body. In the boat, the animal gradually recovered, until it stood up and climbed onto the prow to take stock of its survival. Timba grabbed it, and weighed its flesh in order to work out how many meals it would provide. He put the idea out of his mind, and with a shove, helped the bird to take off.

'Be off with you bird, go back from where you come!'

But the bird turned round and headed back to the boat. The fisherman once again drove it away. Yet again it returned. Ernesto Timba began to despair.

'Get back to your life, you bloody bird!'

Nothing. The bird didn't move. It was then that the fisherman began to wonder: that thing wasn't a bird, it was a sign from God. The warning from heaven would destroy his peace of mind forever.

Accompanied by the animal, he returned to the village. His wife celebrated his homecoming:

'Let's have the bird for lunch!'

Delighted, she called the children:

'Little ones, come and see the dicky-bird.'

Without answering, Timba placed the bird on the mat and went to the back of the house to fetch some wooden boards, wire and reeds. Then he set to work to build a cage so large that even a man could fit inside standing up straight. He put the animal inside and fed it the fish he had caught.

His wife was flabbergasted: the man was mad. Time passed and Timba only cared about the bird.

His wife would ask, pointing at the bird:

'Seeing as how hunger is pinching us, don't you want to kill it?'

Timba would raise his arm, emphatically. *'Never! Whoever touched the bird would he punished by God, would be marked down for life.'*

And so the days passed by, while the fisherman awaited fresh signs of divine intentions. Countless times he lingered in the moist afternoon heat while the river sat there in front of him. When the sun went down, he would go and check the cage where the animal was growing ever fatter. Little by little, he began to notice a shadow of sadness fall over the sacred bird. He realised the creature was suffering because it was lonely. One night he asked God to send the solitary fowl a companion. The following day, the cage had a new inmate, a female. Timba silently thanked the heavens for this new gift. At the same time, anxiety took root in him: why had God entrusted him to keep these animals? What might be the message they brought?

He thought and thought. That sign, that lightning flash of white plumage could only mean that heaven's humour was about to change. If men would agree to dispense their kindness to those messengers from heaven, then the drought would end and the season of rains would begin. It had befallen him, a poor fisherman of the river, to play host to God's envoys. It was his task to show that men could still be good. Yes, that true goodness cannot be measured in times of abundance but when hunger dances in the bodies of men.

His wife, who had returned from the *machamba,* interrupted his thoughts:

'So there are two of them now, are there?'

She came over, sat down on the same mat and, looking long and hard into her companion's eyes, said:

'Husband, the pot's on the fire. I'm asking you for the neck of one of them, just one.'

It was a waste of time. Timba promised severe punishment to whoever mistreated the divine birds.

In time, the couple had chicks. There were three of them, clumsy and ugly, their gullets ever open: enough appetite to empty the river. Timba toiled on behalf of their parents. The household provisions, already so scarce, were diverted to feed the coop.

In the village, the rumour went around: Ernesto Timba was stark raving mad. His own wife, after many a threat, left home taking with her all the children. Timba didn't even seem to notice his family's absence. He was more concerned with ensuring his poultry's protection. He detected a spirit of envy around him, vengeance hatching itself. Was it his fault that he had been chosen? They said he had gone crazy. But he who is chosen by God always wanders off his path.

Then, one afternoon, when he had finished his work on the river, a feeling of uncertainty set his mind aflame: the birds! He set off home at a rush. When he got near, he saw a pall of smoke rising through the trees around his house. He paddled his dugout towards the river bank, jumped out without even tying it up, and began to run towards the scene of the tragedy. When he arrived, all he saw was wreckage and ashes. The wood and wire had been chewed up by the flames. From between the boards a wing, untouched by the fire, sought to save itself. The bird must have hurled itself against the wall of flames and the wing had got away, an arrow ominously pointing towards disaster. It was not swaying to and fro, as is the obsession of dead things. It was rigid, full of certainty.

Timba stepped back, appalled. He shouted for his wife, for his children, and then, on discovering that there was nobody else to shout for, he wept such copious tears of rage that his eyes hurt.

Why? Why had they harmed those birds, pretty as they were? And there and then, amidst all the ash and the smoke, he addressed himself to God:

'You're going to be angry, I know. You're going to punish your children. But look: I'm asking you to forgive them. Let me be the one to die, me. Leave the others to suffer what they are already suffering. You can forget the rain even, you can leave the dust lying on the ground, but please don't punish the men of this land.'

The following day, they found Ernesto hugging the current of the river, chilled by the early morning mist. When they tried to raise him, they found him heavy and impossible to separate from the water. The strongest men were brought to the task, but their efforts were in vain. The body was stuck to the surface of the river. A strange feeling of dread spread among those present. To hide their fear, someone said:

'Go and tell his wife. Tell the others that the village madman has died.'

And they withdrew. As they were climbing the bank, the clouds clashed, the sky seemed to cough sullenly as if it were sick. In different circumstances, they would have celebrated the coming of the rain. Not now. For the first time, their faiths joined together pleading that it might not rain.

Impassive, the river flowed on into the distance, laughing at the ignorance of men. Ernesto Timba, gently lulled by the current, was carried downstream, and shown the byways he had only glimpsed in dreams.

HOW ASCOLINO DO PERPÉTUO SOCORRO LOST HIS SPOUSE

Vivenda da Santíssima Palha was the name on the sign by the side of the road. A path of sand led to the farm, a place which no longer knew the meaning of sweat and toil. In the middle, half hidden by mango trees, the colonial farmhouse measured itself against time. There, in the afternoon shade, Ascolino Fernandes do Perpétuo Socorro would relax on the veranda. Inheritor of the estate, he ruminated over memories, unhurried and without obligations. He recalled Goa, his native land. He rejected the Mozambican in him:

'I am indeed an Indo-Portuguese, Catholic in my faith and in my customs.'

His dress was of the most formal kind, a suit of white linen, shoes of an identical whiteness, and hat of the selfsame colour. Ceremonious, correct, Ascolino embroidered his speech with the brocades of old Portugal which he admired so much. He decorated his repartee with adverbs for no reason or purpose. A long list of them introduced sentences which were spoken incorrectly and with a strong accent:

'Notwithstanding, however, nevertheless, perforce ...'

In Munhava he had established his domains, more dreamt of than firmly fixed. He alone discerned the glory of being Goan, while separating the breeze from the flies during the long afternoons.

He bowed to his visitors, bestowing upon them long silences and green mangoes with salt. Dona Epifânia, his wife, was the one who served them, so thin that one was not even aware she was approaching. When the net doors flapped, one knew she was there. No one had ever witnessed any expression of love pass between them. Did they love each other? If so, they loved without their bodies. Ascolino suffered because of his wife's constant seclusion. He consoled himself but without conviction. Epifânia, he was wont to say, is a clam. If opened, it dies, exposed to the air and to the tides. When the others noted his wife's absence, Ascolino would affirm:

'*Epifane, most sacred spouse indeed. Notwithstanding, howevah, darty years of marriage.*'

Five o'clock in the afternoon was a venerated hour, even more sacred than his wife. Whether or not there were visitors, the ritual was repeated. Vasco João Joãoquinho, faithful and devoted servant, would emerge from the shadow of the mango trees. He wore a khaki uniform which consisted of a tunic and neatly pressed trousers. He would approach, wheeling a bicycle. Ascolino Fernandes, with his eye for protocol, would salute both present and absent friends. The servant would hand him a little cushion which he would arrange on the bicycle frame. He would climb on taking great care not to dirty his trousers on the chain. With these preparations now complete, Vasco João Joãoquinho would mount the saddle, and with a vigorous shove, begin the pageant. Their sally was made all the more difficult by the undulations in the sand. And the two of them, Ascolino and his bicycle chauffeur, would press on, bound for Meneses' bottle store dispensing greetings as they went. The movements of both were correct, only their vehicle did not uphold the by-laws. On they would press, obeying the degenerate will of Ascolino, pedalling against thirst and distance.

On that afternoon the same scenery passed by with the same

men inside it. Vasco chose the grassy parts of the track so the tyres gripped better. Suddenly, the bicycle keeled over and both master and servant fell into the ditch. Ascolino lay motionless in the mud. Vasco picked up the bits and pieces, straightened the handlebars and brushed down his master's hat.

Ascolino recomposed himself with some difficulty. He surveyed the damage and began to chide his servant:

'What have you done, man? You have been spoiling our hat indeed. Who will pay for it perforce?'

'Sorry, boss. I was trying to steer the bicycle clear of that mud back there.'

'Are you not seeing, fellow? I am always telling you: do not brake so suddenly.'

And on they climbed again: Ascolino Perpétuo Socorro, his dignity restored, his hat battered, Vasco pedalling through the sunset. Overhead, the coconut palms lent sound to the breeze.

'Try not to derail the velocipede again, Vasco, will you?'

Reeling through the sands, the servant pushed with all the strength of his legs. But the Goan's thirst could not wait for the minutes to go by:

'Proceed post-haste, Vasco. Pedal harder!'

They arrived at the Bar Viriato, Meneses' store. The bicycle came to a halt by the cement-paved frontage. The master climbed off, brushing the dust off his clothes. He pulled out his pocket watch as he made his way towards his reserved table. Vasco did not enter the front part. Blacks, according to the custom of the time, were only admitted at the rear. In the back yard watered down wine was served. In the bar, in front, the quality was of a different order.

∎

Vasco João Joãoquinho took his time coming in. The others greeted his arrival and asked for stories about him and his boss

Ascolino. Vasco always had a tale to tell, inventing amusing incidents. But he always lingered over the beginning while preparing the condiments of the adventure.

'Well now, Vasco? What happened last night with your boss?'

Vasco considered his words, and chuckled as he thought ahead about the tale he was going to tell.

'You won't believe this one about my boss ...'

'Come on, man! Tell us it.'

And he related the incredible incident of the previous night. Ascolino Fernandes, in the furthest depths of the middle of the night, had started his singsong with the *Fado of the Little Swallows*. Vasco Joãoquinho imitated him, glass in hand:

> *'When a little swallow died*
> *All the little girls cried ...'*

Ascolino sang the whole night through. The little swallows kept dying and his fury kept growing. Until he began to trumpet threats through the open window:

'Now, I'm going to throw the fan out.'

And crashing down came the fan, hurled from the first floor. It smashed into smithereens on the ground, its pieces flying across the yard. Then, another warning:

'Now for the dishes.'

And down into the garden fell pieces of crockery. Gleaming splinters of glass exploded into a thousand moons in the yard of the farmhouse. Ascolino sang ever louder:

> *'When a little swallow died ...'*

There was no sign of Epifânia. Maybe she was shut away in her room. Or perhaps she was crying in the way that only she knew how. The saddest sadness is that which is not heard.

'I'm talking seriously, my friends, because I know all about

sadness. *Our race cries with its body. They don't. They're locked inside their tribulations.'*

'*Listen here, Vasco, don't get off the subject. Go on with the story about your boss.'*

Bits of furniture came travelling through the window. Vasco came over and begged:

'*Please, boss, stop all this.'*

'*Get out of the way, Vasco.'*

'*Oh boss, don't go on, don't wreck the whole house.'*

'*Whose house is it? Is it yours?'*

'*But, boss, have you seen all the junk down here?'*

'*Get out of the way! Hurry! Now, I am throwing the fridge machine.'*

Terrified, Vasco left the yard. Taking a short step and then a longer one to avoid the broken glass, the servant went and hid in the shadows. There, sheltered by the darkness, he waited for the crash. Nothing. The refrigerator wasn't coming.

'*Boss?'*

'*What is it that you are wanting? Nevertheless are you still annoying me?'*

Then he began to sing *fados* again. He bellowed his song; the whole of Munhava was littered with little swallows. He interrupted his artistry and turned towards the inside of the house to insult Epifânia:

'*You don't care about me. It's just prayers from morning to night. This isn't a house for mortals. It's not a farmhouse! It's a church. The Cathedral of Santíssima Palha. Notwithstanding, I tell you what I am going to do: I am going to throw out all the furniture for praying, your crucifix and the altar. Everything out, out of here!'*

Then it was the turn of silence. Vasco Joãoquinho asked himself: is this an interval or the end of the show? Just as he thought it was all over, he heard the noise of a chair being dragged over to the window. It was then that the figure of the

Goan appeared fully, from his knees to his head. His skinny hands tidied his unkempt appearance while he announced solemnly:

'The furniture has all gone. Now it is my turn.'

And before Vasco could say anything, Ascolino Fernandes do Perpétuo Socorro threw himself down from the window. Ascolino's skinniness did not help his speed. He was more like a curtain than a body. When he landed, he didn't get so much as a grunt from the ground. Just a sigh, a little cloud of dust. Vasco, alarmed, ran over to help. He searched for signs of blood, of injury to the body. There were none.

'Boss, did you damage anything?'

'What anything? Help me out of the ground.'

He lifted his boss. When he had reached his full height, Ascolino surveyed the damage around him. Then he walked away through the darkness quietly humming his *fado*.

Everyone at the rear of the Bar Viriato laughed at the story. This time, however, Vasco Joãoquinho arranged his silence with an expression of sadness on his face.

'Hey, Vasco, you always bring us such good stories, man.'

'I didn't invent it. All of what I told you happened. But don't laugh so loud, he might be listening from over the other side.'

But nothing could be heard from the other side. Ascolino was hard at work on the whisky. Separated by only a wall, the other side was still a long way away.

Seated at his reserved table, Ascolino, relishing his own company, recalled Goa, Damão and Diu and spouted adverbs. Notwithstanding, however.

'Please to bring me another helping of whisky.'

Meneses didn't even seem to see Ascolino. He poured out the orders while the sky gradually lost its light. Time slipped by between one glass and another. Ascolino drank with the confidence of a viceroy of the Indies. A finer quality Ascolino than the other Ascolino – the Indo-Portuguese superimposing himself on the Mozambican by means of alcohol. Only one anxiety remained which had not been drowned by whisky: Epifânia. At this stage, his wife must be turning in her sleep, tossed between insults and exhaustion. Ascolino looked at the time, he didn't want to stop for the night on the journey home. Guessing his fears, a Portuguese said:

'Don't hurry yourself, Fernandes. Don't hurry. Your lady's going to get angry with you anyway.'

Ascolino decided to ignore deadlines, to show he was a man, and daring in his delay. If he was downtrodden in life, he excelled in the art of discourse.

'Epifane, she is already being aware of everything. Curry, chacuti, sarapatel, all the good food there is, everything she has been cooking for us to eat upon our arrival. Epifane, most sacred spouse.'

At another table, a group of soldiers awaited their chance. At this point they decided to issue their challenge:

'Goa's gone. Indian mother-fuckers; scum of the earth.'

But Ascolino, to their astonishment, did not show offence. On the contrary, he joined his assailants.

'Yes sir, Indian mother-fuckers indeed. Perforce, however, I am an Indo-Portuguese, defender of the Lusitanian fatherland against its enemies.'

The soldiers eyed each other suspiciously. But Ascolino took the affirmation of his Portuguese loyalty a step further. He climbed onto his chair and swaying this way and that, held forth upon his heroic dreams. A crusade, yes, a crusade to reconquer the name of Goa for Portuguese usage. At its head, commanding the battalions, he, Ascolino Fernandes do Perpétuo Socorro. Behind him, soldiers and missionaries, ships loaded with arms, bibles and some little bottles of whisky.

'This bloke's taking the piss out of us,' concluded one of the soldiers, the biggest one. He got up and walked over to Ascolino, getting the scent of his humours:

'Crusades, what crusades? The only cross you carry is the cross your crossed legs make, your skinny little darkie's legs.'

It was not intentional, perhaps it was because he lost his balance, but Ascolino spilled a few drops of whisky on the other man's uniform. A fist flew through the air, tore through the orator's words and Ascolino collapsed on the ground. The others seized the aggressor, dragged him away, and threw him out of the bar. Ascolino lay there on his back, in surrogate death, one arm raised and holding his glass. Meneses came to his assistance:

'Senhor Ascolino, are you all right?'

'I have been fallen flat.'

'But how did it happen?'

'Abruptly.'

They put the Goan back on his feet. He straightened his creases, and peered into the bottom of his glass. He looked round at the crowd and declared the crusade postponed.

In front of the bar, the Goan prepared his retreat:

'Vashcooo, lessgo!'

While waiting for his chauffeur, he fumbled for his pocket watch, creature of habit that he was. But this time he found the chain, but no watch. Ascolino consulted his non-existent watch and remarked on the lateness of the hour.

'Quick-ly, Vashcooo.'

He arranged the cushion on the bicycle frame before seating himself. The cushion was in place, it was just that Ascolino missed. He fell, tried again, and returned to the ground.

'Vashcooo, switch on the light, switch off this darkness.'

The servant aligned the dynamo with the wheel and gave the pedal a healthy kick. Ascolino was on his hands and knees looking for his own body.

'Did my hat run away?'

Vasco Joãoquinho was also reeling. He picked up the hat and climbed on the bike. Then they both got ready, hindering each other in the process. Meneses enjoyed the spectacle from his window:

'That darkie's stoned out of his mind. Full of whisky and punches.'

Vasco pushed aside pieces of darkness and other obstacles as they set off home. He pedalled along, ringing his bell, *cring, cring.* No longer could ravens be heard or herons seen. Night had levelled colours, erased differences. As they went on, the effects of the Scottish brew began to be felt even more strongly by the Goan, who abandoned his good behaviour once and for all.

'I'm a pale-arsed little darkie, a first-class one if you please.'
And shouting with all his soul: *'Long live Nehru!'*

Some way further on, where the rice plantations end and the coconut palms begin, Ascolino exchanged his servant for his wife and began to call him Epifânia.

'A woman doesn't ride behind. Get up in front.'

Vasco obediently gave up his saddle seat. The Goan, excited, grabbed his servant round the waist.

'Hey boss, get away with you.'

But Ascolino pressed forward with sugary insistence. He tried to kiss his servant who avoided him vigorously. As insistence increased, respect diminished. Vasco now pushed his boss aside:

'Leave me alone, I'm not your woman.' And another, stronger shove sent Ascolino to the ground. Silence among the coconut groves. Only the ravens watched the scuffle inquisitively. The Goan lay spread-eagled on the ground. He asked for a light to see whether the stain on his trousers was puddle water, or whether he'd pissed in his pants. Vasco laughed. Ascolino began to raise himself, reeling, his nose nearly scraping the ground. Then, when finally upright, he examined the surrounding grass:

'Vashcooo, they've stolen the Vivenda da Santíssima Palha!'
'No, boss! We haven't got there yet, there's still some way to

go.'

But Ascolino's mind was made up, and he retorted:

'Vashcooo, we've lost the house. Perforce, you are going to look for it.'

The servant lost his patience and began to pull him along by the armpits. On tow in this fashion, Ascolino saw the road back to front, retreating crab-like. Confusing his coming with his going, he pleaded:

'Vashcooo, don't walk backwards. We are going back to Meneses' store.'

And as if going on ahead, he shouted his order:

'Meneses, give me whisky, and another helping for Epifane, most holy drink.'

And in a generous mood, he turned his head:

'Order whatever you want, Vashcooo. And deduct it from your month's pay. You can drink on this side, there's no need for you to go to the back.'

Tired out with walking backwards, Vasco let go of him. Feeling himself horizontal, the Goan said his prayers and then took his leave:

'Good night, Epifane, most holy wife.'

But Vasco was no longer there. He went back to get the bicycle. Ascolino raised his head with difficulty and seeing his servant loaded down, he hailed him:

'That's it, bring my blanket to cover me with. And cover Epifane too.'

Vasco, in despair, attempted a final warning:

'I don't know, boss. If we don't get back tonight, and sleep here, your lady's going to kick up a big fuss.'

Ascolino agreed. The threat seemed to have had an effect. Propping himself on his elbows, the boss looked straight at his servant and said:

'What's wrong Epifânia? Are you sleeping in khaki trousers now?'

And without further ado, he fell asleep. So heavy was his slumber that Vasco failed to budge him.

∎

Next morning, they were covered by a sheet of insects, leaves and dew. Vasco was the first to arrive back in the world. He was surprised by the sound of a motor nearby. He looked around him, fighting the weight of his eyelids. It was then that he saw, in the near distance, the Vivenda da Santíssima Palha. Could it be that they had slept only a minute or two from home?

In the front yard, all the furniture had been piled up. There were men loading it all onto a lorry. That, then, was the motor he had heard. Dona Epifânia directed the operation like some supreme commander.

The servant hesitated. He looked at his boss, still given over to sleep. Finally, he made up his mind. Vasco Joãoquinho followed the familiar sandy path up to the house. When he got there, he realised what his mistress intended to do. She wanted to leave, to terminate her association with Ascolino without warning or explanation.

'Senhora, don't go away, please.'

The mistress was startled. Then, recovering from her fright, she continued with her removal.

'Senhora, we were late because of the beating the boss got back there in the bar.'

The words of the servant said nothing. His mistress continued to give out her orders. But Vasco Joãoquinho didn't give up:

'Senhora, it wasn't just the business of the beating. We were late because of an accident on the road.'

'An accident?'

Epifânia, suddenly uncertain, began to think. She asked for proof of this truth. Vasco showed her the twisted hat.

She looked at the stains and bit her lip. She chose her words carefully before asking:

'*Was he killed?*'

'*Killed? No, Senhora. He's just lying in the road.*'

'*Is he hurt?*'

'*No, not at all. He's just sleepy. Can I go and get him?*'

Words to be regretted, for once Epifânia had heard them she renewed her determination to leave and the furniture began to be loaded again.

Vasco retraced his steps along the road. Slowly, he returned to the place where he had left his boss asleep. When he got there, Ascolino was already stretching himself. Unable to take the light, he rubbed his eyes, unaware of the noise of the approaching lorry. He sat up and his aching body shrank. The lorry's horn startled him, and in one leap he landed in the ditch. The load passed slowly by, as if opposed to its journey. There before Ascolino's untutored eyes, his life was ebbing away, unrecorded and unnoticed. When the dust settled, Vasco could be seen standing glumly on one side of the road. On the other, Ascolino was climbing out of the ditch. As he looked, the lorry continued further into the distance. Then, brushing the creases in his coat, he asked:

'*What's happening Vasco? Are some neighbours moving from Munhava?*'

'*They're not neighbours, boss. It's the lady, Dona Epifânia herself, who is going away.*'

'*Epifane?*'

'*Yes. And she's taking everything with her.*'

Ascolino looked askance, repeating:

'*Epifane?*'

He stood there churning over his thoughts, kicking at clumps of grass, untidying the scenery. The servant couldn't bring himself to look up. Then, suddenly, Ascolino spoke decisively:

'*Bring the bicycle, Vasco. We are going to pursue that lorry.*

Quickly.'

'But boss, the lorry's a long way ahead by now.'

'Quiet you know-nothing. Load the velocipede, speedily!'

So the servant prepared the seats. On the frame, and without a cushion, sat the boss, while the servant sat on the saddle. And they began to cycle off down the road.

The groove made by the tyre gradually unwove itself in the morning air. No longer could the noise of the lorry be heard through the surrounding rice fields. Ascolino the viceroy led his impossible crusade to try and regain his lost spouse.

'Pedal, pedal quickly. Perforce we must arrive early. When five o'clock strikes we must go back to Meneses' store.'

SO YOU HAVEN'T FLOWN YET, CARLOTA GENTINA?

1. Your honour, let me begin

I are sad. No, I'm not mistaken. What I'm saying is correct. Or perhaps: we am sad? Because inside me, I'm not alone. I'm many. And they all fight over my one and only life. We go along reaping our deaths. But we only have one birth. That's where the problem lies. That's why, when I tell my story, I mix myself up, a mulatto not of races, but of existences.

They say I killed my wife. In real life, I killed one who didn't exist. She was a bird. I let her go when I saw that she didn't have a voice, that she was dying without so much as a complaint. What dumb creature was it that came out of her through the interval of her body?

Very well, your honour, you, a doctor of the laws, have asked me to write down my story, and that's what I'm going to do, a little bit every day. What I'm going to tell you, you're going to use to defend me in court. But you don't even know me. Does my suffering interest you, sir? It doesn't matter to me either. Here I am talking away about this and that, but I don't want anything, I don't want to get out any more than I want to stay. These six years that I've been locked up in this cell have been enough for me to unlearn my life. Now, sir, I just want to be dying. To die is for such a long time, living is too short. I'll stay in between. On my way to death. Do you think that's funny?

I'll explain: the dying are allowed to do what they want. No one laughs at them. They anticipate respect for the dead, they are pre-deceased. When the dying insult us, we forgive them for sure. If they shit in their sheets or spit in their dinner plate, we clean up after them, no questions asked. Please, your honour, help me. Fix it so that I can be dying, sub-dead.

After all, here I am in this prison because I decided to become a prisoner. That's the plain truth, no one pointed the finger at me. Sick of myself, I informed against me. I gave myself up. Maybe on account of being tired of waiting for a time that never came. I can wait, but never get anything. When the future arrives it won't find me. When all is said and done, where am I? Isn't this time the place of my life?

I'm going to leave my thoughts to themselves, and get straight to the story. I'll begin with my brother-in-law Bartolomeu. The night he came looking for me, that was when disaster began to strike.

2. Wings on the ground, embers in the sky

Light was getting thin. Only a glassful of sky was left. In my brother-in-law Bartolomeu's house, they were preparing for the end of the day. He glanced round the hut: his wife bustled about causing the last shadows from the oil lamp to flicker. Then his wife went to bed, but Bartolomeu was restless. Sleep wouldn't come quickly to him. Outside an owl began to hoot calamities. His wife didn't hear the bird warning of death, she was already in the arms of sleep. Bartolomeu said to himself:

'I'm going to make tea: maybe that'll help me to sleep.'

The fire was still burning. He took a stick of wood and blew on it. He shook the crumbs of flame from his eyes and in the confusion dropped the lighted stick on his wife's back. The cry she let out no one had ever heard the likes of before. It wasn't the sound a person would make, it was the howl of an animal. A hyena's voice for sure. Bartolomeu jumped with fright: what am I married to then? A *nóii*? Those women who turn into animals at night and go around doing witches' work?

His wife dragged her burning pain across the floor in front of his distress. Like an animal. What a luckless life, thought Bartolomeu. And he fled from home. He hurried across the village to tell me what had happened. He arrived at my house, and the dogs were very excited. He came in without knocking, without so much as an 'excuse me'. He told me his story just as I am writing it down. At first, I didn't believe him. Perhaps Bartolomeu had mixed his recollections up when drunk. I smelt the breath of his complaint. It didn't smell of drink. It was true then. Bartolomeu repeated the story two, three, four times. I listened to it and thought to myself: and what if my wife is the same? What if she's a *nóii* too?

When Bartolomeu had left, the idea seized hold of my thoughts. And supposing I, without knowing it, were living with an animal-woman? If I had made love to her, then I had traded my human's mouth with an animal snout. How could I excuse such a trade? Were animals ever supposed to rest on a sleeping mat? Animals live and grow strong out in the corrals, beyond the wire. If that son-of-a-bitch of a woman had deceived me, I had become an animal myself. There was only one way to find out whether Carlota Gentina, my wife, was a *nóii* or not. It was to surprise her with some suffering, some deep pain. I looked around and saw a pot full of boiling water. I picked it up and poured the scalding liquid over her body. I waited for the scream but it didn't come. It didn't come at all. She just lay there crying silently, without making a noise. She was a curled up piece of silence there on the mat. All the following day she did not move. Poor Carlota was just a name lying on the ground. A name without a person: just a long, slow sleep inside a body. I shook her by the shoulders:

'Carlota, why don't you move? If you're in agony, why don't you scream?'

But death is a war of deceptions. Victories are just defeats which have been put off. As long as life has a purpose to it, it will build a person. That's what Carlota was in need of: the lie of a purpose. I played the fool to make her laugh. I hopped round the mat like a locust. I clanked cooking pots against each other and spilt the noise over myself. Nothing. Her eyes remained glued to the far distance, gazing at the blind side of darkness. Only I laughed, wrapped up in my saucepans. I got up, breathless with laughter and went outside to give vent to my mad guffaws. I laughed until I was tired. Then gradually, I was overcome by sad thoughts, ancient pangs of conscience.

I went back inside and thought she would probably like to see the light of day, and stretch her legs. I took her outside. She was so light that her blood can have been no more than red dust. I sat Carlota down facing the setting sun. I let the fresh air soak her body. There, sitting in the back yard, my wife Carlota Gentina died. I didn't notice her death immediately. I only knew it when I saw the tear which had stopped still in her eyes. That tear was already death's water.

I stood looking at the woman stretched out in that body of hers. I looked at the feet, torn like the surface of the earth. They had walked so many paths that they had become like brothers to the sand. The feet of the dead are big, they grow on after death. While I measured Carlota's death I began to have my doubts: what illness was it that caused neither swelling nor cries of pain? Can hot water just stop someone's age just like that? This was the conclusion I drew from my thoughts: Carlota Gentina was a bird, of the type that lose their voice in a headwind.

3. Dreams of the soul awoke me from my body

I dreamt of her. She was in the back yard, working at her pestle. Do you know what she was grinding? Water. She was grinding water. No, it wasn't corn, or *mapira,* or anything else. It was water, grains from heaven.

I drew near. She was singing a sad song, it seemed as if she were lulling herself to sleep. I asked the reason for her work.

'I'm grinding.'

'Are those grains?'

'They're your tears, husband.'

And so it was: I saw that there in that pestle was the origin of my suffering. I asked her to stop but my voice could no longer be heard. My throat had gone blind. Just the tonk-tonk-tonk of the pestle, pounding, pounding, forever pounding. Then slowly I began to realise that the noise was coming from my chest, that it was my heart punishing me. Do you think I'm inventing this? Anyone can invent. But from this cell, all I can see are the walls of life. I can feel a dream, a passing whiff of perfume. But I can't grab it. Now I've exchanged my life for dreams. It wasn't just tonight that I dreamt of her. The night before last, your honour, I even cried. It was because I witnessed my own death. I looked down the corridor and saw blood, a river of it. It was orphan blood. Without its father, which was my severed arm. Imprisoned blood like its owner. Condemned. I don't remember how it came to be severed. I have a darkened memory because of these countless nights I've drunk.

And do you know who it was that saved my spilt blood in that dream? It was she. She scooped up the blood with her ancient hands. She cleaned it, lovingly extracted the dirt. She put all the bits together and showed them the way back into my body. Then she called me by that name of mine which I have already forgotten because nobody calls me by it. Here I'm a number, my name is made of digits, not letters.

You asked me to confess truths, your honour. It's true I killed her. Was it a crime? Maybe, if that is what they say. But I fall ill with the uncertainty. I'm not one of those widowers who buries his memories. They are rescued by oblivion. Death hasn't taken Carlota away from me. Now I know why: the dead are all born on the same day. Only the living have separate birthdays. Did Carlota fly? That time I spilled water over her, was it over the woman or the bird? Who can tell? Can you, your honour?

One thing I know for sure: she was left outside her coffin. Those who wept at the funeral were blind. I was laughing. It's true, I was laughing. Because inside the coffin they were weeping at, there was nothing. She had fled, saved by her wings. They saw me laughing like this, but they didn't get angry. They forgave me. They thought it was laughter of the sort which is not an enemy of sadness. Maybe it was sobbing in disguise, the sweat of suffering. And they prayed. As for me, I couldn't. After all, it wasn't a fully deceased dead woman lying there. Rather it was a piece of silence in the form of a beast, that's what it was.

4. I shall learn to be a tree

Writing has made me tired of letters. I'm going to finish in a minute. I don't need a defence any more, your honour. I don't want one. After all, I'm guilty. I want to be punished, I have no other wish. Not because of the crime, but because of my mistake. At the end I'll explain what this mistake was. Six years ago I gave myself up, I arrested me by myself. Now, I myself am condemning me.

I am grateful for everything, your honour. I took up your time, for no payment. You'll call me an ass. I know and accept it. But begging your pardon, your honour, what do you know about me? I'm not like others: I think about what I can put up with, not about what I need. What I can't manage has nothing to do with me. God's failing, not mine. Why didn't God create us already made? Finished, like an animal which, when it has been born, only has to grow. If God made us live why didn't he let us rule our lives?

As it is, even when we're white, we're black. With respect, your honour, you're black too, let me tell you. It's a defect in the race of mankind, this race of ours which is everybody's. Our voices, blind and broken, no longer have authority. We only give orders to the weak: women and children. Even they have begun to be slow to obey. The power of a minion is to make others feel even smaller, to tread on others just as he himself is trodden on by his superiors. Crawling, that's what the job of souls is. If they're used to the ground how is it that they can believe in heaven?

Unfinished, incomplete, that's what we are, and we come to our end when buried. It's worth it to be a plant, your honour. I'm even going to learn to be a tree. Or perhaps a little clump of grass, for a tree wouldn't fit in here. Why don't those witches I was talking about try and be plants, all green and quiet? If that had happened, I wouldn't have had to kill Carlota. All I'd have had to do would be to transplant her; there would be no crime, no guilt.

I'm only afraid of one thing: of cold. All my life I've suffered from cold. Ague of the soul, not the body, that's what I get. Even when it's hot I still get the shivers. Bartolomeu, my brother-in-law, used to say: *'Away from home it's always cold'*. That's true. But I, your honour, what home have I ever had? None. Bare earth, without a here or a where. In a place like that, with neither arrival nor departure, you need to learn to be clever. Not the cleverness they teach you at school. An all-round cleverness, a cleverness with no fixed job in mind, no contract with anybody.

You can see from this last letter, your honour, that I've given up. Why am I like this? Because Bartolomeu visited me today and told me everything just as it really happened. Afterwards I realised my mistake. Bartolomeu came to my conclusion for me: his wife, my sister-in-law, wasn't a *nóii*. He got proof of this over several nights. He spied on his wife to see if she had some other nocturnal occupation. Nothing, she hadn't. She neither crawled round on all fours nor flew off like a bird. And so Bartolomeu was able to prove that his wife was a person.

Then I began to think. If my wife's sister wasn't a *nóii*, then neither was my wife. Witchcraft is a vice of sisters, an illness they are born with. But how could I have guessed it by myself? I couldn't have, your honour.

I am a son of my own world. I want to be judged by other laws, beholden to my tradition. My mistake was not that I killed Carlota. It was that I surrendered my life to this world of yours which does not rest easy with mine. There, where I come from, they know me. There they can decide what my goodnesses are. Here, no one can. How can I be defended if I can't obtain the understanding of others? I'm sorry, your honour: justice can only be done where I belong. When all is said and done, only they can tell that I didn't know Carlota Gentina didn't have wings to fly away with.

Now it's too late. I only notice the time when it has already passed. I'm a blind man who sees many doors. I open the nearest one. I don't choose, my hand merely stumbles across a latch. My life isn't a path. It is a solid stone waiting to become sand. Very slowly, I'm becoming at one with the grains of the earth. When they decide to bury me I'll already be soil. Seeing as I had no advantage in life, this will be my privilege in death.

SAÍDE, THE BUCKET OF WATER

An afternoon of wood and zinc. Sloping roofs brushed by the mist. The watery eyelids of the afternoon seemed to release bats into the air.

In the cane shanty, the landscape was kissed only by death. Saíde was returning home, stumbling over his curses, dragged along by beer, poured down him all afternoon to console his despair.

'Friends? Hell, they're the first to leave a bloke in the shit!'

Bursts of laughter came from open doorways.

'That's right, laugh, you bastards.'

He fumbled in his pockets. Cigarettes: none. Matches: none. His hands impatiently searched his clothes. He felt like a smoke, he needed the strength of a cigarette, the security of preordained gestures.

'Look at the Bucket of Water. His wife hasn't set foot out of the house ever since he took to drink.'

It wasn't true. Women always get the reward of being felt sorry for. Bloody neighbours. The nearest they come is when they want to take a look at your adversities. Apart from that nobody knows who they are.

He went into his house and closed the door. His hand lingered distractedly on the latch, while he gazed round at the emptiness. He remembered the times when he had first met her: those days of Júlia Timane were beautiful ones indeed!

That had been a long time ago. He was sitting by a bus stop waiting for nothing in particular, in the way that only drunks wait. She had walked up and sat down beside him. The *capulana* she wore over her shoulders seemed scarcely enough for such abiding cold. They had started talking.

'I'm Júlia. I'm from Macia.'

'Haven't you a husband?'

'I had one. For the moment I haven't.

'How many husbands have you had?'

'Many. I have children too.'

'Where are these children?'

'They're not with me. Their fathers took them away.'

He offered her his coat to protect her from the cold. She helped him to find his way home. But she had finished up by staying the night. And the other nights too.

When they discovered that he was going with her, they rebuked him. She was secondhand. He ought to choose an untouched woman, to be initiated by his body. He refused to listen. It was then that they began to call him Bucket of Water. Everywhere, his nickname substituted his real name. Water accepts any shape it is given, it hasn't a personality of its own.

In time he began to realise something was wrong: she wasn't giving him children. Nobody could know about this. A man may or may not have a beard. But he must beget children: they are a document which the respects demand to see.

One day he said to her:

'We must have a son.'

'We can't, you know only too well.'

'We must find a way.'

'A way? How? If it's not my fault? They explained the problem at the hospital: you're the one who can't have children.'

'I'm not talking about whose fault it is. I've already studied

the problem and I've found a solution: take on your fuel outside, woman.'

'I don't understand.'

'I'm telling you: sleep with someone else. I shan't get angry. I just want a son, that's all.'

■

That evening she went out. She came back very late. The following evening the same thing happened. This went on for many nights.

He asked: 'Isn't once enough?'

'Don't you want a son? It's best to make sure.'

'Do whatever you think best. But quickly, for I don't want to be put to any shame.'

Júlia became pregnant. He rejoiced in the news. Those first weeks were very happy. Up until the time he woke her up in the middle of the night.

'Júlia. I want to know: who is the owner of this pregnancy?'

'Armando, you swore never to ask.'

'Now I want to know the name. You can't give birth without my knowing the truth about the father of this child.'

Júlia remained silent and settled down once again in bed. He shook her violently.

'Are you going to beat me up?' she asked in alarm.

'If you don't tell me, I will.'

'I won't be the only one to be beaten. You may harm your son.'

He looked at himself: he was on his knees, as if at prayers. A man who demands doesn't assume the position of those who beg. He got up and went to light the oil lamp. In the shadow he spoke to her more calmly:

'Sleep, Júlia, I don't want to hear the name. Even if I ask you for it again, you must never tell me who the person is.'

She smiled, turned down the sheet and showed him the full round moon of her belly.

'*It's your son, Saíde. Yours.*'

The child was born. It was then that he confirmed the suspicion of a feeling: the baby boy was a stranger, a scar on his honour. But a live scar, a whimpering testimony to his inadequacies. Sometimes he loved him and the child was his. At others, the baby was an interloper who rebuffed him.

In the neighbourhood, no one suspected the identity of the father. But Saíde felt more and more insecure: he would look at the child and it seemed to him to know everything. He had wanted a son to hide his shame. Instead, he had a son who threatened his life's secret. The home became increasingly difficult to live in. He became jealous of the attentions his wife devoted to his little rival. The future perturbed him like a darkened road. He beat his wife more and more often, his drunken bouts became ever more frequent. He never hit the little boy. The beatings he wanted to give him were directed at the mother.

∎

He felt the strength of the wind through the doorway and was jolted out of his memories. Every time he recollected, knives got to work in his soul. The past was forbidden to him. And all because of Júlia, that devil of a woman. He closed the door with the decisiveness of rage.

'*You whore!*'

And he set about her with kicks. He wanted to hurt her, to unload all the pain he felt onto her. Cooking pots fell making a loud din. He was undismayed: leaning over the bed he insulted her, spat on her, threatened to kill her stone dead. The neighbours, he already knew, would not come to the rescue. And that night, his fury was greater than ever. He was determined to beat her until she bled. He pulled his belt out and used it with such force of will that he lost his balance and fell over the table. Dishes and glasses were shattered, once again ripping through the silence of night.

Suddenly, he heard a noise at the door. When he looked, whoever it was had just come in. It was Severino, the district warden.

'What do you want, Severino?'

'Calm down, Saíde. What's all this for?'

He was breathing as if feeding many souls.

'Sit down, Saíde.'

He obeyed. With his sighs he quenched the fire in his soul.

'Why are you always doing this? Have you ever heard of anybody beating a woman the way you do?'

He did not answer. He was trying to dampen down the heat inside his breast. He remained like that for a few minutes until he answered:

'I'm not hitting any one.'

Severino did not understand. It must be that he's pissed; he'll start talking about everything under the sun. Saíde insisted.

'There's no one else in this house except for me.'

Severino looked around him suspiciously. It was true, there wasn't anybody else.

'You can search everywhere, Júlia isn't here, she went away long ago. I'm not beating anyone.'

'I'm sorry, Saíde. I thought ...'

And as he was at a loss for words, he decided to leave. He backed out as if the surprise were a snake threatening to attack him.

'Severino?'

'Yes, I'm listening.'

'I don't know why I do this. It's so that you people should think she's still here. Nobody must know that I've been deserted. Every time I deliver a beating, there's no one behind all that *noise. You all think she doesn't go out because of the shame she feels in front of her neighbours. As long as you don't . . .'*

Severino was in a hurry to get out. Saíde stood there, his arms hanging limply at his sides. It was as if his flesh had turned to wood and deep sadness had been chiselled into him. Severino went out, closing the door with the care one shows when not wanting to disturb a child's sleep.

Outside, a crowd awaited news. The warden, with a vague gesture, spread his voice around:

'You can all go. Mama Júlia is well. She asks you to return to your homes and sleep soundly.'

Someone protested:

'But Severino . . . What happened then?'

The warden, with an embarrassed smile, replied:

'Come, my friend. You know what these women of ours are like.'

THE WHALES OF QUISSICO

He just sat there. That's all. Sat stock still, just like that. Time did not lose its temper with him. It left him alone. Bento João Mussavele.

But nobody worried about him. People would pass by and see that deep down he wasn't idle. When they asked what he was doing, the answer would always be the same:

'I'm taking a bit of fresh air.'

It must have really been very fresh when, one day, he decided to get up.

'I'm off.'

His friends thought he was going back home. That he had finally decided to work and start planting a *machamba*. The farewells began.

Some went as far as to contest him:

'But where are you going? Where you come from is full of bandits, man.'

But he did not pay them any attention. He had chosen his idea, and it was a secret. He confided it to his uncle.

'You know, uncle, there's such hunger back there in Inhambane. People are dying every day.'

And he shook his head as if commiserating. But it had nothing to do with sentiment: just respect for the dead.

'They told me something. That something is going to change my life.'

He paused, and straightened himself in his chair: 'You know what a whale is ... well I don't know how ...'

'A whale?'

'That's what I said.'

'But what's a whale got to do with it?'

'Because one appeared at Quissico. It's true.'

'But there aren't any whales; I've never seen one. And even if one did appear, how would people know what the creature was called?'

'People don't know the name. It was a journalist who started spreading this story around about it being a whale or not a whale. All we know is that it's a big fish which comes to land on the beach. It comes from the direction of the night. It opens its mouth and, boy, if you could see what it's got inside ... It's full of things. Listen, it's like a store, but not the ones you see nowadays. It's like a store from the old days. Full. I swear I'm being serious.'

Then, he gave details: people would come up to it and make their requests. Each one depending on what he needed, exactly so. All you had to do was ask, just like that. No formal requisitions or production of travel papers. The creature would open its mouth and out would come peanuts, meat, olive oil. Salt cod, too.

'Can you just imagine it? All a bloke would need is a van, he'd load the things, fill it up, drive it here to the city. Go back again. Just think of the money he'd make.'

His uncle laughed long and loud. It seemed like a joke.

'It's all pie in the sky. There is no whale. Do you know how the story began?'

He made no reply. It was a wasted conversation, but he kept up the good-mannered pretence of listening, and his uncle continued:

'It's those folk there who are hungry. Very hungry. They start inventing these apparitions, as if they were wizardry. But they're just figments of the imagination, mirages ...'

'Whales,' corrected Bento.

He was unmoved. This doubting wasn't enough to make him give up. He would go around asking, he would find a way of getting together some money. And he set about doing just that.

He spent the whole day wandering up and down the streets. He spoke to Aunt Justina who has a stall in the market and with Marito, who has a van for hire. Both were sceptical. Let him go to Quissico first and bring back some proof of the whale's existence. Let him bring back some goods, preferably some bottles of that water from Lisbon and then they might give him a hand.

Then one day he decided to seek better advice. He would ask the local wise men, that white, Senhor Almeida, and the black who went by the name of Agostinho. He began by consulting the black. He gave a brief outline of the matter in question.

'In the first place,' replied Agostinho, who was a schoolmaster, 'the whale is not what it seems at first sight. Whales are prone to deceive.'

He felt a lump in his throat, as his hopes began to crumble.

'I've already been told that, Senhor Agostinho. But I believe in the whale; I have to believe in it.'

'That's not what I meant, my friend. I was trying to explain that the whale appears to be that which it isn't. It looks like a fish but it isn't one. It's a mammal. Just like you and me. For we are mammals.'

'So we are like the whale? Is that what you're saying?'

The schoolmaster spoke for half an hour. He made a great show of his Portuguese. Bento stood with his eyes wide open, avidly taking in the quasi-translation. But if the zoological explanation was detailed, the conversation did not satisfy

Bento's intentions.

He tried the white man's house. He walked down the avenues lined with acacias. On the pavements, children played with the stamens of acacia flowers. Just look at it, everybody mixed together, white children and black. In the old days ...

When he knocked at the wire mesh door of Almeida's residence, a houseboy peeped through suspiciously. With a grimace he overcame the bright light outside, and when he saw the colour of the visitor's skin, he decided to keep the door closed.

'I'm asking to speak to Senhor Almeida. He already knows me.'

The conversation was brief, Almeida answered neither one way nor the other. He said the world was going crazy, that the earth's axis was more and more inclined and that the poles were becoming flatter, or flatulent, he didn't quite understand.

But that vague discourse gave him hope. It was almost like a confirmation. When he left, Bento was euphoric. He could see whales stretched out in rows as far as the eye could see, dozing on the beaches of Quissico. Hundreds of them, all loaded and he reviewing them from an MLJ station-wagon.

With the little money he had saved he bought a ticket and left. Signs of war could be seen all along the road. The charred remains of buses coupled with the wretchedness of the *machambas* punished by drought.

'Now is it only the sun that rains?'

The petrol fumes produced by the bus in which he was travelling seeped in among the passengers, who complained, but Bento Mussavele was miles away, already visualising the coast of Quissico. When he arrived, it all seemed familiar to him. The bay was fed by the waters from the lagoons of Massava and Maiene. That blue which melted away before one's eyes was beautiful. In the background, beyond the lagoons, there was land again, a brown strip which held the fury of the ocean in check. The persistence of the waves was gradually creating cracks in that rampart, embellishing it with tall islands which looked like mountains emerging from the blue in order to breathe. The whale would probably turn up over there, mingling with the grey of the sky at the end of the day.

He climbed down the ravine, his little satchel over his shoulder, until he reached the abandoned beach houses. In times gone by, these houses had accommodated tourists. Not even the Portuguese used to go there. Only South Africans. Now, all was deserted and only he, Bento Mussavele, ruled over that unreal landscape. He settled in an old house, installing himself among the remains of furniture and the ghosts of a recent age. There he remained without being aware of the comings and goings of life. When the tide came in, no matter what the hour, Bento would walk down to the surf and stay there staring into the gloom. Sucking on an old unlit pipe, he brooded:

'It must come. I know it must come.'

Weeks later, his friends came to visit him. They risked the journey on one of Oliveira's buses; each bend in the road was a fright to ambush the heart. They arrived at the house after descending the slope. There was Bento slumbering amid aluminium camping dishes and wooden boxes. A tatty old mattress lay decomposing on a straw mat. Waking with a start, Bento greeted his friends without any great enthusiasm. He confessed to having developed a certain fondness for the house. After the whale, he would get some furniture, of the type that can be stood up against the wall. But his most ambitious plans were reserved for the carpets. Anything that was floor, or looked like it, would be carpeted. Even the immediate vicinity of the house too, because sand is annoying and seems to move together with one's feet. And there would be a special carpet which would extend along the sands, joining the house to the place where the self-same whale would disgorge.

Finally, one of his friends let the cat out of the bag.

'You know, Bento, back in Maputo it's being rumoured you're a reactionary. You're here like this because of this business of arms, or whatever they're called.'

'Arms?'

'Yes,' another visitor chipped in helpfully. 'You know that South Africa is supplying the bandits. They receive arms which come by way of the sea. That's why they're talking a lot about you.'

He began to fret. 'Hey, boys, I can't sit still any more. I don't know who's receiving these arms,' he kept repeating. 'I'm waiting for the whale, that's all.'

They argued. Bento remained in the forefront of the discussion. Who could be certain that the whale didn't come from the socialist countries? Even the schoolmaster, Senhor Agostinho, whom they all knew, had said that all he needed now was to see pigs fly.

'Hold it there. Now you're starting on a story about pigs before anyone's even seen the stupid whale.'

Among the visitors there was one who belonged to the cadres and who said there was an explanation. That the whale and the pigs ...

'Wait, the pigs have nothing to do with ...'

'Okay, leave the pigs out of it, but the whale is an invention of the imperialists to stultify the people and make them always wait for food to arrive from abroad.'

'But are the imperialists making up this story of the whale?'

'They invented it, yes. This rumour ...'

'But who gave eyes to the people who saw it? Was it the imperialists?'

'Okay, Bento, you can stay, but we're going now.'

And his friends left, convinced that there was sorcery at work there. Somebody had given Bento medicine to make him get lost in the sands of that idiotic expectation.

One night, with the sea roaring in endless anger, Bento

awoke with a start. He was trembling as if suffering a bout of malaria. He felt his legs: they were burning. But there was some sign in the wind, some sense of foreboding emanating from the darkness, which obliged him to get up and go outside. Was it a promise? Or was it disaster? He went over to the door. The sand had come away from its resting place and seemed like a maddened whip. Suddenly, underneath the little whirlwind of sand, he saw the carpet, the same carpet he had laid in his dream. If it were true, if the carpet were there, then the whale had arrived. He tried to adjust his eyes as if to discharge his emotion, but giddiness overturned his vision, and his hands sought the doorpost for support. He set off through the sand, stark naked, tiny as a seagull with broken wings. He could not hear his own voice, he did not know whether it was he who was shouting. The voice came nearer and nearer. It exploded inside his head. Now he began to wade into the sea. He felt it cold, burning his tense nerves. Further ahead of him there was a dark patch which came and went like the throbbing heart of a hangover. It could only be that elusive whale.

As soon as he had unloaded the first items of merchandise, he would give himself something to eat because hunger had been vying for his body for a long time now. Only afterwards would he see to the rest, making use of the old crates in the house.

He thought about the work that remained to be done as he advanced through the water, which now came up to his waist. He felt lighthearted, as if anguish had drained his soul. A second voice addressed him, biting his last remaining senses. There is no whale, these waters are going to be your tomb, and punish you for the dream you nourished. But to die just like that for nothing? No, the creature was there, he could hear it breathing, that deep rumble was no longer the storm, but the whale calling for him. He was aware that he could hardly feel anything any more, just the coldness of the water lapping at his chest. What invention was this? Didn't I tell you that you needed to have faith, more faith than doubt?

The only inhabitant of the storm, Bento João Mussavele waded on into the sea, and into his dream.

When the storm had blown itself out, the blue waters of the lagoon subsided once again into the timeless tranquillity of before. The sands took their proper place once more. In an old abandoned house remained Bento João Mussavele's untidy heap of clothes, still warm from the heat of his final fever. Next to them was a satchel containing the relics of a dream. There were those who claimed that those clothes and that satchel were proof of the presence of an enemy who was responsible for receiving arms. And that these arms were probably transported by submarines which, in the tales passed on by word of mouth, had been converted into the whales of Quissico.

How old Jossias was saved from the waters

1. Recollection of the olden days

The earth was conversing with August and old Jossias stood still and listened. The months are all in one another's belly, he thought. And he pictured the arrival of the days, their different clothes and colours. He knew that rain was bound to come soon, he anticipated the drops playing the *marimba* on the sand.

'The water is going to go and read the ground. It's going to lick the wounds of the earth, like some stray dog,' the old man would say.

And he fell back into silence, his eyes raised to measure the clouds as a precaution.

'It looks as if it's just half the rain. It will surely fit comfortably on the land.'

While he made these prophecies, his eyes softened with promises, a procession of green taking charge of his dreams.

'The corn will call me "sir".'

And he already imagined himself a powerful man, grinning in foreglimpsed delight at his future abundance. He was assailed by the memory of the great famine of twenty years before. He began his surrender to sleep, now that his thoughts had lain down in the shadow of that recollection.

He remembered it clearly: the rain-making rituals were carried out in the headman's house. The prayers were words with no beyond: not one drop had been persuaded to fall. For three years the elders had persisted, conversing with the dead who control the rain's pleasure.

Early that morning they had killed the ox. The women had prepared the *ngovo*, or corn liquor.

In the cemetery the elders asked the dead permission for it to rain. After prayers they would give the dead some drink by pouring liquor onto the graves.

'*I'll be the one to carry the pots of* ngovo,' Jossias offered.

They gave him the proud privilege of that delivery. Respectfully, he set out over the baking sand of the tracks. On the way, he took pity on his tired arms and stopped. The pots were heavy. The heat and thirst whispered bad advice to him, bewildering him with invitations.

He drank, closing his eyes to the voice of the liquor. He came back for more three times over. Predictably, the alcohol began to befog his reason. The pots smiled at him, warm and plump. '*They look like Armanda when she dances in that inviting way only she knows how,*' he murmured.

'*You? You are stirring up my blood!*'

He spoke slowly, rolling his words without his head entering that thought. Armanda's voice warned him of the punishment, restoring his sense of judgement. And he once again addressed the pots.

'*Girls, you are ruining my life. Provoking me like this? You'd better fasten your capulanas again. I must finish the task I was told to do.*'

He tried to get up but was too heavy. He drank only half: the rest he spilled down his chest. When he stopped to look, the liquor had all but disappeared. There was a mere trace left at the bottom of the pots. He fell into a panic: how would he explain it to the elders? How would he tell the village that the *ngovo* had deviated from its purpose? He had to find a way of muzzling his mouth, of sealing off the trouble it had uncorked.

He came upon an abandoned well and climbed down into the darkness. At the bottom there was a trace of stagnant water, awaiting his ingenuity. If he added the foul-smelling water to the corn beverage, the clay pots would once again be full. The dead would not notice the difference, for their palate has forgotten the tastier vices.

Like the miners, he thought, as he let himself down the walls of the old well. He was hanging on by his hands, his feet feeling for the bottom when, suddenly, the walls collapsed. They fell, and it was as if the entire sky were dissolving into sand and dust, and the weight of the world were compressing his chest. *'Mother, I shall stay here underneath the bottom of everything, no one will ever find me,'* sobbed Jossias.

And there he lay quite still, buried, sleeping in the suburbs of death, expelled from the light and the fresh air. Hours of time passed and he thought of the never more. The memory of Armanda came to his succour. He clung to the freshness of the recollection; that face was his ultimate faith.

And the others when they came looking for him? Would they guess him to be underground, burrowing the last dregs of his life away like a mole? Would they have the patience to peel the earth until they found him?

But even his hope no longer had a will to it. To be rescued, what for? Drinking sand, sinking in a well, bidding farewell to the world, all that was nothing compared to what would follow. None of them would excuse him for what he had done. Not even Armanda.

When he got out he would have to choose remoteness, to live in the far distance, to grow old without either name or history.

2. All the blue of the floods

What is this? Has God abandoned mankind? Doesn't he care about the earth's misfortune?

So much rain had fallen that even the wells were beginning to spit. Even toads and snakes had lost their homes. And the old man asked:

'Hardship, why don't you take a rest? When afterwards has passed you can come back again ...'

But the way of death is ever full of woes. And it rained even more, the November afternoons got wetter, the pestle and the sleeping mat dripped water together in the yard.

The old man was sitting in the shadow of his groans, only his sighs dreamt. For the rest, it was resignation which conspired to rule him. Is it possible to die so much because of this?

But he had learnt to soak his soul in the balm of the bound-to-be. And he consoled himself:

'Mealie flour is bound to visit me, I know it.'

Gradually, rain water covered the whole area. The rivers clung strongly to the sky and no amount of witchcraft was able to get rid of that water. Maybe the sun, with its last residue of heat, would take away all that blue. But no, the sun slid down the zinc, without drinking almost anything. It passed overhead as diffidently as a stranger.

'The sun's mouth isn't big enough any more,' the old man lamented.

3. The rescue

The water was rising, objects and creatures just had to swim for it. When everything round about was joined to the water like steam, there appeared a motor boat bringing two blacks and a white. It was the white who spoke. What he said was to do with things he had never heard before. What were these words about, after all? Before, they had always been stupid remarks directed at his name, the language of the Portuguese firing insults at his family. Now was this language not like that of the bosses?

'*It must be a ploy to take me away from the* machamba, *to separate me from my things.*'

Or maybe it wasn't like that. The men wanted him to climb into the boat, they had come to save him.

The old man scratched his head, moving his hand from back to front.

'*Go where, if beyond the water all there is is water? Don't you see God wants us turned into fish?*'

The blacks, from behind the white, repeated the same warning, those who didn't leave in the boat would die, that was for sure. The old man smiled, incredulous:

'*Save me, you say? Save me from what?*'

And the old man remembered the accident in the mines of John, fire spreading havoc through the galleries, devouring lives and bodies; yes, that was real dying. When the rescue workers arrived, he sat down like a lost child and cried. But the rescuers did not stop to help him, instead they went on, searching for other, more valuable lives. Another miner pulled him by the arms and shouted to him:

'*Do you want to be firewood, man?*'

Firewood? Wood is firewood even before it burns. To be firewood, he realised, is to die all alone like that, without anyone to weep for us. His number would merely be crossed off the list of contract workers. But smoke entered him by way of sadness and his lungs bade him seek other pastures. If a man saves himself, it is because it is his life's desire. Others are only the fuel of that desire.

And that was how he had remained alive to this day.

They rescued Jossias twice. They saved him from death, but they did not save him from life. For the others, for those who had helped him, there were rewards, their photos appeared in the newspaper. Nobody mentioned that he, Jossias Damião Jossene, continued the same as before, up alongside the bread-line.

'Saving someone should be a complete service,' he had concluded. 'It's no good lifting someone up and then abandoning them without wanting to know the afterwards of it all. It's not enough to be alive. Take my word for it, living is more than that.'

And so that is how Jossias had come to a conclusion on the matter of dying and not dying.

Now in this particular case, what was the point of moving, and where? Beyond, there is only more water, the place this boat came from is water too. It's not even a boat any more, but an island with a motor. If I have to die then I prefer that death which comes swimming right up to the door of my house. The earth under here already has my hands, my life is buried in this ground, all it needs now is my body, that's all.

The rescue team began to get impatient with the old man's ranting. 'What does the fellow want?' asked the white. The others didn't bother to translate, but just laughed. The old man's mad, let's use force to bring him aboard. We haven't got time, there are others to pick up, the old man's out of his mind.

'Let me stay, I can't die far from my life.'

They pulled him along by his armpits, sat him in the rear of the boat and covered him with a blanket.

'Haven't you got a family?'

It was the white who spoke. Family? Maybe you people are my family now, you had to put up with the trouble of rescuing me. He felt like answering but he was trembling too much.

'Ask him in your language if his family isn't somewhere round here in the vicinity.'

They asked him. He took his time in answering, for he wanted to speak good Portuguese. He gripped the old blanket tightly and turned his eyes towards the sea which lay around them, as if trying to discover the things that it covered.

'It's not cold in the water. Why don't you leave me there?'

The others laughed. They placed another blanket round his shoulders and gave him a cup of hot tea. Through his skinny fingers which shakily clasped the aluminium cup, there rose a strange warmth which he was unable to explain. And he began to feel like staying in that boat for good. He wished that his journey would have no end, as if they were saving him from time rather than the waters, as if they had freed him not from death but from his terrible and solitary waiting.

With the eyes of a child, he stared at the darkness swallowing up the land, the evening covering everything with night.

The illusion of night is that it kills the weariness of men, he thought as he closed his eyes.

THE TALE OF THE TWO WHO
RETURNED FROM THE DEAD

It is a truth: the dead ought not to return, to cross the frontier
of their world. They only come and disturb our sadness. We
already know for sure: so and so has gone. We comfort widows,
shed all our tears.

On the other hand, there are those dead who, having died,
persist in coming back. This is what happened in that village
which the waters had wrenched from the earth. The floods
carried the village away, pulled up by its roots. Not even the
scar of the place remained. Many were rescued. Luís Fernando
and Aníbal Mucavel vanished. They perished beneath the
waters, swept along by the river's furious current like a pair
of fish. Their deaths had been taken for a certainty when, one
afternoon, they turned up again.

The living asked them many questions. Then, alarmed, they
called the militia. Raimundo appeared, he who carried his rifle
as if it were a hoe. He was trembling with fear, and he could
find no other words than:

'Show me your papers.'

'You're mad, Raimundo. Put that gun down.'

The militiaman gathered courage when he heard the dead
men speak. He ordered them back.

'Go back from where you came. It's no use trying anything:

you'll be thrown out.'

The conversation was not getting them anywhere. Estêvão, who was responsible for guard duties, arrived on the scene. Luís and Aníbal were allowed in so that they might explain themselves to the authorities.

'You're no longer on our list. Where are you going to live?'

The two apparitions were offended by the manner of their welcome.

'We were swept away by the river. We ended up God knows where, and now you treat us like a couple of infiltrators?'

'Wait, we'll have to speak to the director of social affairs. He is the only one who can deal with your case.'

Aníbal became even more dejected. *'So we've become a case, have we?'* A person is not a divorce, a lawsuit. Nor was it that they had a problem: they just had their whole lives to sort out.

The official arrived on the scene. He was a tubby man, his belly inquisitive, peeping out of his tunic. They were complimented with the respect due to the dead. The official explained the difficulties and the extra burden they represented as two dead people who had returned without warning.

'Look: they've sent us supplies. Clothes, blankets, sheets of zinc, a lot of things. But you two weren't included in the estimate.'

Aníbal became agitated when he heard they had been excluded:

'What do you mean not included? Do you strike people off just like that?'

'But you have died. I don't even know how you came to be here.'

'What do you mean "died"? Don't you believe we are alive?'

'Maybe, I'm not sure any more. But this business of being alive and not alive had best be discussed with the other comrades.'

So they went to the village hall. They explained their story but failed to prove their truth. A man dragged along like a fish only seeks air, he's not interested in anything else.

After some consultation the official concluded rapidly:

'It doesn't matter whether you are completely dead or not. If you're alive, it's worse still. It would have been better to take advantage of the water to die.'

The other, the one with the tunic that played tug-of-war with its own buttons, added:

'We cannot go along to the administrative cadres of the district and tell them a couple of ghosts have turned up. They'll tell us we've got ourselves mixed up in obscurantism. We could even he punished.'

'That's true,' agreed the other. *'We did a political orientation course. You are souls, you're not the material reality that I and all the others with us in the new village are.'*

The fat one added emphatically:

'To feed you, we'd have to ask for an increase in our quota. How would we justify that? By telling them we'd got two souls to feed?'

And there the conversation ended.

Luís and Aníbal left the village hall, confused and baffled. Outside, a crowd had gathered to watch them. The two apparitions decided to look for Samuel, the teacher.

Samuel welcomed them to his house. He explained why they had not been included in the ration quotas.

'The officials here aren't like the ones in other villages. They divert supplies. First they distribute them to their own families. Sometimes, they even say there isn't enough to go round when in fact, their houses are brimming full.'

'Why don't you denounce them?'

Samuel shrugged his shoulders. He blew into the embers to give the fire new strength. Red petals of flame spread the scent of light through the little room.

'Listen, I'll tell you a secret. Someone did complain to their superiors. They say that this week a commission is coming to investigate the truth of such allegations. You should take the

opportunity to explain your case to the commission.'

Samuel offered them a roof and food until the commission of inquiry arrived.

Aníbal sat his thoughts down at the rear of the house. He gazed long and hard at his feet and muttered, as if he were talking to them:

'My God, how unfair we are to our body. What part of it do we take most for granted? The feet, poor things, which drag themselves along to hold us up. It's they that bear both sadness and happiness. But as they are far from the eyes, we ignore our feet, as if they didn't belong to us.

'Just because we are above, we tread on our feet. That's how injustice begins in this world. Now in this case, those feet are myself and Luís, ignored, fallen amongst the dust of the river.'

There was less light than a shadow when Luís came over and asked him what he was muttering about. Aníbal told him about how he had discovered his feet.

'You'd do better to think of how we are going to show these folk that we are real people.'

'Do you know something? In the old days, the forest used to scare me, so empty of people. I thought I could only live with others around me. Now, it's the other way round. I want to go back to where the animals are. I miss not being anybody.'

'Do be quiet now. This is becoming like a conversation between spirits.'

The two stopped talking, fearful of their shaky condition. They began to fidget with things, to scrape their feet on the ground, as if trying to prove the substance of their bodies. Luís asked:

'Can it be true? Might it not be that we really are dead? Maybe they're right. Or perhaps we are being born again.'

'Who knows, brother? It could be any of these things. But what is not right is that you should be blamed, forgotten, struck off the list, rejected.'

It was the voice of Samuel, the teacher. He came over with some mangoes which he gave to the two candidates for life. They peeled the fruit, while the teacher continued to speak:

'It's not fair that they should forget that, whether you're alive or dead, you still belong to our village. After all, when we had to defend it against the bandits, didn't you take up arms?'

'That's true. I even got this scar from an enemy bullet. Here, look.'

Aníbal got to his feet in order to show the others proof of his suffering, a deep groove that death had carved in his back.

'Everyone knows that you deserve to be counted among the living. It's fear alone that causes them to keep quiet, to accept lies.'

Standing there like that, Aníbal clenched his fist as if to squeeze out his anger. Drops of the sweet-sad juice of the mango fell to the ground.

'Samuel, you know about life. Don't you think it would be better if we left, if we chose another place to live?'

'No, Aníbal. You must stay. You are bound to win in the end, I'm sure. After all, a man who leaves because he is beaten, no longer lives. He will find nowhere else to begin again.'

'And you, Samuel, are you one of those who doesn't believe we are alive?'

'Be quiet, Luís. Let Samuel here advise us.'

'These people who bedevil you are bound to fall. It is they who do not belong here, not you. Stay, my friends. Help us in our plight. We too are not being considered: we are alive but it is as if we had less life, it's as if we were only halves. We don't want that.'

Luís got up and peeped out into the darkness. He walked round in a circle, returning to the centre, and coming near to the teacher:

'Samuel, aren't you scared?'

'Scared? But these people must fall. Wasn't this why we

fought, to get rid of such scum?'

'*I'm not talking about that,*' replied Luis. '*Aren't you scared that they will catch us here with you?*'

'*With you? But do you really exist? Surely, I can't be with people who don't exist.*'

They laughed, got up and left through the two doors of the house. Aníbal, before taking his leave, said: '*Hey, Samuel! Long Live the Revolution!*'

■

Three days later, the commission arrived. It was accompanied by a journalist who had become interested in the story of Luís and Aníbal. He had promised to investigate the affair. If the matter could not be resolved, he would expose the activities of the village officials in his newspaper.

The commission met for two days. Then the villagers were summoned to a general assembly. The room was packed out with people who had come to hear the verdict. The chairman of the commission announced its solemn conclusions:

'*We have closely examined the situation of the two individuals who arrived in the village, and have reached the following formal decision, namely that comrades Luís Fernando and Aníbal Mucavel should be deemed members of the population in existence.*'

Applause. The meeting seemed more relieved than happy. The speaker continued:

'*But the two apparitions would be well advised not to leave the village, or life, or anywhere else again. We have shown clemency this time, but will not tolerate this behaviour next time.*'

The meeting now applauded with real conviction.

Next day, Luís Fernando and Aníbal Mucavel began to see to the question of the documents that would prove they were alive.

THE GIRL WITH A TWISTED FUTURE

Joseldo Bastante, the village mechanic, used his ears to seek an answer to his life's problems. When a traveller passed by, when a car stopped, he would come near and capture conversations. It was in this way that he managed to hear of some prospects for his eldest daughter, Filomeninha. For one whole week, news kept coming from the city of a young man who was achieving great success twisting and turning his body like a snake. The lad had been engaged by an impresario to show off his skill at turning his rear into his front. He roamed the country and everyone ran to see him. And so the young man earned enough money to fill boxes, suitcases and cooking pots. All this thanks to his being able to fold and rotate his spine along with his nether regions. The contortionist was mentioned time and time again by lorry drivers and each one added a twist to the elastic talents of the boy. They even went as far as to tell how, in one show, he had tied himself up with his own body, as if it were a strap. The impresario had had to help untie the knot; if he hadn't, then the lad would have been belted up to this day.

Joseldo thought about his life, his twelve children. Where would he find a future to share among them? Twelve futures, where? And so he took the decision: Filomeninha would be a contortionist, displayed and advertised along the highways and byways of afar. He ordered his daughter:

'*From this moment on, you're going to practise bending yourself, to get your head as far as the floor and vice versa.*'

The girl began her gymnastics. She progressed too slowly for her father. In order to hasten his preparations, Joseldo Bastante brought from the workshop one of those enormous petrol drums. At night he would tie his daughter to the drum so that her back and the curve of the recipient would cling to each other like a courting couple. In the morning, he would pour hot water over her before she had woken up properly:

'*This water is for your bones to become soft, flexible.*' When they unbound her, the girl was bent over backwards, her blood flow irregular and her bones disjointed. She complained of pains and suffered from dizziness.

'*You can't wish for riches without sacrifices,*' was her father's reaction.

Filomeninha was crumpling up for all to see. She looked like a hook without any more use, an abandoned rag.

'*Father, I can feel a lot of pain inside me. Let me sleep on the mat.*'

'*No, little daughter. When you are rich you will surely sleep even on a mattress. Here at home we shall all lie in comfort, each one on his own mattress. You'll see, we'll only wake up in the evening after the bats have stirred.*'

Time passed, and Joseldo was still waiting for the impresario to pass through the town. At the garage, his ears were like antennae listening for news of the showman. In the newspapers, his eyes hunted for clues as to the whereabouts of his saviour. In vain. The impresario was amassing riches in some unknown location.

Meanwhile, Filomeninha was getting worse. She was almost unable to walk. She began to suffer from bouts of vomiting. She seemed to want to cast her body out through her mouth. Her father warned her not to succumb to such weaknesses:

'If the impresario turns up he mustn't find you in this state. You're supposed to be a contortionist and not a vomitist.'

The weeks went by, heightened by Joseldo Bastante's anguish. In such a small place, what happens is whatever passes through. An event is never native. It always comes from outside, it shakes souls, inflames time and then beats a retreat. It goes away so quickly that it doesn't even leave embers with which the residents might rekindle the fire if they so wished. The world possesses places where its timeless rotation stops and rests. This was such a place.

Time went filling up with nothingness until one evening Joseldo heard from a lorry driver news of the appearance of his lucky star: the impresario was in the city preparing a show.

The mechanic left his work and rushed home. He told his wife:

'Make Filomeninha put on a new dress!'

His wife replied, puzzled:

'But the girl hasn't got a new dress.'

'I'm thinking of your new dress. Yours, woman.'

They stood the girl on her feet and clothed her in her mother's dress. It was big and long, and it was obvious that their sizes were not the same.

'Take off your scarf. Artists don't cover their heads. Wife, put her hair in plaits while I go and get the money for the train fare.'

'Where are you going to get the money from?'

'That's none of your business.'

'Joseldo?'

'Don't keep on at me, woman.'

∎

Some hours later they left for the city. On the train, the mechanic gloated over his thoughts: a fruit is not harvested in a hurry. It takes its time, between passing from sour-green to ripe-sweet. If he had looked for an answer, as others wanted, he would have lost this opportunity. To those in a hurry he replied proudly: to wait for is not the same as to sit around waiting.

Lulled by the rhythm of the carriages, Joseldo Bastante continued to surrender his little daughter to the fate of the stars, the fortune of those who are immortal. He looked at the girl and saw that she was trembling. He asked her the matter. Filomeninha complained of the cold.

'What cold? With all this heat, where's the cold?'

And he searched for the cold as if temperature had a body which might come and touch him in the twinkle of an eye.

'Don't worry, little girl. When we get some smoke in here, it will get warmer.'

But the girl's shivers became ever more extreme, until they were even stronger than the rocking of the train. Nor did the oversize dress hide her shuddering. Her father took off his coat and placed it around Filomeninha's shoulders.

'Now try and stop trembling or you'll make my coat burst its stitches.'

They arrived in the city and began to look for the impresario's office. They walked down endless streets.

'Hell, daughter, so many street corners! And all the same.'

The mechanic dragged his daughter along, stumbling into her.

'Filomeninha, stand up straight. They'll surely think I'm taking you to the hospital.'

Finally, they came across the house. They went in and were told to wait in a small room. Filomeninha fell asleep in her chair, while her father entertained himself with dreams of wealth.

The impresario received them only at the end of the day. He did not beat about the bush.

'I'm not interested.'

'But, sir ...'

'There's no point in wasting my time. I don't want it. Contortionism is out, it's no longer a sensation.'

'It isn't? Just look at what my daughter can do with her head ...'

'I've already told you, I'm not interested. This girl is sick, that's what she is.'

'This girl's what? This girl's got an iron constitution, or rather a rubber one. She's just tired from the journey, that's all.'

'The only thing I'm interested in now are guys with steel teeth. Those sets of teeth you people sometimes have, strong enough to gnaw wood and chew nails.'

Joseldo smiled humbly and said he was sorry that he couldn't be of service: 'I'm a mechanic, that's all. I use my hands to fiddle about with screws, not my teeth.'

They left. The impresario remained sitting in his big chair, amused by that girl, so skinny inside her borrowed dress.

On the way back, Joseldo bemoaned his fate. Teeth, now it's teeth they want! Beside him, Filomeninha dragged herself along, shuffling her steps. They boarded the train and waited for it to pull out. Her father gradually became calmer. He appeared to be watching the bustle of the station, but his gaze did not reach beyond the murky glass of the window. Suddenly, his face lit up. Taking his daughter by the hand, he asked, without looking at her:

'It's true, Filomeninha: you have strong teeth! Isn't that what your mother says?'

And as he didn't get an answer, he shook the child's arm. It was then that Filomeninha's body fell, twisted and weightless, onto her father's lap.

PATANHOCA, THE LOVESICK SNAKE CATCHER

Patanhoca it was who killed the Chinawoman Mississe, owner of the store in Muchatazina. Now as to the reason why he killed her, I can't tell you that. People talk a lot, each one according to his whim. When I asked, they gave me an answer. So I'm going to tell you the story. Or rather, pieces of the story. Torn pieces like our lives. We can join the bits but never complete the picture.

Some say it was nobody who killed her. She died just like that, from inside her body, on account of her blood. Others got as far as to see the wounds through which the poison entered the dead woman.

I don't want to present the truth, for I never knew it. If I invent, then it's life that's to blame. After all, the truth is no more than the mulatto daughter of a dishonest question.

I'll start with Mississe.

1. The widow of distances

Mississe was a widow, a Chinese one, a woman of secrets and mysteries. Her shop was situated at the point where the roads end and all that is left are the unpaved tracks of the poor. There was no set time for opening and closing: her mood dictated this. It was she who decided what time of day it was.

Happiness stepped out of her life and forgot to return. Sadness was a closed padlock on Missise. They even said it was Chinese bewitchment and that her far-off homeland, travelling in clouds of vapour, was tormenting her soul.

Nobody knew how she had come there, how she had abandoned her people. And China, as everyone knows, is a distance away. The journey is such slowness that a man has time to change colour. Her neighbours and customers wondered to themselves about her dead husband. And at night, whom did Missise share the cold with? Who was it who snuffed out her darkness?

When she had arrived in Muchatazina, she was still young. Pretty, say those who knew her then. The Portuguese came to visit her beauty on the sly. They failed to enter her favour, remained substitutes of nobody. The widow wrapped herself in a cloak of sourness, becoming ever more widowed. The Portuguese, rich ones even, would come out of there with heads bowed. They would pause in the garden, taking advantage of the shade of the many cashew trees. To distract their frustration they would tear the fruit from the branches. The cashew is the blood of the sun suspended, its fiery sweetness the juice we drink. Then they would walk away, venting their threats.

On Saturdays the widow would indulge herself in bazookas, large bottles of beer, first one, then another, and then more and more. She would finish when the beer had wetted all her blood.

The store gave off brightness, the generator chugging away to push out that light. Fumes and mysteries would seep from the window, the Chinawoman's incense drugging the moons. It was at such times that the pain of this woman could be heard. Screams echoed in the corridors, her voice spiralled down a dark well. One night they distinguished words in her wailing: *'My children! Give me back my children, murderer!'*

So there were children after all? How could that be if no one knew of them? The neighbours listened in astonishment to her lament. The widow groaned, screamed, howled. They tried to go to her assistance, to wipe away her furies, but no one could get near. Shadow was ever present. Death was the only garden round her house, enclosing her widow's despair.

2. Patanhoca, the snake mechanic

Patanhoca was a sad figure, robbed of life's good fortune. Something had torn his lips away, leaving his mouth with no above and no below. His teeth never unclenched. His mouth, because of the way it never blinked, was like a hyena's envy. Can a living creature keep his whole soul behind his teeth? Certainly this was Patanhoca's punishment. It was said he was the devil who had come to Muchatazina. This was a lie. Who said what the devil's face looked like? Is it ugly? On the contrary, the devil is as beautiful as can be, so as to deceive us into choosing backwards. A man like that is not tempted by women: he loves snakes, crawling animals and things which don't demand beauty. The snake catcher had taught himself to be a bachelor.

Morning, evening and other times too, Patanhoca would shut himself away with his snakes. A snake mechanic, he would scrape the rust off their scales, and nurture their poisons. His was the art of those who have lost the skill of living, the devil's lore. It wasn't even worth looking for the truth behind his life's condition. Did Patanhoca really know the secret of snakes? The answer has no document or testimony. But the doubters, if in fact there were any, were never heard.

When the evenings began to disperse the daylight, that was when he would go out, when darkness cradled the oil lamp. The paths were already pitch black but Patanhoca would set his steps in the direction of the store.

When he arrived at his destination he put out the lamp and began the task of spreading his sorcery. His perch was there in her yard, he, an owl drawn towards the lights of Mississe. What was Patanhoca's motive for always spending the night there? Were his lingerings just distraction? There was a reason, and that was love.

Shame manacled the snake catcher's passions. Looking was the only reward reaped from the shadows and the silences. To reveal the heart without showing the body, to dispense help and kindnesses: that is what João Patanhoca had decided to do in the secrecy of his life. Isn't a widow more alone than anyone else? Where is the arm to defend her?

That arm was Patanhoca. His powers kept thieves away from the store. Every night, so they say, he would set his snakes free around the house. So many of these snakes were there that the sand was poisoned under the blanket of night. You didn't need to be bitten. It was enough for somebody to step into the yard. In the morning, no one could enter or leave before the snake owner's prayers had given the go-ahead. His words swept the yard clean and abolished the frontier. All this, all this guard work, Patanhoca did without asking for anything in return. He would rivet his eyes on the widow, but they were no longer eyes. They were the servants of Chinese whimsies.

3. First night: the invitation

Then one night the widow opened the door. Was she naked? Or was it a play of light which eliminated her clothes? She waved to him. Patanhoca stayed where he was without revealing himself. Then she beckoned him. Her voice was a mother's:

'Come out of the dark, come in!'

He did not move, guardian of fears, unschooled in matters of happiness. He had never had any. She called him again, this time more hoarsely. She went down the steps, and pushed forward into the darkness. She tasted the smell of the mixtures and potions spreading their terror. She had never set eyes on such a smell before.

'*Get back inside Mississe!*'

This was Patanhoca's order. It was the first time he had spoken. The words came out spitting and scraping, without the shape lips could provide. The crickets fell silent, the night air stifled. The widow pretended she hadn't heard and went on without turning. Again Patanhoca shouted his warning:

'*Be careful! Snakes!*'

Then she stopped. He came nearer, keeping to the dark side. He held out a little cloth pouch:

'*Warm up this tea: it's your medicine.*'

'*No, I don't need it.*'

'*What do you mean you don't need it?*'

'*All I want is for you to come and stay here.*'

'*Stay where?*'

'*To live here, together with me. Stay, João.*'

He shuddered: João? His eyes closed, pained: can a word, such a trifle, do so much harm to a man?

'*Don't say that name again, Mississe.*'

She advanced further, wanting ever more strongly to lean against his shadow.

'*João? It's your name. Why can't I say it?*'

Silence gave the crickets their leave. Men and animals speak in turn, such is the law of nature.

Can a man weep? Yes, if you awaken the child he has inside him. Patanhoca wept, but he couldn't shed tears, for he had no lips.

'*Why don't you come back again?*'

'*I'm Patanhoca, snake catcher. It's not just a name I was given. I've got a snout, not the face of a person.*'

'*No, you're João. You're my João.*'

He explained his sorrows, said his life was shattered and that when you want to pick up the pieces, it's always too late. The Chinawoman wearied of his lament:

'Then let me out. Release me from this nightly prison, these terrors, these snakes encircling my life.'

In his fury he threw the little pouch to the ground and moved away from the circle of light to which he had brought his sadness.

4. Second night: the revelation

The next night, Patanhoca returned earlier. She was already seated on the steps, like a queen, smothered in perfumes. Her bangles robbed her of age, and made her skin glow. Patanhoca forgot to cover his shame in the darkness, and approached the woman from the back. He called her but she didn't flinch.

'Mississe?'

The widow looked up and he shuddered. There before him were her twenty years, there was the prize sought by all the hunters of desires.

'Mississe, you're chancing your luck. The snakes will bite you.'

She moved up one step and invited him:

'Sit here, João. Let's talk.'

Back he stepped.

'No. Speak from there, I'm listening.'

'João, come nearer. I promise I shan't look at you. I'll speak to your back.'

He accepted. He remained coiled in his body.

'Well then?'

'There is no other man, nor will there be. Just you, you alone.'

'Why did you ruin my life, Mississe?'

'Let's not talk about that problem, please.'

'We must talk.'

She paused. The memory pained her, and it wasn't saliva she felt in her mouth any more – it was blood pushing out her words.

'You killed them, João.'

'That's a lie, it was the snakes.'

Her nerves started to play on her, and her mouth stumbled in anger:

'And who brought the snakes? Wasn't it you? I warned you, I begged you so many times: take them away from here, make them vanish into thin air. But you always answered that you were an artist. An artist of what?'

'I was, I am. It was just on that night I was drunk. My secrets fled me, that's what happened.'

She cried, didn't even hide her face. The moon wreathed her tears. Pearls were born. The warmth of the real ones faded with envy. Clumsily, he tried to put right past insults.

'And who were they? Children without any future. Mulatto-Chinese, a race without a race. People make children in order to better them ...'

'Be quiet, Patanhoca!'

She raised both her body and her voice, the two suddenly mingled in one. She ran inside and slammed the door, sobbing.

Patanhoca, standing, his hands together on his chest, apologised without effect. Mississe's accusing voice reached him:

'Everyone thinks you're good, but that's not true. They think you help me, with your snakes all around my night. I know, only I know the snakes are to hem me in. You want to imprison me forever, so that I won't run off with other men.'

He retreated slowly, hurting himself on her words. But that pain was almost good to feel and, from time to time, he dwelt on what she said.

'You are evil, Patanhoca. It wasn't you who chose the snakes, but they who chose you.'

He gave up and moved away, his soul reeling within. Jealousy of others, jealousy of the living, that was his wickedness. The others, whether they were handsome or ugly, could trade with each other by day. Only he didn't have the right currency. The others smoked, kissed, whistled, had a right to be greeted and bidden good day. Only he had nobody to grow tired of. That Chinawoman Mississe had stolen the fire which we can kindle in others.

5. Third night: the counsel of sleep

It was night, the last but one, and Patanhoca was still in his house. He lay on his mat ordering his thoughts:

'It's true. I killed those two little children, but I didn't mean to. That night, drink confused my hands. I swapped the medicines round. But that Chinawoman got her own back on me.'

And he closed his eyes as if that crippling memory hurt him, she giving vent to her furies upon his head, smashing the bottle, cramming his flesh with glass. Blood and beer flowed in one and the same froth, her screams passed out on the ground where he was made night. Everybody thought he had died. Even she did, she who had left him, his wounds and his glass, to the night mist. She moved to a suburb of the city and opened her business.

He had crawled through the darkness, hands and voices protecting his thread of life and leading him along paths that he alone knew. He tried to forget the Chinawoman but he couldn't. He launched the boat of his life in other waters: the same current took hold of it.

He decided to move to her area, he trapped himself as if the hunter of his own destiny. He found her and saw that he had not yet been replaced. Mississe showed her suitors the street, even those who were rich and powerful. Could it be that she was waiting for him?

Fear and shame inhibited him from revealing himself. He appeared through his snakes, sent to dispel the threat of thieves. Whether she took her time to understand, Patanhoca never found out. She did not display any change, but continued, a widow without expectations. Did her calmness belie her?

Such were the questions the snake catcher of Muchatazina, João Patanhoca, pondered on, as he laid his tiredness to rest. He fell asleep awaiting the counsel of dreams. He listened with attention to his visions. They told him the following: she had repented, forgiven him. He would be taken back, once again João, once again a name and a face. Once again loved.

6. The last night

Mississe had once more caused his heart to rejoice. She stood there in the cascade of light, extinguishing the stars. She alone glowed, her white blouse and skirt, her tousled hair dripping onto her shoulders. Patanhoca overflowed from his body: then it was true what the dream had said! She was prettifying herself to celebrate his return.

'Tonight, João, let's have fun.'

He made no reply, he was afraid he might snarl and shame the João she was calling. With a movement of the head, she beckoned him towards the corridor:

'Come in, João, let's drink.'

He climbed up the stone steps, shook the dust off his feet at the entrance, walked across the carpets, excusing himself at every turn. On a cupboard in the living room, a large photograph of their happiness was exhibited, a picture of them both and their two children commemorating life together.

He seated himself awkwardly. She served the glasses. It wasn't beer, but one of those wines that make you feel dizzy before you even drink it. He unravelled memories, sweet trifles flowed between them, from one glass to another. He began to lose his inhibitions and drink dribbled shamelessly down his chin.

'*I'm going to stop drinking, Mississe. I'm seeing the world go by at high speed.*'

She wore a strange smile, which was too placid.

'*No, João. Drink your fill. I want you to drink. Afterwards, I have a request.*' An adversary of empty glasses, she filled another one. João was puzzled by the request, worried by that afterwards she promised. Hopes and fears crossed within him and he said what he didn't want, ever wanting what he did not say.

'*Mississe, it wasn't the medicines that I swapped round. It was myself I swapped. Now, am I João or Patanhoca?*'

She took his hands, made them one and spoke:

'*João, please, listen: go to your house and bring me that medicine you know about. I want to take it tonight.*'

So this was the request? Or maybe it was a trap, hopes tricking him.

'*I can't woman. I'm pissed; I have no legs to find my way with.*'

'*Go, João. You know the way with your eyes closed.*'

He looked around him: the linen tablecloth, the photograph, things from times that had fled them, they were there, silent witnesses to their disjoined lives. Mississe persisted. She got up and leaned her hot flavoured body against him, placing her hands on Patanhoca's sweating back. He felt uneasy, unable to take any more.

He got up abruptly, turned towards the corridor and went. He found it difficult to keep to the line of his route. At the end, almost repentant, he turned round:

'*But listen here: what medicine is it, Mississe? The snake vaccine?*'

She didn't answer, remained with her back to him, clearing away the plates and glasses.

'*Do you know, Missise? The only remedy, do you know what it is?*'

And he laughed, snorting loudly. She looked at him, saddened. How hard it was to look at that laugh he wore, but which didn't belong to him.

'*Missise, I'm telling you: the proper medicine is that wine we've just finished.*'

'*It's late. Hurry up João.*'

He struggled down the steps and walked off into the night. She still seemed to say something he didn't understand; he shook his head, confused. Could it be that he had heard her correctly? Going back to China, was that what she had said? I yearn for the land about to be born? Ravings of a Chinawoman, he concluded quietly.

He smiled sympathetically. The old woman must be drunk, poor thing, she even deserved it. This is what João Patanhoca thought as he stumbled along the path. He felt pity for her. After all, she was the widow of a man who was still alive, he himself. And so many years had passed since she had last taken her lace blouse from the cupboard, so many years since she had spread the white tablecloth on her table for visitors.

THE EX-FUTURE PRIEST AND HIS WOULD-BE WIDOW

Life is a web weaving a spider. Whether the creature believes himself a hunter in his own home or not, it matters little. The instant turns round and he becomes the quarry in an intruder's trap. This will be proved in the following tale which occurred in real though humble surroundings.

It concerned Benjamim. Ever since he was little, he had been a devotee of absences, he had lived parallel to heaven. Others played, celebrating the insignificant nothings of childhood. Only Benjamim withered among the Scriptures, amid saints and incense. Even his parents, who wished him sober and orderly, thought it too much.

'Go and play, Ben. Take advantage of your years.'

But Ben, unhearing, went on shedding his boyhood. His body matured into an age beyond his own. Nights filed by, bent themselves concave for the benefit of boys and girls. Only our friend's hands remained joined, stuck together, immaculate. Benjamim lived a life more lofty than the souls.

Until one day Anabela appeared, Anabelissima. She was pure candy, capable of publishing desires in the most prudish of eyes. Anabela fell for Benjamim. The poor man didn't even react to her: with a hedgehog's skill he rolled himself into an ever tighter hall. The girl sent him love notes, messages more sighed than scribbled. Anabela unwrapped herself before his eyes. But it's always like that: when there's a chance in the air there isn't the ware. And for every forward woman a timid man. Let us T our crosses. Take each case on its merits.

The whole neighbourhood, meanwhile, entertained its thousand mouths with the tale of the romantic disencounter. In a nearby bar, people commented:

'Women? The more they wiggle their hips, the more they close their heart.'

'I know what it is she wants: cash, a fat wallet. But the only good thing that's free is rain.'

'No, it's not a matter of money. After all, think of Henrique, a mulatto just like her, he was turned down when he offered her the ring.'

There was only one truth though: Anabela, coveted by all, only had eyes for Benjamim. While he, taciturn, followed his vows. He wanted to enter the Seminary, to study padreology. While he waited, his only concerns were his devotions. Ben was ever devoteful.

Anabela's attacks became more persistent. It seemed that the more difficult her catch, the more keenly she pursued it. Who knows whether desire does not feed off impossibilities? Anabela began to visit him at unhidden hours. Many saw her leaving Benjamim's house, brazen, indiscreet. The girl seemed to be inviting scandal. Even when pronouncing his name, her voice slid along: 'Benjamim: Bendyoumee?' People started murmuring. For how long would the lad hold out, the zealot fend off the zealous?

'He won't stand it. Is any man rust-proof?'

But appearances are more powerful than events. And surprise of surprises: Anabela's belly began to swell. Anabela, the self-same Anabela.

Her father, the esteemed Juvenal, then took preventive measures against his dishonour. After all, everybody knew what had happened. Juvenal was a much feared man. They awaited the consequences. A finger on the bell of Benjamim's front door announced the storm:

'Senhor Benjamim?'

'Yes? What do you want?'

'I want to know the date.'

'What date?'

'The date of the wedding.'

'Wedding?' 'Whose wedding?'

'Yours, Senhor Benjamim. The date of your marriage to my daughter Anabela.'

The cassava began to grow sour. Ben became a stranger in his own home. A citizen struggling for survival, he managed to mumble a protest. But the other continued:

'You're a seminarist? So what? I know them well: they're the worst!'

Juvenal, a father-in-law on the eve of his making, was not about to accept argument and lies: the child in the womb was beyond doubt, legitimate and unconditional. And so the man went away, leaving Benjamim on the threshold of night. His thoughts were drained of memory, speechless. When all is said and done, no sadness can be explained for it is a wound beyond the body, a pain on the far side of sentiment. And Benjamim's anguish was a flood covering everything. He imagined himself under the towel of darkness, as if life and death were symmetrical to him. All because of a mistake, his dream had been shattered. No longer was he to be a priest, his only ambition. And he would have to marry someone who only inspired anxiety in him. Deprived of earthly succour, Benjamim prayed. And he did so with such burning fervour that he wore through all his trousers at the knees. Even the ones from his wedding suit had to be sewn up.

∎

Inevitably they were married. Anabela and Benjamim, and vice versa. Along with them, their families were joined in matrimony, names and destinies crossed paths. Their lives began to mingle with each other, and they became mutual witnesses of their intimacies. Their mornings to their nights were full of misunderstanding. He, virginious, only kept his kneecaps busy, with his continual genuflexions. She ever yearning for night-long dances, and other distractivities.

And then in the end, her pregnancy was not consummated. Not that she had an abortion or miscarriage. Nothing like that. Anabela just disembellied mysteriously. Benjamim asked no questions: better to feign ignorance. And that's how it was.

Anabela meanwhile grew tired of parading her beauty without Ben exercising his masculine functions. So she decided to consult a neighbour, Bila by name, an elderly retired nurse.

'What's the matter, little neighbour?'

She replied that it was a very intimate problem, and the neighbour invited her in. Anabela, embarrassed, occupied a meagre edge of chair. She cast her eyes nervously round the room:

'I'm sorry, Senhor Bila. I haven't yet found a deaf wall ...'

The nurse smiled benevolently, reassuring the girl. Let her speak freely: his were the most trustworthy of walls. Anabela confessed the reason for her unhappiness: the half-baked Benjamim. The old man listened to her words, her tears, her sighs. At the end, he summed it all up.

'You mean, he husbanded you but doesn't exercise sovereignty.'

She approved of his conclusion but did not agree with his next judgement:

'It's something that's plain to see, Anabela. I can see that you're not a complete wife. You always look a little downcast.'

She raised her hand, trying to interrupt, but Bila went on:

'Ben surprises me, so sturdy in his body.' And then he laughed: *'He's like a sack of coal: he looks strong but can't stand up*

straight.'

'It's not what you think, Senhor. I just want you to help poor Ben.'

'I'm sorry, Anabela, but it's not possible.'

He divulged his limitations: as a nurse he knew nothing, as a neighbour he could do less still.

'These things don't lie within the scope of hospitals.'

Bila got up. He pulled out a handkerchief and wiped his face. Then, he went to the window and looked out at nothingness. He settled himself inside his coat before speaking.

'The cure for these ills can only he found in tradition. But you city people are already beginning to deny ...'

'I don't deny anything. Ben would just never agree because of his religion.'

'But what do you mean? Is loving your own woman against any religion?'

'No, but this business of witchcraft ...'

'Leave the matter with me, Anabela. I will persuade Ben; I have known him for a long time.'

The nurse explained the procedure; the stricken husband would begin by bathing in an infusion of roots.

'It is to wash away his bewitchment.'

Anabela was dubious, she wanted details. Bewitchment? Yes, for that was where her husband's misfortune stemmed from. The roots would wash poor Ben clean of his bewitchment. After that, Bila continued, he would be vaccinated.

'Then that's where you as a nurse come in, Senhor Bila.'

The neighbour shook his head. It was a traditional vaccine, made from the dusts of the fire, the ashes from the bone of a lion.

'A lion? Where can you find lions nowadays?'

'They're old lions, colonial ones. Guaranteed quality.'

The vaccine would be administered by an old witch he knew, capable of such arts as to be able to inflame an old anthill with passion. Even foreign aid workers went to consult her. The witch, according to the neighbour, had several international caps to her name. But Benjamim would have to move, with both luggage and soul, to the witch's residence.

'A training course, as some people might call it.'

The final test would be done with the old woman herself. If Benjamim had been properly cleansed, he would never again waste a chance with the lovely Anabela.

'Sleep with the old woman, my Benjamim?'

There was no alternative, said the nurse. Sores in the mouth are healed with saliva. She argued her fears:

'I've heard it said that there are men who only manage to do it with old women, those of very advanced age. With young women, they can't.'

Anabela went home full of doubts. A nightmare tormented her for many nights. She dreamt that on falling asleep she became an old woman, covered in wrinkles and scales. She aged at the precise moment that she fell into sleep. Her husband remained unaware of such changes from beauty to hideousness and vice versa. In one such dream however, after they had fulfilled their love, she fell asleep while he contemplated her with passion. Then, before his very eyes, the astonishing transformation took place. Her smooth skin crinkled, her fresh young body withered. He was startled, almost abandoned by the breath of life. He rushed next door to consult Bila.

'I need a medicine man to undo the spell cast over Anabela.'

Bila answered with a question: how did he know whether Anabela was not in fact an old woman who made herself young during the day?

'What difference does it make?'

'A lot, Ben, a lot. If your woman is the one you saw asleep, then you will be stuck with a wrinkled hag for the rest of your life.'

'But I want to undo the wizardry.'

'Very well. But afterwards don't say I didn't warn you.'

Still in the depths of the dream, Anabela awoke one misty morning. Looking at herself in the mirror, she saw that she was shrivelled up. She looked as if she had just died and then suddenly changed her mind. She shook the mirror until she saw her face shatter into splinters, but each piece of glass confirmed her manifold wrinkles. She washed herself in lukewarm water and rubbed herself with herbal creams. To no effect. The wrinkles persisted, stubborn, invincible. And when she tried to leave the room, her torpid legs failed her.

Anabela would awaken from the nightmare, covered in sweat. She would run to the mirror to check her appearance. The mirror reflected her, smooth and resplendent. She would sigh with relief, consoled by reality.

The bad dreams continued even after Benjamim's departure to the witch's house. Anabela could not imagine what arguments the nurse had used to convince her husband. But the truth is that Benjamim packed a small suitcase and set off without saying a word. He remained on his cure for three weeks. Anabela counted the days on the fingers of her despair. Would he come back normal? Or would he bring new habits from his intimacy with the old woman? He arrived at last. Anabela stood looking askance, without asking anything. Benjamim was pale, more overturned than returned. He sat down on the bed and stared at his wife for a long time. She was puzzled by his behaviour. What soul was there behind this man?

They sat there in silence for some time. Then Ben signalled her to come closer. Anabela got up, already feeling the volcano of her desires smouldering in her breast. She knelt before her husband:

'What is it, Ben?'

His arm wandered drunkenly in the vicinity of her bosom. She smiled and came nearer. Benjamim whispered something, it seemed more like a sigh than a word. The chill of an invisible hand caused the young wife to shiver.

'*I want,*' he said.

She began to unbutton herself, her dress appeared to tremble under her fingers. She came and sat next to him, waiting. Another whisper slipped past Benjamim's lips:

'*I want ...*'

'*So do I, my darling.*'

'*I want water. Give me some water, Anabela.*'

A deep disappointment ran through her flesh. She sat still, between disbelief and frustration. In the midst of her delay, Benjamim suddenly got up. But before he could take a step, he had an attack of dizziness and collapsed on the floor with less substance than a mat.

They picked him up and lay him in bed; they tried in vain to wake him up. But Benjamim remained on the other side of his eyelids: his breathing was irregular. Anabela wept for her husband in that vegetable state, speaking to him tenderly as if he could still hear her. She spent sleepless nights, tending the creature who lay there beside her.

Time passed beyond lapse. One night, when the moon had already unfurled, Anabela fell asleep, vanquished by tiredness. In the depth of her slumber, however, she felt a shiver as if someone were touching her. She lay quite still, waiting. There was no doubt about it: they were hands practising the art of tenderness. Now they were enveloping her waist and filling her with a warmth which for so long had been wasted in sighs. Her heart began to beat faster: who could be the author of such desires? Benjamim? No, it couldn't be him if he had never dared, even before the accident. So she pretended to sleep and her anonymous lover unfolded himself in the mirror of her body; sea and shore flowed into each other. With her eyes still shut, she received this intruder, this picklock of her unhappy solitude. The sightless encounter repeated itself night after night. With closed lids, she would welcome the stranger. They loved each other with fury but without speaking. She was scared that Benjamim might wake up and catch her unknown lover in the act. Night hour followed night hour replete with moans, and the deep sighs of those who are losing their very life.

Until one day, Bila the nurse, on his daily visit to the patient, announced:

'Benjamim has begun to twitch his fingers. Tomorrow he will wake up completely.'

There was cheering and laughter. Everyone rejoiced. Everyone except Anabela. Her indifferent expression was noticed by her in-laws. The mother, saving appearances, said:

'Poor mite. She's so exhausted she can't even react.'

The young wife had, in fact, taken on the grey countenance of a widow. And when she accompanied her visitors to the door, she could be seen to be holding back the onrush of tears. The nurse, anxious, called her aside.

'What's wrong, Anabela? Don't you feel well?'

She did not reply. She turned her face and the dyke of her intimate bitterness burst. She accepted a handkerchief and tidied her appearance. Then she pulled herself together, and said in a flickering voice:

'Can't you leave him to sleep for a few more days? Only a few more days?'

The nurse raised his head, surprised. She explained herself:

'It's just that I wanted to be with him a bit longer. I wanted to so much, Senhor Bila.'

'With him? Who?'

Once again tears fell. The neighbour in embarrassed consent was less of a nurse, and more of a priest. Believing he had received the confession of an indiscretion, he set the young wife at ease:

'Very well, my child. I understand perfectly: you're so pretty, so sought after. How could you keep yourself to yourself for so long?'

And they both went to the room of him who lay on the verge of life. While the nurse prepared the syringes, she bent over her husband. Maybe he, the secluded and bashful Benjamim, was the only one who heard the secret she surrendered to him. Anyway, the nurse glimpsed something resembling a smile at the corner of Benjamim's mouth. And smiling too, he injected him with fresh depths of slumber.

THE BARBER'S MOST FAMOUS CUSTOMER

Firipe Beruberu's barbershop was situated under the great tree in the market at Maquinino. Its ceiling was the shade of the crab apple. Walls, there were none: which is why it blew all the cooler round the chair where Firipe sat his customers. A sign on the tree trunk displayed his prices. On it was written: '7$50 per head'. But with the rising cost of living, Firipe had amended the inscription to: '20$00 per headful'.

On the ageing timbers there hung a mirror, and next to it, a yellowing photo of Elvis Presley. On a crate, by the bench where the customers sat waiting, a radio shook to the rhythm of the *chimandjemandje*.

Firipe would weed heads while talking all the while. Barber's talk about this and that. But he didn't like his chitchat to tire his customers. When someone fell asleep in the chair, Beruberu would slap a tax on the final bill. Underneath the prices listed on his sign, he had even added: 'Headful plus sleep – extra 5 escudos'.

But in the generous shade of the crab apple tree there was no room for anger. The barber distributed affabilities, handshakes. Whoever let his ears wander in that direction heard only genial talk. When it came to advertising his services, Firipe never held back:

'I'm telling you: me, I'm the best barber there is. You can walk anywhere round here, look into every neighbourhood: they'll all tell you Firipe Beruberu is the greatest.'

Some customers just sat there patiently. But others provoked him, pretending to contradict him:

'That's fine sales-talk, Master Firipe.'

'Sales-talk? It's the truth! I've even cut top-quality white man's hair.'

'What? Don't tell me you've ever had a white man in this barber's shop ...'

'I didn't say a white had been here. I said I'd cut his hair. And I did, you take my word for it.'

'Explain yourself, Firipe, come on. If the white didn't come here, how did you cut him?'

'I was called to his house, that's what happened. I cut his, and his children's too. Because they were ashamed to sit down here in this seat. That's all.'

'I'm sorry, Master Firipe. But it can't have been a rich white. It must have been a chikaka.' Firipe made his scissors sing while, with his left hand, he pulled out his wallet.

'Ahh! You folk? You're always doubting and disbelieving. I'm going to prove it to you. Wait there, now where is the ...? Ah! Here it is.'

With a thousand cares he unwrapped a coloured postcard of Sidney Poitier.

'Look at this photo. Can you see this fellow? See how nice his hair is: it was cut here, with these very hands of mine. I scissored him without knowing what his importance was. I just saw that he spoke English.'

The customers cultivated their disbelief. Firipe replied:

'I'm telling you: this fellow brought his head all the way from over there in America to this barbershop of mine ...'

While he talked, he kept looking up into the tree. He was keeping a watchful eye in case he had to dodge falling fruit.

'These bloody crab apples! They make a mess of my barber-shop. And then there are always kids round here, trying to get at them. If I catch one, I'll kick him to pieces.'

'What's this, Master Firipe? Don't you like children?'

'Like children? Why, only the other day a kid brought a sling and aimed it at the filthy tree, hoping to shoot down an apple. The stone hit the leaves and, mbaaa! it fell on top of a customer's head. Result: instead of that customer having a haircut here, he had to have a head shave at the first-aid post.'

Customers changed, the conversation remained the same. From out of Master Firipe's pocket, the old postcard of the American actor would appear in order to lend truth to his glories. But the most difficult to convince was Baba Afonso, a fat man with an impeccably groomed heart, who dragged his haunches along at a slow pace. Afonso had his doubts:

'That man was here? I'm sorry, Master Firipe. I don't believe a bit of it.'

The indignant barber stood there, arms akimbo:

'You don't believe it? But he sat right there in that chair where you're sitting.'

'But a rich man like that, and a foreigner to boot, would have gone to a white man's salon. He wouldn't have sat down here, Master Firipe. Never.'

The barber feigned offence. He could not have his word doubted. Then he resorted to a desperate measure:

'You don't believe me? Then I'll bring you a witness. You'll see, wait there.'

And off he went, leaving his customers to wait with bated breath. Afonso was calmed down by the others.

'Baba Afonso, don't be angry. This argument, it's only a game, nothing more.'

'I don't like people who tell lies.'

'But this one isn't even a lie. It's propaganda. Let's pretend we believe it and have done with it.'

'As far as I'm concerned, it's a lie,' fat old Afonso kept saying.

'Okay, Baba. But it's a lie that doesn't harm anyone.'

The barber hadn't gone far. He had walked no more than a few steps to talk to an old man who was selling tobacco leaf. Then the two of them returned together, Firipe and the old man.

'This is old Jaimão.'

And turning to the tobacco seller, Firipe ordered:

'You tell them, Jaimão.'

The old man coughed up all his hoarseness before attesting.

'Yes. In truthfully I saw the man of the photo. It was cut the hair of him here. I am witness.'

And the customers showered him with questions.

'But did you get to listen to this foreigner? What language did he speak?'

'Shingrish.'

'And what money did he pay with?'

'With copper coin.'

'But which type, escudos?'

'No, it was money from outside.'

The barber gloated, self-satisfied, his chest puffed out. From time to time the old man breached the limit of their agreement and risked using his own initiative.

'Then, that man went in the market for to buy things.'

'What things?'

'Onion, orange, soap. He bought baccy leaf too.'

Baba Afonso leapt from his chair, pointing a chubby finger at him:

'Now I've caught you: a man like that wouldn't buy baccy leaf. You've made that up. That category of fellow would smoke filter cigarettes. Jaimão, you're just telling lies, nothing more.'

Jaimão was taken aback by this sudden attack. Fearful, he looked at the barber and tried one last line of argument:

'Ahh! It's not a lie. I remember even: it was a Saturday.'

Then there was laughter. For it wasn't a serious fight, their scruples were little more than playfulness.

Firipe pretended to be upset and advised the doubters to find another barber.

'Okay, there's no need to get angry, we believe you. We accept your witness.'

And even Baba Afonso gave in, prolonging the game:

'I expect that singer, Elvis Presley, was also here in Maquinino, having his hair cut ...'

∎

But Firipe Beruberu did not work alone. Gaspar Vivito, a young cripple, helped him with the clearing up. He swept the sand with care, so as not to spread dust. He shook out the cloth covers far away.

Firipe Beruberu always told him to take care with the hair clippings.

'Bury them deep, Vivito. I don't want the n'uantché-cuta *to play any tricks.'*

He was referring to a little bird that steals people's hair to make its nest. Legend has it that once the owner's head has been raided, not a single whisker will ever grow on it again. Firipe blamed any decrease in his clientèle on Gaspar Vivito's carelessness.

Yet he could not expect much from his assistant. For he was completely crippled: his rubbery legs danced a never ending *marrabenta*. His tiny head tottered lamely on his shoulders. He slobbered over his words, slavered his vowels, and smeared his consonants with spittle. And he tripped and stumbled as he tried to shoo away the children who were collecting crab apples.

At the end of the afternoon, when there was only one customer left, Firipe told Vivito to tidy up. This was the hour when complaints were received. If Vivito could find no way of being like other folk, Firipe paid more attention to jokes than to barbering skills.

'*Excuse me, Master Firipe. My cousin Salomão told me to come and complain at the way his hair was cut.*'

'*How was it cut?*'

'*There's not a hair left, he's been completely plucked. His head is bald, it even shines like a mirror.*'

'*And wasn't it he who asked for it like that?*'

'*No. Now he's ashamed to go out. That's why he sent me to complain.*'

The barber took the complaint in good humour. He made his scissors click loudly as he spoke:

'*Listen, my friend: tell him to leave it as it is. A bald man saves on combs. And if I cut off too much, I won't charge.*'

He circled the chair this way and that, then stood back to admire his talent.

'*There you go, get off the chair, I've finished. But you'd better take a good look in the mirror, otherwise you might send your cousin to complain later.*'

The barber shook the towel, scattering hairs. Then the customer joined his protests to those of the plaintiff.

'*But Master Firipe, you've cut off almost everything in front. Have you seen where my forehead reaches to?*'

'*Ahh! I haven't touched your forehead. Talk to your father, or your mother, if you want to complain about the shape of your head. It's not my fault.*'

The malcontents joined forces, bemoaning their double baldness. It was an opportunity for the barber to philosophise on capillary misfortunes:

'*Do you know what makes a person go bald? It's using another man's hat. That's what makes a man lose his hair. I, for instance, I won't even wear a shirt if I'm not sure where it's come from. Much less trousers. Just think, my brother-in-law bought a pair of underpants second-hand ...*'

'But Master Firipe, I can't pay for this haircut.'

'You don't have to pay. And you, tell your cousin Salomão to pass this way tomorrow: I'll give him back his money. Money, money ...'

And that's how it was: a dissatisfied customer earned the right not to pay. Beruberu only charged for satisfaction. Standing from morning to nightfall, weariness began to burden his legs.

'Hell, what a dog's life! Ever since morning: snip-snip-snip. I've had enough! Living's hard, Gaspar Vivito.'

And the two of them would sit down. The barber in his chair, his assistant on the ground. It was Master Firipe's sundown, a time to meditate on his sadness.

'Vivito, I'm worried that you may not be burying the hair properly. It looks as if the n'uantché-cuta is losing me customers.'

The boy replied with choked sounds, he spoke a language that was his alone.

'Shut up, Vivito. Go and see if we made much money.'

Vivito shook the wooden box. From inside there was the jingle of some coins. Their faces lit up with a smile.

'How well they sing! This shop of mine is going to grow, mark my words. In fact I'm even thinking of putting in a telephone here. Maybe later, I'll close it to the public. What do you think, Vivito? If we only take bookings. Are you listening, Vivito?'

The assistant was watching his boss, who had got up. Firipe walked round his chair, talking all the while, enjoying imagined futures. Then, the barber looked at the cripple and it was as if his dream had had its wings shattered and had plummeted into the dark sand.

'Vivito, you should be asking: but how will you close this place if it hasn't got a wall? That's what you should he saying, Gaspar Vivito.' But it wasn't an accusation. His voice lay prostrate on the ground. Then he went over to Vivito and let his hand ripple over the boy's dangling head.

'I can see that hair of yours needs cutting. But your head won't stand still, always moving this way and that, fiddle-de-dee, fiddle-de-daa.'

With difficulty, Gaspar climbed up into the chair and put the cloth round his neck. Agitated, the boy pointed to the darkness round about.

'There's still some time for a scissorful or two. Now see if you can sit still, so that we can hurry.'

And so the two preened themselves under the great tree. All the shadows had died by that hour. Bats scratched the surface of the sky with their screeches. Yet it was at this very hour that Rosinha, the market girl, passed by on her way home. She appeared out of the gloom and the barber stood hesitant, totally enveloped in an anxious look.

'Did you see that woman, Vivito? Pretty, too pretty even. She usually goes by here at this hour. I sometimes wonder whether I don't linger here on purpose: dragging time until the moment she passes.'

Only then did Master Firipe admit his sadness to himself, and another Firipe emerged. But he didn't confide in anyone: as for the mute Vivito, could it be that he understood the barber's sorrow?

'It's true, Vivito, I'm tired of living alone. It's a long time since my wife left me. The bitch ran off with another. But it's this barber's profession too. A fellow's tied here, can't even go and take a look at what's happening at home, control the situation. And that's what happens.' By this time he was masking his rage. He diverted the human grief from himself and imposed it upon the creatures of the earth. He threw a stone up into the branches, trying to hit bats.

'Filthy animals! Can't they see this is my barbershop? This place has got an owner; it's the property of master Firipe Beruberu.'

And the two of them chased imaginary enemies. In the end

they stumbled into each other, without a heart to be angry. Then, exhausted, they let out a chuckle, as if forgiving the world its insult.

■

It happened one day. The barbershop continued its sleepy service, and on that morning, just as on all the others, gentle banter flowed from one topic to another. Firipe was explaining the sign and its warning about the tax on sleeping.

'Only those who fall asleep in the chair have to pay. It often happens with that fat one, Baba Afonso. I start putting the towel round him and he starts snoozing straightaway. Now me, I don't like that. I'm not anybody's wife to have to put heads to sleep. This is a proper barbershop.'

At that point two strangers appeared. Only one of them entered the shade. He was a mulatto, nearly white in colour. Conversation died under the weight of fear. The mulatto went up to the barber and ordered him to show his papers.

'Why my papers? Am I, Firipe Beruberu, disbelieved?'

One of the customers came over to Firipe and whispered to him:

'Firipe, you'd better do as he says. This man's from the PIDE.'

The barber bent over the wooden crate and took out his papers:

'Here are all my bits of plastic.'

The man examined his identity card. Then, he screwed it up and threw it on the ground.

'Hey, barber, there's something missing in this card.'

'Something missing, what do you mean? I've given you all my papers.'

'Where's the photograph of the foreigner?'

'The foreigner?'

'Yes, the foreigner you sheltered here in your barber's shop.'

Firipe was puzzled at first, then he smiled. He had realised what the fuss was about and prepared to explain:

'*But officer, this business of the foreigner is a story I made up, a joke ...*'

The mulatto pushed him, silencing him suddenly.

'*A joke, let's see about that. We know only too well there are subversives here from Tanzania, Zambia, wherever. Terrorists! It's probably one of those you put up here.*'

'*But put up, how? I don't put anyone up, I don't get mixed up in politics.*'

The policeman inspected the place, unhearing. He stopped in front of the sign and read it clumsily under his breath.

'*You don't put anyone up? Then explain what this here means: "Headful plus sleep – extra 5 escudos". Explain what this sleep means ...*'

'*That's just because of some customers who fall asleep in the chair.*'

The policeman was already growing in his anger.

'*Give me the photo.*'

The barber took the postcard from his pocket. The policeman interrupted his movement, snatching the photo with such force that he tore it.

'*Did this one fall asleep in the chair too, did he?*'

'*But he was never here,*' I swear. Christ's honour. That's a photo of a film star. Haven't you ever seen him in films, the ones the Americans make?'

'*Americans, did you say? Okay, that's it. He's probably a friend of the other one, the one called Mondlane who came from America. So this one came from there too, did he?*'

'*But this one didn't come from anywhere. It's all a lie, propaganda.*'

'*Propaganda? Then you must be the one in charge of propaganda in the organisation ...*'

The policeman seized the barber by his overall and shook

him until the buttons fell to the ground. Vivito tried to pick them up, but the mulatto gave him a kick.

'*Get back you son-of-a-bitch. We'll arrest the lot of you before we finish here.*'

The mulatto called the other policeman and whispered something in his ear. The other one walked back down the path and returned some minutes later, bringing with him old Jaimão.

'*We've already interrogated this old man. He's confirmed that you received the American in the photograph here.*'

Firipe, smiling feebly, almost had no strength left to explain.

'*There, you see officer? More confusion. It was me who paid Jaimão to testify to my lie. Jaimão is mixed up in it with me.*'

'*That he is, to be sure.*'

'*Hey, Jaimão, admit it: wasn't it a trick we agreed on?*'

The old wretch turned this way and that inside his tattered coat, baffled.

'*Yes. In truthfully I saw the man of which. In that chair he was.*'

The policeman pushed the old man and handcuffed him to the barber. He looked round with the eyes of a hungry vulture. He faced the small crowd which was silently witnessing the incident. He gave the chair a kick, smashed the mirror, tore up the poster. It was then that Vivito became involved and began shouting. The cripple clutched the mulatto's arm but soon lost his balance, and fell to his knees.

'*And who's this? What language does he speak? Is he a foreigner too?*'

'*The boy's my assistant.*'

'*Assistant, is he? Then he'd better come along too. Okay, let's go! You, the old man and this dancing monkey, get moving. Walk in front of me.*'

'*But Vivito ...*'

'*Shut up mister barber, the time for talking's finished. You'll see, in prison, you'll have a special barber to cut your and your*' *little friend's hair.'*

And before the helpless gaze of the whole market, Firipe Beruberu, wearing his immaculate overall, scissors and comb in the left-hand pocket, trod the sandy path of Maquinino for the last time. Behind him, with his ancient dignity, came old Jaimão. Following him lurched Vivito with a drunkard's step. Bringing up the rear of this cortège were the two policeman, proud of their catch. Then, the humdrum haggling over prices ceased, and the market sank into the deepest gloom.

The following week, two guards arrived. They tore out the barber's sign. But as they looked round they were struck by surprise: nobody had touched anything. Instruments, towels, the radio and even the cash box were just as they had been left, waiting for the return of Firipe Beruberu, master of all the barbers in Maquinino.

EVERY MAN IS A RACE

Asked what his race was, he replied:
  'My race is me, John the Birdman.'
  Invited to explain himself, he added:
  'My race is me myself. A person is an individual humantity.
Every mn is a race, Officer.'

(Extract from the bird seller's statement)

Rosa Caramela

Our passions are kindled when the fuse to our heart is lit. Our most lasting love is rain, between the cloud's flight and the prison of a puddle. We are, after all, hunters who spear ourselves. And the well-aimed throw always carries with it a trace of the thrower.

Little, if anything, was known about her. Ever since she was a little girl, folk had known her as the hunchback cripple. We called her Rosa Caramela. She was one of those people who are given another name. The one she had, her natural name, didn't suit her. Re-baptised, she seemed to fit better into the world. Nor were we willing to accept other permutations. She was Rosa. Subtitle: Caramela. And we would laugh.

The hunchback was a mixture of all the races, her body crossed many a continent. Barely had she been delivered into life than her family withdrew. Ever since then, her dwelling was barely visible to the naked eye. It was a hovel made of haphazard stones, without measurement or care. Its wood had never been turned into planks: tree trunk, pure matter, was what remained. Lacking both bed and table, the hunchback didn't attend to herself. Did she ever eat? Nobody ever saw her with any victuals. Even her eyes were ill fed, having that scrawny look that conveyed hope of being gazed upon one day, and the self-contained weariness of one who had once dreamed.

She had a pretty face, in spite of it all. Detached from her body, she might even have kindled desires. But if you stood back and glimpsed all of her, then her prettiness was cancelled out. We used to see her wandering along the pavement, her steps so short that her feet scarcely crossed each other. She found her diversion in the public gardens: she would talk to the statues. Of all her illnesses this was the worst. Anything else she did involved secret and silent matters, no one paid any attention at all. But talking to statues, no, nobody could accept such a thing. For the spirit she invested in her conversations was enough to give you a fright. Was she trying to heal the scars of the stones? She consoled each statue with a mother's inclination.

'There now, let me clean you. I'm going to take this dirt of theirs off you.'

And she would wipe their limbs, frozen in stone, with a filthy cloth. Then she would go on her way, fleetingly visible when passing through the circle of light of a street lamp.

By day, we forgot she existed. But at night, the moonlight would remind us of her crooked outline. The moon seemed to stick to the hunchback, like a coin to a miser's pocket. And she, in front of the statues, would sing in a hoarse, inhuman voice: she would entreat them to emerge from their stony abode. She dreamed wide awake.

On Sundays, she retired, and was nowhere to be seen. The old woman would disappear, jealous of those who filled the gardens, disturbing the peace of her territory.

Nor did anyone ever try to explain Rosa Caramela's behaviour. The only reason that was ever given was the following: once upon a time Rosa had been left stranded at the entrance to the church, a bunch of flowers in her hand. Her fiancé, whoever that might have been, was late. He was so late that he never turned up. He had warned her: I don't want any fuss. It'll be just the two of us. Witnesses? God alone, if he's not too busy. And Rosa pleaded:

'But what about my dream?'

She had dreamed of a reception all her life. A dream of glitter, a cortège, and guests. A moment that was to be hers alone, she a queen, pretty enough to inspire envious thoughts. A long white dress and the veil straightening her back. Outside, the hooting of a thousand cars. And now, there was her sweetheart depriving her of her fantasy. She brushed her tears aside with the back of her hand – what other use does it have? She complied. Let it be as he wanted.

The hour came, the hour went. He didn't come, much less arrive. The bystanders wandered off, taking their sniggering and mockery with them. She waited and waited. Nobody had ever waited so long as she. Only she, Rosa Caramela. She sat there with only the step to comfort her, a stone suffering the weight of her disenchantment with the world.

A story people tell. Does it contain the sap of truth? What seems likely is that there was no sweetheart. She had extracted it all from her imagination. She had invented herself a wife-to-be, Rosita beloved, Rosa wedded. But while nothing happened, the outcome still pained her greatly. She was crippled in her reason. In order to cure her ideas, they put her away. They took her to a hospital and didn't want to know her any more. Rosa never got visitors, nor did she receive any medicine from any quarter. She paired off with herself, dispeopled. She became a sister to the stones, so often did she lean against them. Walls, floor, ceiling: only stone gave her any size. Rosa landed, with the flightiness of those in love, upon the cold floor tiles. Stone was her twin.

When she was discharged, the hunchback set off in search of her mineral soul. It was then that she fell in love with statues, solitary and sure of themselves. She dressed them with tenderness and respect. She brought them drink, came to their assistance on rainy days, or when it was cold. Her favourite statue was the one in the little garden in front of our house. It was a monument to some colonial figure whose name was no longer legible. Rosa whiled away many an hour contemplating that bust. An unrequited love: the statued man remained ever distant, never deigning to give the hunchback any attention.

From our veranda we could watch her, we, under the tin roof, in our wooden house. Above all, it was my father who would watch her. A silence would descend upon him. Was it the hunchback's madness that caused our good sense to fly away? My uncle would joke, in order to save us from our state:

'She's like the scorpion that carries its poison in its back.'

We shared our laughter among ourselves. Everybody, that is, except my father. He remained intact, solemn.

'No one can understand the degree of her tiredness, you see. Always lugging her back around on her back.'

My father concerned himself a lot with other people's tiredness. He himself couldn't be bothered with matters of fatigue. He would sit there and make use of life's many tranquillities. My uncle, a man of diverse resources, would advise him:

'Brother Juca, find yourself a way of making a living.'

My father didn't bother to reply. He even seemed to become more firmly ensconced, an accomplice of his old chair. Our uncle was right: he needed a salaried occupation. His only initiative was to hire out his own shoes. On Sunday, his team's supporters would pass by on their way to the football.

'Juca, we've come because of the shoes.'

He nodded ever so slowly. *'You know the contract: take them and then, when you come back, tell me what the game was like.'*

And he would bend to take his shoes from under the chair. He would stoop with such effort that it was as if he were picking up the floor itself. He would lift the shoes and look at them in feigned farewell:

'This is hard for me.'

It was only because of the doctor that he stayed behind. He had been forbidden excesses of the heart, rushes of blood.

'My lousy heart.'

He thumped his chest to punish the organ. Then he addressed his shoes once more:

'Look you here, my little shoes: make sure you come home on time.'

And he took his payment in advance. He sat with a set expression counting the notes. It was as if he were reading a fat book, of the type that like fingers more than they do eyes.

My mother: she was the one who stepped out into life. She would leave very early on her business. She would arrive at the market when the morning was still small. The world became visible as the sun came up. My mother would set up her stall before any of the other women. Among the piles of cabbages, her face could be seen, fat with sad silences. There she would sit, she and her body. In the struggle for life, Ma escaped us. She arrived home and left in the dark. At night, we would listen to her complaining to Father about his idleness.

'Juca, do you think about life?'

'Indeed I do, a lot even.'

'Sitting down?'

My father spared himself in his replies. She, and she alone, lamented:

'Me all alone, on the job, here at home and out there.'

Gradually, their voices would fade away down the hall. From my mother, there were still some sighs to come, as her hopes swooned. But we didn't put the blame on our father. He was a good man. So good that he was never right.

And so, life went on in our little neighbourhood. Until, one day, we got the news: Rosa Caramela had been arrested. Her only crime: venerating a colonialist. The militia chief explained the sentence: yearning for the past. The hunchback's madness concealed other, political motives. That was the commander's judgement. If that were not so, what other reason would she have to oppose, with bodily violence, the statue's demolition? Yes indeed, because the monument was a foot from the past tripping up the present. It was a matter of priority that the statue should be circumcised, for the nation's honour.

Consequently, old Rosa was taken away, to cure her of her alleged mentality. Only then, in her absence, did we realise how much she contributed to the making of our landscape.

For a long time, we heard no news of her. Until one afternoon, our uncle tore open the silence. He had come from the cemetery, from Nurse Jawane's funeral. He climbed the little steps up to the veranda and interrupted my father's repose. Scratching his legs, my old man blinked hard, sizing up the light.

'So have you brought my shoes?'

My uncle didn't answer straightaway. He was busy helping himself to some shade, curing his sweat. He blew on his lips, tired. On his face, I noticed the relief of someone who has just returned from a funeral.

'Here they are, good as new. You know, Juca, these black shoes were really useful!'

He fumbled in his pockets, but the money, always quicker to enter, was reluctant to come out. My father stopped him:

'I didn't hire them out to you. We're of the same family, our shoes are related.'

My uncle sat down. He pulled over the bottle of beer and filled a large glass. Then, with the skill of knowledge, he took a wooden spoon and removed the froth to another glass. My father drank the froth from the glass. Forbidden liquids, the old man only indulged in fizz.

'It's light, this froth. The heart doesn't even notice it go by.'

He consoled himself, his eyes looking straight ahead as if he were extending his thought. That self-absorption was nothing but a pretence.

'Was the funeral full?'

While he unlaced the shoes, my uncle described the flood, crowds trampling on the flowerbeds, all there to bid farewell to the nurse, poor man, who also died by his own hand.

'But did he really kill himself?'

'Yes, the fellow strung himself up. By the time they found him he was already stiff, he looked like a lump of starch on the end of a rope.'

'But why did he kill himself?'

'How should I know? They say it was because of women.'

They fell silent, the two of them, sipping at their drink. What pained them most was not the fact but the motive.

'To die like that? It's better to pass away.'

My old man took the shoes and examined them suspiciously:

'Is this earth from there?'

'What, that there?'

'I'm asking you if it's from the cemetery.'

'Maybe.'

'Then go and clean it, over there. I don't want the dust of the dead hereabouts.'

My uncle went and sat on the bottom step, brushing the soles. Meanwhile, he continued to talk. The ceremony was going on, the priest was saying the prayers, reviving their souls. Suddenly, what happened? Along came Rosa Caramela, all dressed in mourning.

'Has Rosa come out of prison?' my father asked, astonished.

Yes, she'd come out. During an inspection tour of the gaol, they'd given her an amnesty. She was mad, she'd committed no more serious crime than that. My father insisted, surprised:

'But she, at the cemetery?'

My uncle went on with his account. Rosa, all in black from

her back down. Like a raven, Juca. She came in like a grave digger, glancing at each tomb. She seemed to be choosing her hole. You know, Juca, in the cemetery no one lingers when visiting graves. We pass by in a hurry. Only that hunchback, the old girl ...

'*Tell the rest,*' my father cut in.

The story went on: Rosa right there, in the middle of everybody, began to sing. The bystanders stared at her in educated astonishment. The priest kept up his prayer, but people were no longer paying any attention. It was then that the cripple began to undress.

'*You're lying, brother.*'

Cross my heart, Juca, may I be had by two thousand knives. She undressed. She began taking off her bits of cloth, at greater leisure than today's heat. Nobody laughed, nobody coughed, nobody did anything at all. When she was naked, de-clothed, she came over to Jawane's grave. She raised her arms, and threw her clothes on to his tomb. The sight scared the crowd which retreated a few steps. Then Rosa prayed:

'*Take these clothes, Jawane, you'll need them. For you're going to be stone like the rest of them.*'

Eyeing those present, she raised her voice, she seemed larger than a mere creature:

'*And now: am I allowed to fancy him?*'

The onlookers fell back, you could hear the dust speak.

'*What was that? I can fancy this dead man! He no longer belongs to time. Or am I forbidden him too?*'

My father left his chair, he seemed almost offended.

'*Rosa spoke like that?*'

'*It's the truth.*'

And my uncle, by this time in the spirit of the thing, imitated the hunchback, her twisted body: and this one, can I love him?

But my old man didn't want to listen.

'*Shut up, I don't want to hear any more.*'

Suddenly, he hurled the glass through the air. He wanted to get rid of the froth but, in a mistaken lapse, he let go of the whole glass. As if in apology, my uncle went and picked up the pieces of glass, scattered on their backs all over the garden.

That night, I couldn't sleep. I went and sat my restlessness down in the garden in front of the house. I looked at the statue, it was off its pedestal. The colonialist was lying with his whiskers next to the ground, it was as if he had climbed down himself, burdened by fatigue. They had uprooted the monument but forgotten to take it away, the job needed finishing. I felt almost sorry for Beardy, all soiled from the pigeons, covered in dust. I stoked myself up, and came to my senses: am I like Rosa, placing feelings in lumps of stone? That was when I saw Caramela herself, as if summoned by my ruminations. I sat frozen, stock still. I wanted to run away, but my legs refused me. I shuddered: was I turning into a statue, becoming the subject of the cripple's passion? What a horrible thought, my mouth might escape me for ever. But no. Rosa didn't stop in the garden. She crossed the road and reached the steps up to our house. She stooped and cleaned the moonlight away from them. She put her belongings down in a whisper. Then, tortoise-like, she withdrew into herself, perhaps getting ready to sleep. Or maybe sadness was her only intention. For I heard her weep, in a murmur of dark waters. The hunchback was overflowing, as if it were her turn to become a statue. I wandered endlessly in such thought.

Then it happened. My father, in painstaking silence, opened the door to the veranda. Slowly, he approached the hunchback. For a few seconds, he leant over the woman. Then, moving his hand as if he were dreaming his gesture, he touched her hair. Rosa didn't react at first. But soon, she began to emerge from herself, her face in the fullness of light. They looked at each other, both of them gaining beauty. Then, he whispered:

'Don't cry, Rosa.'

I could hardly hear, my heart thumped in my ears. I drew nearer, ever concealed behind the darkness. My father was still speaking to her, in a voice I had never heard before.

'It's me, Rosa. Don't you remember?'

I was in the middle of the bougainvillaea, its thorns were tearing me. I didn't even feel them. Fear pricked me more than the branches. My father's hands sank into the hunchback's hair, they were like people, those hands, like people drowning.

'It's me, Juca. Your sweetheart, don't you remember?'

Gradually, Rosa Caramela emerged from cover. Never had she existed so much, never had a statue merited such eyes. Softening his voice still more, my father called her:

'Let's go, Rosa.'

Without wanting to, I had left the bougainvillaea. They could see me, I placed no obstacle between us. The moon even seemed to sharpen its shine when the hunchback got up.

'Let's go, Rosa. Pick up your things and let's go.'

And off they went, the two of them, deep into the night.

THE PRIVATE APOCALYPSE OF UNCLE GEGUÊ

'Father, teach me about existence.'
'I can't. I only have one piece of advice to give.'
'And what is that?'
'Have fear, my son.'

A man's story is always badly told. That's because a person never stops being born. Nobody leads one sole life, we are all multiplied into different and ever changeable men. Now, as I unravel my memories, I learn my various languages. Even so, I can't understand myself. For, as I discover myself, I cause my own night to fall, as if there were things only visible to the fully blind.

I was born of no one, it was I who delivered myself. My parents disowned the inheritance of their lives. They left me in the world still smothered in blood. It wasn't their wish to see me grow from a crawling creature into a young boy, dribbling my snot, skinny even in my cough.

The only person I had in the world was my uncle, Geguê. It was he who watched over my growth. I owe it to him alone. No one else could tell you what I was like. Geguê was the solitary keeper of that bottomless chest where I went seeking my treasure, the shattered pieces of my childhood.

Not that he ever brought me much: an old crust of bread, a clean bit of rubbish. He never talked about where he scratched a living. His words were few, rain that didn't even moisten the ground, water which was sorry for having fallen. He relied on dreams:

'Tomorrow, tomorrow.'

That was the instruction he gave me: lessons of hope when the future had already grown feeble. For I came along at a time when life's paths had grown weary. My uncle protected me as I bided my time, and suggested that other lights were shining in the distance.

'We'll get up early and go yonder. Tomorrow.'

There was no early, much less a yonder. And tomorrow was still the previous day. Uncle invented missions. A poor man can't bribe his way to his fate. He invents expectations for himself, unreachable places and times.

One day, he brought me an army boot. Large, of a size to have space left over. I stood gazing at that lonely old boot, with a hovering foot. I hesitated between left and right. Does a shoe without a partner fit any foot?

'Don't you like it?'

'Yes, I do.'

'Well then?'

'The lace is missing,' I lied.

Geguê lost his temper. His patience was very brittle.

'Do you know where that boot comes from?'

That old beetle crusher had history's guarantee: it had trudged through the heroic times of the independence struggle.

'Those are veteran boots! You can be sure.'

Then he cursed me: I had no respect, no loyalty to the fatherland. I was destined to weep, humiliated and downtrodden. Or was I waiting for the roads to soften, so as to be able to stroll along without a care?

'*You don't want to wear it then?*'

He picked up the boot and threw it far away. Then a strange thing happened: hurled into the air, the boot seemed to have found its wings. It flew along in rapid gyrations. Had Uncle Geguê challenged the spirits of war?

That night, whether or not because of the angry scene, I lay fingering the darkness, my teeth chattering. Fever choked my body, setting my breast ablaze. I dreamed with my eyes open. More than open: alight. I dreamed of my mother, it was she, I know, although I had never set eyes on her. But it was she, for there was no other sweetness like it. She held my arms and called me: son, my son. I trembled, for those words had never come to rest in my soul. What did she want? Nothing, she was just coming to ask me to be good. Not to turn my back on my heart. My good behaviour – that would be her reward. Mother, I called, Mother, take me away from here. But she couldn't hear me, it was as if my words fell to the ground before reaching her. She went on with her counsel, stressing the value of goodness. Mother, I'm so cold, take me to you. Then she offered me the tender shelter of her hands. At that moment, as if by some enchantment, I shed my orphanhood.

Suddenly, a noise brought me back to my body. It was Uncle Geguê. His hands lay between mine, just as I had left them. That comfort was his treatment, the best remedy he knew: he summoned back memories more remote even than my own birth.

'*Uncle, my mother was here, wasn't she?*'

'*Be quiet, and drink this water.*'

The illusion had given me another fever: I yearned for her presence, and grew impatient for a new apparition. While I sipped my drink, I felt a sweat flowing inside me, as if my blood were turning to water. I submerged myself in that hidden river, and abandoned my senses. At the end of it all, on the frontier of light, there was a vague presence, a nothing without end: my mother. Why had she visited me from the depths of my fever? And what was that evil she was warning me of?

Next morning, I woke up far away from the night before. I looked at the blue all around me. Uncle Geguê was right after all: morning did exist. There it was, with the sun uncovering different colours and beauties. I wanted to share my feelings, but Geguê had already gone. So I rejoiced on my own. I had vanquished my illness and returned from my visit to hell. I gazed at the heavens, looking for God. But my eyes couldn't reach that far. My mother's words echoed within me, as if she were some divine voice. How could she speak like that? She was no one, silence was her only tool.

I stopped thinking about it. Whoever had kindled the question inside me would give me the answer. I stumbled off down the path. Where was I going with such feeble steps? I'd do better to rest, to gather my strength. But there was some secret motive pushing me along. Before I realised it, I was standing under the *mafurreira* tree, on the very spot where the boot had landed. But it was no longer sleeping there. A passer-by explained: your uncle was here together with Comrade Secretary. They had a bit of a meeting and discussed the matter of the boot. The Secretary then reached his decision: this boot is of too great a historical significance, it mustn't end up on the rubbish dump. Geguê had agreed, you couldn't throw away such an important piece of heritage. But Comrade Secretary corrected him:

'That's where you're wrong, Geguê: we must get rid of the filthy thing.'

'Get rid of it? But isn't the boot very historical?'

'Precisely because of that,' answered the Secretary.

'But we mustn't do it before the public eye.' The less Geguê understood, the more he expressed his agreement:

'Of course, of course.'

'Do you know what we're going to do, Geguê my friend?'

'What's that, Comrade Chief?'

'We're going to drown that boot in the marshes.'

And off they went. The passer-by hadn't seen them again. I went back home and waited for Geguê. Night fell and he still hadn't returned. I began to get worried: had there been a round-up? That uncle, the man who had provided my life with shade, had he been taken? He who had never had a fixed job, had he been carried off to Niassa, as part of the campaign against nonproductive elements?

In the anguish of waiting, I took stock of myself. When all was said and done, that man was very much of a father to me now. And I looked upon him as a son would, regardless of whether I had issued from his body. Such were my thoughts when I saw him coming. He walked round the house, as was his custom: the beetle always circles its hole twice before going in. When he emerged into the light, I saw what a surprise he had brought: he was wearing a red armband, with the letters GV in black on it.

'Yes, sir. A revolutionary guard. I'm one of them too now.'

My uncle, a guard? It wasn't possible. I could imagine him being one of those who were kept under guard, for to be honest, if he inspired anything at all, it was mistrust. The way he earned his living was worthy of ample suspicion. If I didn't ask any questions, it was in order not to stain my filial sentiments. I preferred not to know. But what was this business of serving as a revolutionary guard? Surely, it was a provisional arrangement. Yet he was adamant: he was one of them. With his red band over his ragged shirtsleeve, my uncle barked his commands:

'Left right, left right.'

Seeing his skinny body puffed up with pride, as he marched along at a dignified stumble, I bent double with laughter. He looked at me seriously:

'They're going to train me, didn't you know?'

He went on talking. Even so, I had my doubts. Was it true? That they should give the key of the door to the thief himself? How could he be a defender of the Revolution?

'*Am I supposed to call you Comrade Uncle?*' I asked.

'*You must understand,*' he answered. '*You can't stay lowly all your life. Do you know who it was who chose me? It was the Secretary, the man himself. He's known me for years, we are cousins, almost of the same family.*' Then he ended up by making threats: people aren't going to forget the name of Fabião Geguê in a hurry.

Next afternoon he was off. He went to the militia barracks for training. He stayed there for weeks, and came back home with no more skills than he'd left with. He didn't even know how to fire a gun. All he could do was march up and down: left right, left right.

His body was in a sorry state on account of the tiredness he'd been given. He looked at me and sighed. Then, he lay down and closed his eyes.

'*Uncle, are you going to sleep like that? Take your uniform off at least.*'

'*Shut your mouth. If I got tired in my uniform, I must rest in it too.*'

He told me to warm up some tea. He didn't want to go to sleep with his stomach awake. '*As it is, I can't tell my back from my belly,*' he complained.

'*I can't make tea, Uncle. We have no leaves.*'

'*It doesn't matter, we'll just drink it as it is: water tea.*'

But when the water boiled, he was already asleep. I was dozing off too when I heard shadows. A woman emerged from a silhouette, her *capulana* on her back. She protected her face with her arm, and coughed because of the smoke rising from the fire. When she noticed me, she pointed at the ground:

'*Is that Geguê?*'

I nodded. She was about to shake the sleeping man, but I

sensed problems, and stopped her:

'*Don't wake him, Mother. He's a bit unwell.*'

She turned her face. Her cheeks were fully revealed in the light. Then I saw she was not a mother. She was just a girl of my own years. She was beautiful, with eyes that invited desire, her skin radiant with body.

'*My name is Zabelani.*'

She was the mistress of her name. She spoke in a whisper, her voice was born of wings rather than her throat. My uncle must have been awake but he did not stir. He lay there quietly, with a dead man's competence. The girl decided to sit down. Little could I have imagined the skill with which she placed such a rotund body on the tiniest of wooden boxes. The seat swayed but did not complain.

'*And you, who are you?*'

'*I'm Geguê's nephew.*'

She was silent, as if she were no longer there. Then, rubbing her arms, she asked me to feed the fire. '*The fire's feeling cold,*' she said.

'*Have you come to stay with us?*' I asked.

Yes, that was her intention. She told her story: she had come, fleeing from the terrors of the countryside. The world was coming to an end there, in open suicide. Her parents had disappeared in some unknown whereabouts, carried off by bandits. She told me all this without shedding the briefest of tears.

'*Now I've come to stay here. Geguê is my uncle as well.*'

I prepared a mat, and gave her a blanket. She fell asleep straightaway. Morning was already high and still she slept. Uncle Geguê gazed at her dried-up body and shook his head:

'*This girl will throw your good sense off balance, boy.*'

He came at me with proverbs: two trees block the way. Together, you two will cause me big problems. While we broke our hunger he gave me veiled advice. It's the sea that causes islands to be round, he said. That girl's beauty is your doing, nephew of mine. Women are an endless territory, and when we journey through them, we always get lost.

'But, Uncle, I haven't even looked at the girl.'

Geguê went on. Quantity and variety were valid company. But I should never spend anything on a woman. Whether through the bride price of olden days, or through traditions of more recent making: I should avoid alliances. Which is the best family? The unknown relatives of strangers. Only those ones count. With the others, our blood relatives, we have debts from the day we are born. Uncle Geguê did not accept the values of tradition, those family ties which made neighbours of our existences.

The days passed. I saw very little of my uncle. He left home early, occupied in secret matters. For sure, they weren't legal. Meanwhile, I went around with Zabelani. As time went by, I began to understand Geguê's warning. That girl was driving me to feverish ditherings. Because of her I was vertigo's apprentice. My whole body yearned but I feared opportunity. Was that love of mine a state of eternal arrival? Or were Fabião Geguê's words once again being confirmed: the woman of our life is always in the future?

One Saturday afternoon, I took Zabelani to one of those places that only I knew. We walked along under the coconut palms, we wandered among their wavering necks. Their tops swayed in the breeze, going this way and coming that. The oxen spread themselves among the long grass, while snipe let fly sudden flashes of whiteness against the landscape. Zabelani slowed down, languid. Our hands touched, brushed against each other lightly in distraction. She stopped and asked me: show me where the river flows. I pointed far ahead. She stepped back and nestled against me. Until all her forms matched my body. I felt my skin and nerves becoming one. Then she let her skirt slip to the ground and, slow as the moon, she turned to face me. That instant was a deep one, almost eternal. Apart from the river, all that could be heard was the sound of our breathing.

When we got home, Uncle Geguê called me aside. I expected a scolding, but he took his time, chewing on a blade of grass.

'Are you fucking that dame?'

'Uncle, don't talk like that ...'

'I shall, to be sure.' Then he spat: 'Whores!'

He ordered Zabelani to pack her things immediately. She was to be taken away, separated from me, put somewhere only he knew about. I gave vent to my anger, ranting and raving. My uncle no longer recognised me. I cursed his dishonesty, his habit of shirking work. I even tried to get my hands on him, but he held my arms. To write you the truth, I tendered more tears than I did words. He lowered my hands, binding me to myself once again. Exhausted by my sobbing, I calmed down. We sat down, a sad smile came to his face. Anger gathered up its bitter feelings, and the atmosphere returned to its sluggishness.

'You know, my boy? I'm going to tell you something: work is a very infinite thing.'

He coated his truth with sweetness – it wasn't that that thing in him was laziness. He was just making a living out of life's waywardness, without wasting his strength. I shouldn't ill judge his parsimony: in this life, only the present suffer. The absentee's advantage: he never wears himself out.

'Take the case of an ox, little nephew. In the water, you might think an ox was nothing at all, isn't that so? But no, he just lazes in the current. The cleverness of an ox is to make the water do the work in his journey.'

I smiled sleepily. Weeping is a sure guarantee of total fatigue. Afterwards we cease to care. Geguê was taking away the one I loved. But I no longer resisted him. Surrendering to my eyelids, I only had a tiny patch of soul left.

'That's right, little nephew: sleep. For tomorrow morning,

good and early, I'm going to teach you how to get by in life.'

Geguê woke me up early. He told me to wash and get ready. I looked around, Zabelani had already been taken away. I stood there, lacking the nerve to ask. Nor did Geguê's face give any encouragement. I sat down and listened to him. His plan was simple: go to Aunt Carolina's house, break into the hen house, steal the said hens. Then set fire to the back of it.

'But, Uncle ...'

'Go, and don't delay.'

He added: this is just the beginning. There would be other houses. My job was to sow confusion, spread fear. Geguê was coming into his own, boosted by a uniform, promoted in his powers.

'But Uncle, how can you, a militiaman ...'

'Do you think the militia exists only when there's peace?'

I abandoned myself. At first, I suffered his threats. If I refused, he would take charge of the consequences. I shouldn't forget that Zabelani's fate was in his hands. Later, I listened to his promises: if I accepted, I wouldn't have reason to be sorry.

I set off, but I did so without myself. I carried out acts of wickedness, so many that I couldn't even remember the first ones. After committing such huge cruelties, I began to fear myself. Because I had all but gained a taste for it, I began to pride myself in my actions.

One thing surprised me about my evil deeds: I never suffered from any remorse. I'd go to bed and sleep at night. Where, then, was my conscience? My uncle gave me the answer:

'There aren't any good people in this world. There are only wicked ones who are lazy.'

Geguê's word was enough to convince me. For when it comes down to it, how can there be any good in a world which no longer expects anything? I kept repeating to myself – there are those who desire and those who hope. Now, in the area where we lived, there was no desire or hope any more.

At long last my mother's dream could be explained. It wasn't even a dream, but the mirage of a dream. I, it turned out, had been born without principle, devoid of love. How could my mother teach my retarded heart? Only Zabelani might have sweetened my being. But I was forbidden her recollection by my uncle. Love weakens men, you will be given other tasks, braver missions. After some time, my uncle gave me a rifle. I looked at the weapon, sniffed the barrel, the scent of death.

'*Take a piece of cloth, cover your face. No one will know who you are.*'

Geguê was not punished by his conscience. It was all as lighthearted as his habitual laugh.

'*This'll put the wind up them.*'

With that weapon, I brought my wickedness to perfection. I broke into cattle pens, I emptied bottle stores. When I wasn't stealing things, a handkerchief over my mouth, I was a militiaman's auxiliary. I was at once a policeman and a burglar. For good effect, my uncle even gave me his red armband. With this, I was able to dispense punishment. What I really enjoyed was to take charge of the road. Take chickens out of baskets, demand to see travel permits, untie goats. And to ask awkward questions when examining identity cards:

'*Is this photo yours?*'

'*Yes, it is, if you please.*'

'*But it's too light.*'

'*It's not my fault. That's how it came out.*'

I enjoyed their stutterings. I complicated matters:

'*Or is it that you're ashamed of your race?*'

At the end of it all, I would issue penalties: loading stones, digging holes, hoeing the earth. Little by little, as a result of Uncle Geguê's and my work, a war was born. Thereabouts, no one was the master of time-honoured circumstances any more. A house, a car, property: everything had become all too mortal. As soon as it was had, it burned. A yearning for days gone by was abroad among the older folk.

'*We might as well have ...*'

And they all sighed: if only there were a law, whatever that might be. But one which offered people protection in their human anxieties. Some were bitter, adding up the sum total of their sacrifices:

'*Is this what we fought for?*'

Until one afternoon, I got a warning. It was a sign, brief, but which spelt itself out to me word by word. I was walking along the path through the marshes. There was a group of men there fishing for *ndoé*. I always liked to watch them at this task, for it is the only type of fishing done on land rather than in the sea. The men bring spears and stab at the ground, seeking the holes where the *ndoé* lives in time of drought. It's a pretty sight: suddenly, a silvery fish leaps out of the dark mud. Such is the *ndoé*, a watery creature that understands the air, breathing both inside and outside it.

At that point, however, I felt a tightness in my chest. I sat down. It was as if death were speaking within me with its quiet hissing. The men had speared a fish. The creature wriggled and writhed, gleaming as it caught the light. It's no use expecting a *ndoé* to drown: you have to cut its head off. That's what those folk proceeded to do, placing it on a stone. On this occasion, the sight of it fled from my eyes, reality no longer accommodated me. While the blood oozed on the mud, I got the signal. There it was, in the middle of the slime: the soldier's boot. The same one I had spurned, the same one my uncle had hurled into the marshes. It seemed to have grown beyond its size, lost the notion of its frontiers. Over it, the blood had spilled, like the red of a flag.

The fishermen noticed the boot, picked it up and examined it. They looked at me, shrugged their shoulders, and threw the boot away. It fell next to me with a solemn thud. Then, I picked it up, and washed it in the puddle, both inside and out. I applied great care to it, as if it were a child. A little orphan child like myself. Afterwards, I chose a clean patch of ground and gave it its due burial. While I invented the ceremony, I seemed to sense the sound of a military band, the fluttering of a thousand flags.

It was already late when I got home. I wanted to tell Geguê about the burial. I wasn't ever able to. The moment I arrived, he pressed me with heavy urgency:

'Give me my share! Where's my share?'

I didn't understand. But he was simmering away in the sauce of his anger, and wasn't speaking any language at all.

He insisted. He searched through my things, fumbled around in my bag. He didn't find what he was looking for.

'But Uncle, I promise I didn't do anything.'

He held his head in his hands. He doubted himself, he doubted me. He kept repeating: a rogue doesn't cut another rogue's hair. Seeing him sitting there, vanquished, I decided to console him. My heart raced as I stroked his shoulder. Geguê gave in, and accepted my truth. Then, he explained: there were some more bloody goings-on in the area. Other ruffians were on the increase, soldiers of no one. Robberies were spreading, conspiracies and felonies, bestialities. Death had become so common that only life inspired terror. To avoid notice, survivors imitated the dead. As they couldn't find enough victims, the bandoleers dragged the corpses from their graves in order to hack them about again.

'You haven't been going around with them, have you nephew? You haven't joined these bands, have you?'

I shook my head. But my voice wouldn't even utter a sound.

My throat had tightened, I stuttered silences. How could my sufficiencies produce such crimes? My uncle just stood there, gazing at my reply without moving. He didn't believe me.

'So tell me: what was it you were burying out there in the mud?'

'I was burying the boot.'

He was surprised: the boot? But hadn't it been put to rest at a time beyond memory? What was it I saw in that boot, what did I have to say to such a piece of flotsam? He began to list his doubts, one after the other. He asked me to promise to forget such rubbish. I promised.

'Uncle, now I would like to know something: where is Zabelani's house?'

He hesitated, I insisted. It was vital to go and get the girl, save her from the bandits. It may be that it's too late, who knows? Geguê mumbled, indecisive. 'These are dangers that surpass your strength, nephew.'

'Uncle, please tell me.'

He skirted the subject: these were not times conducive to love. How could I woo her in such a deathly place?

'Uncle, let's save Zabelani.'

At last he appeared beaten. He began to curse my obstinacy – can you warn a lizard that the stone under him is hot? You're not worth the trouble. If your mother could see you.

'Never speak to me of my mother again!'

Geguê was astonished. I had come to hate that absence. My mother's shadow was an unbearable burden to me. You can't miss someone who never existed. It behoved me to kill that absence, to be a native of myself, alone assume my birth.

'That girl, Uncle, that girl, she's the only mother I have now.'

My uncle got up, turned his back on me. Was he concealing his tears? I let him retire with dignity, I didn't even peep at him. He went into the house and brought out his gun. Taking my hand, he placed some cartridges in it.

'This time you're taking cartridges, live ones.'

Then he told me where Zabelani lived. We stood there for some time, holding hands. I was puzzled by Geguê, and that heartfelt emotion of his. My uncle seemed to be taking his leave of me.

I hurried along doleful tracks in the sand, wondering whether time had not stolen a march on me. And, indeed, it had. Zabelani's neighbours told me what had happened: the girl had been taken away that very night. They had burned the house down and stolen anything of value. Could the bandits have carried out such a sordid piece of work on their own account?

'Tell me friends, who do you suspect?'

Someone showed those bandits the way, the bystanders told me. No, there was no doubt about it: they had seen who it was. It was one of those militiamen. They couldn't see his snout, but he must have been a friend, a relative. Because Zabelani, when she saw him, had come out willingly, with open arms. What was more, it seemed strange that they should know exactly where to find the girl, wasn't that so? Such were their words. I returned home, my spirits staggering along behind me. My feet dragged, as if they wished to delay the execution of all my pent-up fury. I passed through the marsh, there where the boot slumbered in its subterranean dwelling. I arrived in our backyard when darkness had already fallen. Inside, a spirit lamp was burning, my uncle wasn't asleep. I stopped near the door, and called his name. He appeared in the doorway, dragging his slippers. With the spirit lamp in the background, all you could see were his outlines. The rest was shadow, not even his face was visible. My uncle was disappearing inside his very silhouette, and this helped me to gather my strength. I raised the gun, and took aim through the distortions of my tears. Then Geguê spoke. His words didn't even register in my mind, so moistened were my feelings.

'Shoot, son, shoot.'

My eyes escaped me. But then my hatred showed me the way – that was the right moment to act. In a few seconds, I visited every moment of my life. There was Geguê straddling my life, sole comfort in my profound dejection. Does any bird dismantle its nest?

But my uncle loomed large, full of insistence. Never had he made such a humble request:

'Shoot, nephew. It is I who am asking you.'

The shot deafened me. I heard nothing, I saw nothing. To this day, I have my doubts as to whether I hit him, whether I cut the thread of his life. For at that very moment, my eyes filled with all the water I never shed in previous sadness. And I fled from that spot, running as far as my legs would take me.

Now I think to myself: it's not even worth my while knowing where that bullet came to rest. Because it happened inside me: I was issuing from myself in birth once more, I was giving new life to my orphanhood. When it came to it, I was firing at that whole lapse of time, killing the belly inside us, where the dead shadows of this old world are born.

ROSALINDA'S JOURNEY TO NEVERNESS

You must understand: we lack the competence to stow our dead away in a place called eternity.

Our dead refuse to accept their final condition: in their disobedience, they invade our daily lives, they intrude upon us from that territory where life's law of exclusion should hold sway.

The most serious consequence of such promiscuity is that death itself, held in scant respect by its lodgers, loses the fascination of total absence. Death ceases to be the most irrevocable and absolute difference between beings.

Rosalinda was a woman of some rearguard, well furnished in her seating area. A lady of generous corporation, of flesh both inside and beyond her clothes. She suffered from such volume that she would sit down on top of her own weight, unsurpassed. Once upon a time, she had been slender, one of those women who facilitate love. In its time, her slimness had met with success. But then, ever since she had been widowed, she had shunned amusement, oblivious to life. Nowadays, Rosalinda wearied herself waiting for time to go by: she would chew *mulala* until her spittle turned orange. Fat women don't grow angry with life: they are like oxen, who never expect misfortune.

As the afternoons shed their heat, her routine would be the same. She would visit the cemetery. And what was more, she would do that every single day. Her dead husband Jacinto's grave was on the far side of the cemetery. It matched the position he had always occupied, at the back end of life. With her small step, Rosalinda would advance among the underground dwellings, hesitating as if her own shadow caused her pain. When she reached the spot, she would kneel down, her bended knees consigning the rest of her legs to defeat. And there she would remain, in the solitary company of the dead man.

Thus the days gradually lay themselves to rest, the sweat of years dripped away as surely as the years added up. Rosalinda became her own ancestor, so many were the relatives caught up in the big sleep. Only she remained, with her backdated thoughts. Kneeling there by the grave, she recalled:

'Jacinto, you son-of-a-bitch.'

With a tender gesture, she would smooth the sand, caressing her memories. God might punish him, God might fall sick. But who could explain why she missed those times of suffering, why she enjoyed the sweet taste of bitter memories?

'You shackled my life, and all you provided me with were beatings.'

She was right: Jacinto had only sworn fidelity to the bottle. If he had in fact departed on his journey, his soul must have travelled in the shape of a bottle. Apart from that, he had multiplied himself in matters of love, rewarding himself with many women. By the time he got home, the hour was improper and his lips were blind. At this hour, he would say, I'm only good for studying the bottom of a glass. He would speak like that in order to offend her. For he had enrolled at night school, fulfilling a promise of reform. He went to classes, but only for a few nights. My little Rosalinda, let me explain myself. Life isn't worth the effort. I'm not a man for school, letters tire me out.

I'm a fruit, Rosalinda. A fruit, just like a cashew. Does anyone teach a fruit how to ripen? Answer me that, Rosalinda. Does it take someone to explain things to a cashew? No one. The only lessons it gets are from the soil. In the same way, it's enough for a man to keep his feet on the ground, to make use of all his roots. Not like those folk who leave the land and go to foreign parts. They end up not even feeling the ground they tread. They are like tinder wood: it takes a spark to set them ablaze.

Rosalinda knew where this was leading. This was the talk that preceded blows, the preface to a beating. No sooner did the bottom of the bottle hove into sight, than words gave way to kicks. Afterwards, he would storm out, sick of being a husband, tired of being a person.

It would be true to say that Jacinto only caused Rosalinda's heart the expense of suffering. Even on his deathbed, his eyes, but recently deceased, obstinately peeped out at the world. They couldn't see anything any more. Silence ruled the room, not a word dared to move. But just as someone was about to close the dead man's eyelids, a voice ordered:

'Don't close his eyes.'

The fright sent a chill through everybody. Rosalinda looked down, avoiding the grime of shame.

'That man is still waiting for someone.'

So that was how Jacinto sank into the abyss, with his eyes open, alert to any encounters the future might bring. Though aware of his eternal infidelities, Rosalinda set aside the most perfumed clothes for him. Just as she had done in his life, tidying his appearance before he went out:

'Are you going out to meet women all creased up like that? Let me tidy you up and make you handsome.'

Is the mouth the heart's hiding place? In this case, no. She tarted up her husband with honest goodwill. Far be it that other women should think she did not fulfil her wifely duties. Let them respect her proud work while they enjoyed Jacinto.

Now that his life had been interrupted, Rosalinda recalled it all with brave benevolence. With his passing, she forgave him everything: women, drink, long absences. Goodwill surfaced immediately during the first prayer, there at the graveside. As she prayed, her soul softened. After the amens, she realised she was in love, for the first time, right there at the tail end of life. Jacinto, in spite of everything, my Jacinto.

'True love is more than for ever.'

Death without cure, love without remedy. How much of an orphan is there in a widow, when it comes down to it? How much are we stripped of existence, only to be left holding our umbilical cord? The others were astonished by the tubby Rosalinda. So it was only after the man died that she crowned him king of her heart? Yes. Also, it was only now that she had total control of Jacinto, only now did he belong wholly and exclusively to her. Those staring eyes that he had taken away with him were, after all, destined for her alone. Only for me, Rosalinda compensated herself. Never again would he share himself with another body. Jacinto was guaranteed her by means of an imagined oath of devotion. Only a portrait could have been as faithful as that.

She was more and more convinced by her sad consolation: Jacinto's death was nothing more than the marriage she had always dreamed of. The others, her rivals, had vanished, the wanton hussies. Suddenly, they were but a puff of some forgotten breath. A loose woman is never kept. Rosalinda now understood: the life they had led together was merely a betrothal, the product of an incomplete decision. And she accepted, without any pain, the memory of past insults:

'Your name, Rosalinda, is a double lie for you are neither pretty nor a rose.'

She smiled as she remembered. She sighed as her soul emptied on an ebb tide. Here, in this overdue present, she devoted her whole self to Jacinto in a subterranean love. The fat lady overflowed like the juice of a fallen fruit. She no longer knelt down. That was a widowsome gesture. What was more, she began to prettify herself, putting a glow on her recent marriage.

But then there came a day. Rosalinda was buying flowers when she saw a beautiful girl arrive with dainty step. The stranger walked up to Jacinto's grave and prostrated herself, in a display of grief. Rosalinda was puzzled. Her eyes became concerned, not seeing so much as guessing. That one was a cocksure young lady, an up-stager: you could see she'd never worn a *capulana,* never chewed *mulala.*

'That one must be Dorinha, the last of his other women.'

The widow drew nearer but without letting herself be seen. She didn't stray from her footprints. She paused at a nearby grave, and stood there peeping, ambushed in her own contemplation. The other exhibited but a handful of tears, no great weight of sadness. Rosalinda cursed that woman as she navigated through her sorrows.

'As for you, Jacinto, I bet you're laughing down there under the ground. You enjoyed your life to the full, you son-of-a-bitch: but your fooling about is over now.'

Rosalinda made up her mind, quick and decisive. She set off for the undertaker's and asked him to change the coffin's place, to swap the 'here lies'.

'Madam wishes to transfer the mortal remains?'

Then, the undertaker showed her the lengthy paperwork that would be more than a match for her. The widow pressed her point: it was only a tiny change, just a few metres. The man explained, there were the proper channels, time lapses before submissions could be granted. The widow gave up. But she only pretended to be beaten. For a new thought now filled her. She returned in the evening, taking her nephew Salomão with her. When her intentions became clear, the little boy got scared:

'But, Auntie, what do you want us to do? Is it to dig Uncle Jacinto up?'

No, she assured him. It's just to swap the neighbouring gravestones. Even so, Salomão was trembling more than the flame of a spirit lamp. The widow led the way, doing the digging herself:

'I always said: a flame craved never lights.'

The translapidated Jacinto must have been surprised by all this coming and going. Now, only I know which is the real gravestone, you rogue. Rosalinda brushed death's dust from her and administered an appropriate pardon to herself. She hoped that God would turn a blind eye to her tricking of the intruder. Let the other one, the would-be widow, devote her snivelling to the neighbour in the next grave. For Jacinto's eyes, those eyes which the earth abstained from eating, were meant for Rosa and Linda alone.

It happened as she had foreseen. On the following day, the intruder turned up and surrendered her feelings to the wrong grave. Rosalinda feasted on laughter, as she watched the delusion. She made the sign of the cross, more for herself than for God:

'In life they deceived me. Now it's my turn.'

Rosalinda, the posthumous spouse, was getting her own back. And for some time, repayment continued in this fashion. Then, one day, she thought to herself: before, I never managed to do anything. I was nothing at all. But now, I can feel my power. Rosalinda filled herself with belief, she moved around in the regions beyond death, there where destiny no longer existed. And in this way, she believed she possessed an understanding which had no bounds. As she wandered through the ruins of the cemetery, Rosalinda let out loud cackles.

'Come on, Jacinto, let's drink xicadju.'

She would pour the liquor into an invisible glass, and avail herself of hidden caresses. After a while, she would begin to remonstrate:

'Leave your books, husband. What do you want to study for now?'

And she would push the invisible. Her laughter gained no respect, but caused the quiet corners of the cemetery to tremble for a while. But then others, more obedient in matters of gravity, began to display concern at her unruliness. The widow was ignorant of the ways of sadness, her cackling disturbed the sacred repose of the souls.

So they took the fat woman away, she who was a widow before she had been a spouse. They took her away to a shadowy place where she turned into absence. Rosalinda had finally reached neverness.

THE BIRD-DREAMING BAOBAB

Birds, all those who know of no abode on the ground.

That man will always remain in shadow: no memory will be enough to save him from the dark. To be true, his star was not the Sun. Nor did he come from a country called life. Maybe that was why he lived with all the caution of an outsider. The bird seller didn't even have a name to shelter him. They called him the birdman.

Each morning, he would pass through the white folks' neighbourhood carrying his enormous cages. He made these cages himself, from such flimsy material that they didn't even look like a prison. What they did look like were winged cages, cages that might fly away. Inside them, the birds fluttered around in a twinkle of colour. A cloud of twitters enveloped the bird seller, so loud that they made the windows rattle:

'Mother, look, here comes the dicky-bird man!'

And the birds would flood the streets. Joyfulness was exchanged: the birds shouted and the children chirped. The man would take out a mouth organ and put sleepy melodies to tune. The whole world was filled with stories.

Behind their curtains, the settlers tut-tutted at such abuses. They sowed suspicions among their children – who did that black think he was? Did anyone know his credentials? Who had authorised those grubby feet to dirty the area? No, no, and no again. The black ought to return to his proper place. But the birds, they're so sweet – the children insisted. The parents took on sterner airs: enough said.

But the order was not destined to be greatly respected. One little boy more than all the others disobeyed it, and devoted himself to the mysterious birdman. That was Tiago, a dreamy child, whose only gift was to pursue his fancy. He would wake up early, put his nose to the window pane waiting for the bird seller to come by. The man would come into view and Tiago would rush down the stairs, thirty steps in five jumps. Feet bare, he would go down the street and disappear among the swarm of birds. The sun would sink and there would be no sign of the lad. At Tiago's home, people would start to give their worries a polishing:

'Barefoot, just like them.'

The father planned his punishment. Only the mother's soft heart brought relief to the little boy's arrival, in the fullness of night. The father insisted on an explanation, even if it were but the outline of one:

'Did you go to his house? But does that good-for-nothing have a house?'

His dwelling was a baobab, the empty hollow inside its trunk. Tiago told them: it was a sacred tree, God had planted it upside down.

'See what that black has been filling the child's head with.'

The father turned to his wife, heaping blame on her. The lad continued: 'It's true, Mother. That tree is capable of great sadness. The old men say that a baobab can commit suicide in despair by way of fire. Without anyone setting it alight. It's true, Mother.'

'What nonsense,' the lady of the house soothed.

And she would draw her son away from his father's reach.

Then the man would decide to go out, and join his rage to that of the other settlers. At the club there was clamour from all: the birdman's visits had to be stopped. Measures could not include death by killing, nor anything that might offend the eyes of women and children. In a word, the cure would have to be thought about.

The following day, the bird seller repeated his joyful invasion. Even the settlers hesitated: after all, that black was bringing with him birds of a beauty never before seen. No one could resist their colours, their chirping. The sight was like nothing else in this true and natural world. The bird seller bowed in nameless modesty, disappearing from himself out of humility.

'These are truly excellent birds, these ones with their wings all ashow.'

The Portuguese began to wonder: where in the name of magic did he get such miraculous creatures? Where, if they themselves had already brought the most distant bush-land to heel?

The bird seller dissembled, answering with a chuckle. The whites began to fear their own suspicions – might that black have a right to enter a world which was closed to them? But then they set about paring down his merits: the fellow lived in trees, among the birds. They were like creatures of the wild, was the general conclusion.

Whether because of the scorn of the powers that be, or because of the admiration of the meek, the birdman became a topic of conversation in the concrete part of town. His presence began to fill the length of a conversation, unsuspected empty moments. The more people bought from him, the more their houses were filled with sweet song. Such music fell strangely on the settlers' ears, proving that the area they lived in had little in common with the land around them. Could it be that the birds were eroding the residents' sense of self, turning them into foreigners? Or was it the black who was at fault, that son-of-a-bitch who insisted on existing, unaware of the duties of his race? The traders ought to realise that there was no room for his bare feet in those streets. The whites were concerned at such disobedience, blaming it on the times. They yearned jealously for the past, when creatures could be tidied away depending on their appearance. The bird seller, by overstepping himself in such a fashion, was leading the world towards other awareness. Even the children, thanks to his seduction, were forgetting their behaviour. They were becoming more like children of the street than of the home. The birdman had even made inroads into their dreams:

'Pretend I'm your uncle.'

And they all joined the family, all became related, relatively speaking.

'Uncle? Have you ever heard of a black being called uncle?'

The parents were determined to arrest their dreams, their tiny, boundless souls. The command was issued: the street is out of bounds, you can't go out any more. Curtains were drawn, the houses shut their eyelids.

Order seemed to rule once again. That's when things began to happen. Doors and windows opened by themselves, furniture appeared turned back to front, drawers were swapped round.

At the Silvas' house:

'Who opened this cupboard?'

No one, no one had. Old man Silva got angry: everyone in the house knew that firearms were kept there. With no sign of having been forced, who could the burglar have been? Such was the indignant plaintiff's doubt.

At the Peixotos' house:

'Who scattered grass seed among my papers?'

No one, nothing, not anyone, came the reply. The Peixoto supremo warned: you know very well what type of documents I keep in that drawer. He listed their secret functions, their confidential matters. Let the spreader of grass seed own up. Bloody birds, he mumbled.

At the mayor's residence:

'Who let the birds in?'

Nobody had. The governor was unable to govern his temper: he had come across a bird inside a cupboard. Solemn municipal discussion papers covered in bird droppings.

'Just look at this one: bird shit in the middle of the official seal.'

In the wake of all these occurrences, a general uproar gripped the area. The settlers held a meeting in order to try and reach a decision. They assembled at the home of Tiago's father. The lad slipped out of bed and stood at the door listening to their grim threats. He didn't even wait for the sentence to be passed. He rushed off through the bush in the direction of the baobab. There, he found the old man settling himself by the warmth of the fire.

'They're coming to get you.'

Tiago was gasping for breath. The bird seller was not put out: he knew, he was waiting for them. The little boy tried harder, for never before had the man meant so much to him.

'Run away, there's still time.'

But the bird seller set himself at ease, in sleepy langour. He stepped serenely into the trunk and there he tarried. When he came out, he was wearing a tie and a white man's suit. Once again he sat down, clearing the sand underfoot. Then he paced up and down, surveying the horizon.

'Run along, boy. It's night time.'

Tiago lingered. He glanced at the birdman, awaiting his gesture. If only the old man were like the river: still but moving. But he wasn't. The bird seller belonged more to legend than to reality.

'And why did you put on a suit?'

He explained: he was the natural offspring of that land. It

was his duty to know how to receive visitors. It was for him to show respect, the duties of a host.

'As for you, go, go back home.'

Tiago got up, reluctant to leave. He looked up at the huge tree, as if he were asking it for protection.

'Can you see that flower?' asked the old man.

And he recalled the legend. The flower was where the spirits dwelt. Whoever harmed the baobab would be persecuted for the rest of his life.

The settlers began their noisy arrival. They surrounded the place. The little boy fled, hid, and watched. He saw the birdman get up and greet the visitors. The beating started straightaway, with cudgels and kicks. The old man didn't even appear to be suffering, a vegetable were it not for the blood. They bound his wrists and pushed him up the dark road. The settlers followed behind, leaving the boy alone in the night. The child hesitated, now stepping forward now back. Then it happened: the flowers of the baobab fell, like stars of felt. Their white petals turned red on the ground.

Suddenly, the boy made up his mind. He dashed off through the bush after the procession. He tailed their voices and learnt that they were taking the birdman to gaol. When it became pitch black behind the wall next to the prison, Tiago began to suffocate. Was it any use praying? If the world around him had stripped itself of beauty. And in the heavens, just as in the baobab, no star glittered with pride any more.

The birdman's voice reached him from beyond the prison bars. Now he could see his friend's face, and all the blood which covered it. Interrogate the fellow, squeeze him hard. That was the order which the settlers left behind them as they withdrew. The guard saluted obediently. But he didn't even know what secrets he was supposed to drag out of the old man. What madness could they prove against the old street hawker? And now, standing there all alone, the figure of the prisoner seemed free of all suspicion.

'May I have permission to play? It's a tune from your part of the world, boss.'

The birdman put the harmonica to his lips and tried to blow. But he recoiled from the effort with a wince.

'They beat me a lot around the mouth. It's a pity, otherwise I'd play.'

The policeman became suspicious. The harmonica was hurled out of the window, and it fell near where Tiago was hiding. He picked the instrument up, and stuck its pieces together again. Those pieces were like his soul, starved of a hand that might make it whole. The lad curled up in the warmth of his own roundness. As he set off into sleep, he put the instrument to his lips and blew, as if he were playing his own lullaby. Who knows whether the birdman, shut away inside, didn't hear the sound of such comfort?

He awoke in a kingdom of chirping. The birds! An infinity of them covered the whole police station. Not even the world, in its universal dimensions, seemed a big enough perch. Tiago approached the cell, surveyed the gaol. The doors were open, the prison deserted. The bird seller had vanished without trace, the place had lost all recollection of him. He called the old man, but was answered by the birds.

He decided to return to the tree. There was no longer any other place where he might go. No street, nor house: only the baobab's belly. As he walked along, the birds followed in a twittering cortège, high in the sky. He arrived at the birdman's abode, and looked at the ground covered with petals. They were no longer red, having returned to their original whiteness. He entered the trunk, putting distance between himself and time. Was it any use waiting for the old man? For sure, he had vanished, a fugitive from the whites. Meanwhile, he began to blow on the harmonica once more. He lulled himself in its rhythm, no longer with an ear to the world outside. If he had paid due attention, he would have noted the arrival of a host of voices.

'*That black son-of-a-bitch is inside the tree.*'

Vengeful steps surrounded the baobab, crushing the flowers underfoot.

'*It's the fellow, along with his mouth organ. Play away, you scallywag, for you'll soon be dancing!*'

Torches were put to the trunk, and the flames licked the ancient bark. Inside, the boy had unleashed a dream: his hair was growing into tiny leaves, his legs into timber. His wooden fingers dug root-like into the soil. The boy was in transit to another realm: he was turning into a tree, consenting to the impossible. And from the dreaming baobab, there rose the birdman's hands. They touched the flowers, the corollas curled: monstrous birds were born and released, petal-like, on the crest of the flames. The flames? Where were they coming from, invading the remotest frontier of the dream world? That was when Tiago felt the sting of the blaze, the seduction of ash. Then the boy, a convert to the ways of sap, emigrated once and for all to his newfound roots.

THE RUSSIAN PRINCESS

'... It was enough for the existence of gold in Manica to be rumoured, and for it to be announced that a railway would be built to transport it, for pounds sterling to appear out of the blue in their tens of thousands, opening shops, establishing steamship lines, organising overland transport, investing in industrial enterprises, selling liquor, seeking to exploit in a thousand and one ways not so much the gold, but the very exploiters of the future gold ...'

António Ennes, *Moçambique*,
Government Report, Lisbon, 1946.

Forgive me, Father, I'm not kneeling right, it's my leg, you know. This skinny little leg of mine which I wear on my left side, doesn't hold my body up properly.

I've come to confess the sins of long ago, blood pounded in my soul, it frightens me just to think about it. Please, Father, listen to me slowly, be patient. It's a long story. As I always say: an ant's journey is never a short one.

You may not know, but this town was once favoured by another life. There were times when people came here from far away. The world is full of countries, most of them foreign ones. The heavens are so full of flags now that I don't know how the angels can fly about without bumping into a length of cloth. What did you say? Get to the point? Yes, I'm getting there. But don't forget: I asked for more than a little piece of your time. It's just that a life goes by slowly, Father.

Let me continue then. At that time, there also came to the town of Manica a Russian lady. Nadia was her name. Rumour had it she was a princess there where she'd come from. She was in the company of her husband Yuri, a Russian too. The couple came because of the gold, like all the other foreigners who came here to dig up the riches of this land of ours. That man Yuri bought the mines, in the hope of becoming rich. But as the old men say: don't run after the hen with salt already in your hand. Because the mines, Father, were the size of dust, a single puff was enough and there was almost nothing left.

At the same time, the Russians had brought with them relics of past sustenance, luxuries from times gone by. Their house, if you were to see it, was full of things. And folk working for them? Why there were more than many. As for me, being an *assimilado,* I was head servant. Do you know what they called me? General Commissioner. That was my rank, I was someone. I didn't do any work: I told people to work. The boss's requests, it was I who attended to them, and they always spoke to me politely, with respect. Then I would take their requests and bellow orders at the domestic staff. Yes indeed, I shouted. That was the only way to make them obey. No one labours for the joy of it. Or could it be that God, when he expelled Adam from Paradise, didn't do so with a kick in the pants?

The servants hated me, Father. I felt that rage of theirs whenever I stole their days off from them. I didn't care, I even liked not being liked. I grew fat on their anger, I all but felt like a boss. I've been told that a taste for giving orders is a sin. But I think that it's this leg of mine that counsels me in my wickedness. I have two legs: one of a saint, the other the devil's own. How can I follow but one road?

Sometimes, I would catch snatches of the servants' conversation as I passed their huts. They would be ranting over a host of things, their talk bristling with teeth. I would approach them and they would fall silent. They didn't trust me. But I felt flattered by their suspicion: I commanded a fear that made them so small. They got their own back by making fun of me. They would forever be imitating my limp. They would fall about laughing, the rascals. I'm sorry for using oaths in a place of respect. But that old anger of mine is still alive. I was born with the defect, it was a punishment God had in store for me even before I took on a person's shape. I know God is good, without a fault. But Father, even so: do you think he was fair to me? Am I insulting the Holy Father? Well, I'm confessing. If I'm causing offence, increase my penance afterwards.

Very well, I'll continue. In that house, the days were always the same, sad and silent. Early in the morning, the boss would be off to the mine, the gold farm, as he called it. He would only return at night, in the thick of night. The Russians never had visitors. The others, the English, the Portuguese, never stopped by there. The princess lived enclosed in her sadness. She would dress formally even inside the house. You could even say she visited herself. She always spoke in murmurs, so that to listen to her, you had to put an ear right up next to her. I would approach her slender body, with a skin the whiteness of which I'd never seen before. That whiteness often attended my dreams, and even today I tremble at the fragrance of that colour.

She used to linger in a tiny room, gazing at a glass clock. She would listen to the hands dripping the minutes away. It was a clock from her family, and she only trusted me to clean it. If that clock were to break, Fortin, it would mean my whole life would break too. She would always tell me that, warning me to take care.

One of those nights, I was in my hut lighting the spirit lamp.

Suddenly, I was startled by a shadow behind me. I looked, and it was the mistress. She was carrying a candle and came slowly towards me. She peeped round the room, as the light danced into the corners. I stood there tongue tied, ashamed even. She was used to seeing me in the white uniform I wore for work. There I was in my pyjama trousers, devoid of a shirt and of decorum. The princess walked round me and then, to my astonishment, sat down on my mat. Can you believe it? A Russian princess sitting on a mat? She remained there a myriad of time, just sitting stock still. Then she asked, in that way of hers when she spoke Portuguese:

'So you live here?'

I had no answer. I began to wonder whether she was ill, whether her head wasn't changing places.

'Lady, it's better that you go back to your house. This room is not good for you.'

She didn't reply. Then, she asked another question:

'And for you, it's good?'

'It's enough for me. All we need is a roof to shut out the sky.'

She corrected my certainties. It's animals, she said, that hide away in lairs. A person's house is a place to stay in, a place where we sow our lives. I asked if there were blacks where she came from and she laughed her fill: Oh! Fortin, you ask some funny questions! I was surprised: if there weren't any blacks, who was it that did the heavy work in her country? Whites, she answered. Whites? She's lying, I thought. After all, how many laws are there in the world? Or is it that misfortune was not distributed to people according to their race? No, I'm not asking you, Father, I'm just discussing it with myself.

That's how we talked that night. At the door, she asked to see the compound where the others slept. At first, I refused. But deep down, I wanted her to go there. For her to see that their adversity was far worse than mine. And so I complied: we went out into the darkness in order to see the place where those of the houseboy rank lived. Princess Nadia was filled with sadness at the sight of such living space. She spoke with so much expression that she began to switch her words, jumping from Portuguese to her own dialect. Only now did she understand why the boss never let her go out, or dispense favour. It was just so that I wouldn't see all this poverty, she said. I noticed she was crying. Poor lady, I pitied her. A white woman, so far from those of her race, there, in the middle of the bush. Yes indeed, for the princess, the whole place must have been bush, or suburbs of bush. Even the big house, all clean and tidy in obedience to their customs, even her house was a bush dwelling.

On the way back, I stepped on one of those *micaia* thorns. The barb pierced deep into my foot. The princess tried to help me, but I pushed her away:

'*You mustn't touch it. It's this leg of mine, lady ...*'

She understood. She began to console me, saying that it was no defect, that my body merited no shame. In the beginning, I didn't like it. I suspected she felt sorry for me, that she was showing commiseration, and nothing more. But then I surrendered to her gentleness, and forgot the pain in my foot. It was as if that leg were no longer mine as it walked along.

From that night on, the lady began to go out often, to visit her surroundings. She would take advantage of the boss's absence, and tell me to show her the way. One of these days, Fortin, we must leave early and go as far as the mines. Those desires of hers scared me. I knew the boss's orders which forbade the lady to go out. Until one day, the beans were spilled:

'*The other servants told me you've been going out with the lady.*'

The bastards had groused on me. Just to prove that, like them, I would bow before the same voice. Envy is the worst snake: it bites with the teeth of the very victim. Which is why, at that moment, I retreated:

'*It's not me who wants it, boss. It's the lady who orders it.*'

You see, Father? There I was in a trice, informing against the lady, betraying the confidence she had placed in me.

'It's not going to happen again, do you hear, Fortin?'

We stopped taking to the streets. The princess begged me, urged me. Just for a bit of a distance, please, Fortin. But I didn't have the spirit for it. And so the lady was once again a prisoner in the house. She looked like a statue. Even when the boss arrived, after darkness had fallen, she just sat there benumbed, looking at the clock. What she saw was time, which only reveals itself to those in life who have no presence. The boss didn't even bother with her: he would march straight up to the table, and order drink to be brought. He would eat, drink, and then start all over again. He never even noticed the lady, it was as if she belonged to some lower form of existence. He didn't beat her. Blows are not the stuff of princes. Assault or murder are not things they carry out, they hire others. It's we who are the labour of their grubby whims, we who are destined to serve. I only ever delivered a blow, gave a hiding, when told to by others. The only folk I ever beat up were those of my own colour. Nowadays, when I look around me, I have nobody I can call a brother. Nobody. These blacks don't forget. It's an embittered race the one I belong to. You, Sir, are black, you can understand. If God is black, Father, I'm done for: I'll never be forgiven. Never ever! What did you say? I can't speak of God? Why, Father, is it that he can hear me down here, so far from heaven, and me so tiny? Can he hear? Wait, Father, let me just make myself more comfortable. My devil of a leg, it never wants to obey me. That's better, now I can confess some more. It was as I said. Or rather as I was saying. There was no history in the Russians' home, nothing happened. Nothing but the lady's sighs and silences. And the clock drumming away in that emptiness. Until one day, the boss hounded me with shouts:

'Call the servants, Fortin. Quickly, everybody outside.'

I summoned the houseboys, the servants and also the fat

cook, Nelson Máquina.

'Let's go to the mine. Hurry, climb onto the cart.'

We got to the mine, we were given spades and we started to dig. The roof of the mine had collapsed yet again. Beneath the earth we were treading on, there were men, some already stone dead, others taking leave of life. The spades rose and fell nervously. We saw arms appear, sticking out of the sand, they looked like roots of flesh. There was shouting, a confusion of orders and dust. Next to me, the fat cook pulled at an arm, summoning up all his strength to unearth the body. But blow me if it wasn't a loose arm that had already been torn from its body. The cook fell over with that piece of death gripped in his hands. Sitting back clumsily, he began to laugh. He looked at me and that laugh of his filled with tears, the fat man was sobbing like a lost child.

I couldn't stand it, Father, I threw in the towel. It was a sin but I turned my back on that tragedy. There was too much suffering. One of the servants tried to grab me, insulted me. I turned my face, I didn't want him to see that I was crying.

That year, the mine caved in a second time. The second time too, I abandoned the rescue attempts. I'm no good, I know, Father. But you've never seen a hell like that one. We pray to God to save us from hell after we die. But, when all is said and done, hell is where we live, we step on its flames, and we bear with us a soul full of scars. It was the same there, it looked like a field of sand and blood, we were frightened even to set foot on it. For death buried itself in our eyes, pulling our soul along with its many arms. Is it my fault, tell me frankly, is it my fault that I gave up when it came to winnowing bits of people?

I'm not a man given to rescues. I'm a person who is happened to rather than who happens. I was thinking about all this as I walked back. My eyes didn't even ask the way, it was as if I were walking in my own tears. Suddenly, I remembered the princess. I seemed to be listening to her voice asking for help. It was as if she were there, at the corner of every tree, on her knees and begging as I am now. But once again I refused to dispense life, I distanced myself from goodness.

When I got back to my hut, it pained me to hear the world round about, full of the beautiful sounds of nightfall. I hid myself in these selfsame arms of mine, I shut off my thoughts in a darkened room. It was then that her hands came to me. Slowly my arms, wilful snakes that they were, disentangled themselves. She spoke to me as if I were a child, the son she had never had:

'It was an accident at the mine, wasn't it?'

I nodded without a word. She uttered some curses in her own language and went out. I went with her, for I knew she was suffering more than I. The princess sat down in the main lounge and waited for her husband in silence. When the boss arrived, she stood up slowly, and in her hands appeared the glass clock. The one she told me to take such care with. She raised the clock high above her head and, with all her strength, hurled it to the ground. The glass shattered and spread all over the floor in shimmering grains. She continued, breaking other pieces of china, doing everything unhurriedly and without a single cry. But those shards of glass were cutting her soul, I knew. As for the boss, he shouted all right. First in Portuguese. He ordered her to stop. The princess took no notice. He shouted in their language and she never even heard. And do you know what she did then? No, you can't imagine it, even I can hardly believe the events I witnessed. The princess took off her shoes, and looking her husband in the eye, began to dance on top of the pieces of glass. She danced and danced and danced. How she bled, Father! I should know, I cleaned it. I got a cloth and wiped the floor as if I were caressing the lady's body, bringing comfort to all her wounds. The boss ordered me to go, to leave everything as it was. But I refused. I've got to clean this blood away, boss. I answered him in a voice that didn't even seem my own. Was I disobeying him? Where did that strength come from that rooted me to the ground, imprisoned in my own will?

So that's how it was, the impossible made true. A length of time passing in a single flash. I don't know whether it was because of the glass, but the next day, the lady fell ill. She lay there in a separate room, she slept alone. I would make the bed while she rested on the sofa. We would talk. The subject never changed: recollections of her homeland, childhood balm.

'This illness, lady, for sure it's caused by longings.'

'All my life is there. The man I love is in Russia, Fortin.'

I bustled around, feigning inattention. I didn't want to know.

'His name is Anton, and he is the only ruler of my heart.'

I'm imitating the way she spoke, but it's not to make fun of her. That's the way I remember her confession of such a love. Confidences followed, she forever yielding up to me memories of her hidden passion. I was afraid that our conversations might be overheard. I would hurry with my tasks so as to get out of the room. But one day, she handed me a sealed envelope. It was a matter of the greatest secrecy, no one should ever suspect. She asked me to post the letter in town.

From that day on she never stopped giving me letters. One after the other, first one, then another, and yet another. She wrote as she lay there, the writing on the envelope shook with her fever.

But Father, do you want to know the truth? I never posted those letters. Nothing, not a single one. That's the sin I bear and must suffer. It was fear that inhibited me from the obedience I owed her, fear of being caught with such frenzied proof in my hand.

The poor lady would look at me with warmth, trustful of a sacrifice that I wasn't even making. She would give me her correspondence and I would begin to tremble, as if my fingers were holding a flame. Yes, that's the right word: a flame. For that was the very fate that awaited all those letters. I threw them all into the kitchen stove. It was there that my lady's secrets were burned. I would listen to the flames, which sounded like her sighs. God bless me, Father, just telling you my shame makes me sweat.

And so time passed. The lady's strength deteriorated. I would enter her room and she would look at me, almost pierce me with those blue eyes of hers. She never asked whether an answer had arrived. Nothing. Only those eyes, stolen from the sky, looked at me inquiringly and in mute despair.

The doctor now came every day. He would come out of the room, shaking his head in misbelieved hope. The whole house lay in gloom, the curtains ever drawn. Only shadows and silence. One morning, I saw the door open just a crack. It was the lady peeping out. With a gesture, she summoned me in. I asked if she was feeling better. She didn't reply. She sat down in front of the mirror, and covered her face with that perfumed powder, so deceiving death's colour. She painted her mouth but took a long time getting the colour right on each lip. Her hands were trembling so much that the red smudged her nose and her chin. If I were a woman I would have helped, but being a man I just stood there looking, bashful.

'Are you going out, my lady?'

'I'm going to the station. We're both going.'

'To the station?'

'Yes, Anton is arriving on the next train.'

And, opening her bag, she showed me a letter. She said it was his reply. It had taken a long time, but it had arrived in the end, she waved the envelope as children do when they're scared you may deprive them of their fantasy. She said something in Russian. Then she spoke in Portuguese: Anton was coming on the train from Beira, he was going to take her far away.

She was raving, of course. The lady was feigning an idea. How could an answer have come? If I was the one who collected all the mail? If many a day had gone by since the lady left the house? And, what was more: if the lady's letters had been posted in the stove?

Supported by my arm, she started off down the road. I was her walking stick until we were near the station. It was here, Father, that I committed my worst sin. I'm very hard on myself, there are things I don't accept in me. Yes indeed, I'm the person I defend myself least from in everything. That's why this confession is such a weight off my conscience. I'm counting on God to defend me. Am I not justified, Father? Listen on then.

The princess' skin was right up against my body, I was sweating her sweat. The lady was in my arms, abandoned to me entirely. I began to dream that she was running away with me. Who was I if not Anton himself? Yes indeed, I cast myself in the role of the author of the letter. Do you think I was an intruder? But at the time, I agreed to it. For if my lady's life was devoid of any worth, what did it matter if I helped in her ravings? Who knows? Maybe this madness might heal the wound which was stealing her body away from her. But do you see, Father, the pretence I had taken on? I, Duarte Fortin, General Commissioner of all the domestic staff, was running away with a white woman, and a princess into the bargain. As if she would ever want someone like me, a man of my colour and unequal legging. There's no doubt about it, I have the soul of a worm, and I shall have to crawl around in the next world. My sins require many a prayer. Pray for me, Father, pray for me a lot! For the worst, the worst is yet to come.

I was carrying the princess along by a roundabout route. She wasn't even aware of the diversion. I took the lady down to the riverbank and laid her on the soft grass. I went to the river to fetch some water. I bathed her face and her neck. She replied with a shiver, and her mask of powder began to dissolve. The princess gasped for breath. She looked around and asked:

'The station?'

I decided to lie. I told her it was right there, just nearby. We were in the shade only in order to hide from the others, who were waiting in the station yard.

'We mustn't be seen. We had better wait for the train in this hiding place.'

She, poor soul, thanked me for my cares. She said she had never met such a kindly man before. She asked me to wake her up when the train came; she was very tired, she needed rest. I sat there looking at her, enjoying her close presence. I saw the buttons on her dress and imagined the warmth that lay underneath. My pulse gathered pace. At the same time, I was scared. And supposing the boss were to catch me right there in the middle of the grass with his lady? It would just be a question of pointing the dark muzzle of his shotgun at me and firing. It was the fear of being shotgunned that deterred me. I lingered there, just looking at that woman in my arms. It was then that my dream once again began to escape me. Do you know what, I felt, Father? I felt that she no longer had her own body: she was using mine. Do you understand, Father? She had a white skin that was mine, that mouth of hers belonged to me, those blue eyes were both mine. It was as if her soul were distributed between two opposite bodies: one male, the other female; one black, the other white. Do you doubt me? You can take it from me, Father, that opposites are the most alike. If you don't believe it, see here: isn't fire most like ice? They both burn, and in both cases, a man can only penetrate them when he's dead.

But if I were her, then I must be dying in my second body. That was why I felt weakened, listless. I dropped down beside her and we stayed there, the two of us, without moving. She, with her eyes closed. I, trying to stave off my slow drift into sleep. I knew that if I closed my eyes, I would never again open them upon life. I was already deep inside myself, I couldn't sink further. There are moments when we are very like the dead, and that semblance gives the dead encouragement. That's what they can never forgive: we who are alive being so like them.

And do you know how I saved myself, Father? By digging

my arms into the warm earth, just as those dying miners had done. It was my roots that bound me to life, that's what saved me. I got up, sweating all over, full of fever. I decided to get out of there, without delay. The princess was still alive and gestured to try and stop me. I ignored her plea. I returned home, all the while with that same anxiety I had felt when I abandoned the survivors at the mine. When I arrived, I told the boss: I found the lady under a tree near the station, she was already dead. I accompanied him so he could see for himself. There in the shade, the princess was still breathing. When the boss bent down, she grabbed him by the shoulders and said:

'Anton!'

The boss heard the name that didn't belong to him. Even so, he kissed her brow lovingly. I went to fetch the cart and, when he picked her up, she was dead, as cold as things. Then, from her dress fell a letter. I tried to pick it up but the boss was quicker. He looked at the envelope in surprise and then glanced at me. I stood there with my chin in my chest, fearful that he might ask questions. But the boss screwed up the paper and put it in his pocket. We went home in silence.

On the following day, I ran away to Gondola. I've been there ever since, working on the trains. From time to time, I come up to Manica and pass the old cemetery. I kneel by the lady's grave and ask her to forgive me for I know not what. Actually, that's not true, I do know. I ask her to forgive me for not being the man she was waiting for. But that's only a pretence of guilt, because you know what a lie this kneeling of mine is. Because while I'm there, in front of her grave, all I can remember is the scent of her body. That's why I've been confessing this bitterness of mine to you, which has stolen my taste for life. It's not long now before I shall leave this world. I've even asked God to let me die. But it seems God doesn't listen to such requests. What did you say, Father? I shouldn't say such resigned things? But that's the memory I have of myself. Widower of a wife I never had. It's just that I feel so wretched. The only happiness that warms me, do you know what it is? It's when I leave the cemetery and go and walk among the dust and ashes of the old Russian mine. The mine is now closed, it died along with the lady. I go there by myself. Then I sit down on an old tree trunk and look back at the road I have trodden. And do you know what I see then? I see two different sets of footprints, but both issued from my body. One set is large, a man's feet. The others are the print of a small foot, a woman's. They're the princess' footprints, walking alongside mine. They are her prints, Father. There is no certainty greater than the one I have of that. Not even God can correct me of such certainty. God may not forgive me my sins and I may run the risk of having hell as my fate. But I don't care: there, in hell's ashes, I shall see the print of her footsteps, forever walking on my left-hand side.

THE BLIND FISHERMAN

'Each man's boat is in his own heart.'
Makua proverb, from northern Mozambique.

We live far from ourselves, in distant make-believe. We vanish into concealment. Why do we prefer to live in this inner darkness? Maybe because the dark joins things, sews together the threads of separation. In the warm embrace of night, the impossible wins us to suppose we can see it. Our fantasies come to rest in such illusion.

I write all this, even before I begin. Written with water by someone who wants no memories, which are ink's ultimate purpose. All because of Maneca Mazembe, the blind fisherman. It happened that he emptied both his eyes, two wells dried up by the sun. The way he lost his sight is a story that defies belief. There are tales that get harder to understand the more they are told. After all, many voices only produce silence.

It happened one fishing trip: Mazembe was lost in the endless deep. The storm had taken the little boat by surprise, and the fisherman drifted boundlessly, ad infinitum. The hours passed, summoned away by time. With neither net nor provisions, Mazembe placed all his faith in waiting. But hunger began to make a nest in his belly. He decided to cast his line, but without any hopes: the hook had no bait. And nobody has heard of a fish that kills itself out of choice, biting an empty hook.

At night, the cold ripened. Maneca Mazembe covered himself with himself. There's nothing more snug than one's body, he thought. Or can it be that babies, inside their pregnancy, suffer cold?

The week went by, full of days. The boat stayed above the line of the water. The fisherman survived above the line of life. As his hunger grew, he felt his ribs in the frame of his body:

'I'm no longer myself.'

It's always like that: one's judgement grows thin more quickly than one's body. It was within that thinness that Maneca's decision took root. He pulled out his knife and held his face firmly. He took his left one out, and left the other one for other tasks. Then he stuck the eye on the hook. Disinterred, it was already a foreign body. But he shivered as he looked at it. That disinherited eye seemed to stare at him, hurt in its orphan's solitude. Which is why the hook, upon piercing his estranged flesh, hurt him more than any thorn can maim.

He cast the line and waited. He could already imagine the size of the fish, drowning in the air. Yes, for it isn't every day that a fish can get his teeth into such a titbit. And he laughed at his own words.

After many false starts, the fish arrived. Fat and silvery. In fact: has anyone ever seen a skinny fish? Never. The sea is more generous than the earth.

That's what Mazembe thought as he avenged his hunger. He cooked the fish in the middle of the boat. Take care, for one day it will catch fire with you in it. That was his wife Salima's warning. Now, with his stomach satisfied, he smiled. Salima, what did she know? Slim, her frailty was that of the reeds, which surrender to the lightest breeze. Nor could he understand how she could muster such strength upon lifting the mortar stick so high. And lulled by the thought of Salima, Maneca wilted into sleep.

But you can't tell the height of a tree by the size of its shadow. Hunger, obstinate as ever, returned. Mazembe wanted to row, but he couldn't. Strength no longer came to help him. It was then that he decided: he would pluck out his right one. And so, once again, he became his own surgeon. The fisherman was enclosed by darkness. The doubly blind Mazembe entrusted his fingers with sight. Once more he cast his line into the sea. He hardly had to wait before feeling the tug which announced the biggest fish he had ever caught.

In his provisional respite from hunger, his arms regained their competence. His soul returned from the sea. He rowed and rowed and rowed. Until the boat hit something, darkness meeting darkness. Judging by the waves, murmuring in infantile ripples, he guessed he must have reached a beach. He got up and shouted for help. He waited several silences. At last, he heard voices, people approaching. He was surprised: those voices seemed familiar to him, the same as those from where he came. Could it be that his arms had recognised the way back, without the help of his sight? He was pulled by many hands helping him to get out of his boat.

There was weeping and bewilderment. All wanted to see him, no one wanted to look at him. His arrival spread joy, his aspect sowed horror. Mazembe had returned shorn of that which goes furthest towards making us what we are: the eyes, windows which reveal the light of our soul.

After that, Maneca Mazembe never again put to sea. Not that it was his desire to remain in such an unliquid exile. He would insist: his arms had proved that they knew the water's paths. But no one would let him go. Every time, his wife would refuse to give him his oars.

'*I must go, Salima. What are we going to eat?*'
'*Better poor than a widow.*'

She would put him at rest, they would catch clams, *magajojo*, shells you could get food from and sell. Like that, they would hold their misery at bay.

'*I can fish too, Maneca, in the boat ...*'

'*Never, woman. Never.*'

Mazembe blew a storm: she was never to repeat such an idea. He might be blind but he hadn't lost his male status.

Times passed. During the long morning, the blind man would stock up on the sunshine. As his mind rode the waves, his dreams fed their images to him. Until, when the day was at its height, his daughter would lead him to the caress of some shade. There they would serve him his food. Only his children were allowed to do this. For the fisherman had given himself over to one sole war: to reject the cares of his devoted wife, Salima. To accept her support was, for Mazembe, the most painful humiliation. Salima offered him tenderness, he shunned it. She called his name, he muttered an answer.

But as time deepened, hunger set in. Salima would creep out, more punctual than the tides, picking up the husks of wretchedness, too many shells for so little food.

Salima then announced to her husband: no matter how much it pained him, she was going to take the boat out the next day. She was going fishing, her body concealed powers unknown to him. Mazembe forbade it, in despair. Never! Where have you ever seen a woman fishing, ordering a boat about? What would the other fishermen say?

'*Even if I have to tie you to my foot, Salima, you are not going out to sea.*'

With his word said and done, he shouted for his children. He walked down to the beach. All his skinniness was tautened by the bow of his body. The tide was low and the vessel was reclining lazily with its belly in the sand.

'*Come, children. Let's haul this boat up.*'

He and his children pushed the boat up on to the dunes. They took it to where the waves never reached. Mazembe shook his hands, slandering his wife.

'*Don't you try anything with me, Salima.*'

And turning to the boat, he declared:

'*Now you're going to be a house.*'

From that day on, Maneca Mazembe lived in the boat, a mariner of dry land. He, along with his vessel, was like a turtle, turned on its back, incapable of returning to the sea. And in that lengthy solitude, Mazembe abandoned himself to neglect.

Until one random morning, Salima approached the boat and stood contemplating her husband. He was in a choice state of dishevelment, his face full of many a day's beard. The woman sat down, and settled a saucepan of rice in her arms. She spoke:

'*Maneca, it's a long time since you gave me a good hiding.*'

Who knows, she volunteered, maybe that bitterness of his was due to his abstinence? Perhaps he needed to feel her tears, lord and master of her sufferings.

'*Mazembe, you can beat me. I'll help: I'll stay still and not dodge at all.*'

The fisherman silently ran along the paths of his soul. He knew women's traps. So he let the conversation drift rudderless:

'*I don't even know the time of day. Nowadays, I never know.*'

Salima persisted, almost in supplication. Let him beat her. The man, after more than a few instants, got up. He stumbled over her, gripped her arm in an accusing clinch. Salima sat awaiting his conjugal violence. His hand came down, but it was to take hold of the saucepan. With a sudden gesture, he threw the food to the ground.

'*Never again bring me food. I don't need anything from you. Ever again.*'

The woman sat among the rice and sand, the world dissolved into grains. She watched her husband returning to the boat and noticed how alike they were growing, man and thing: he deprived of light, it yearning for the waves. As Salima was turning to leave, she was stopped short by his calls:

'Woman, I'm asking you to bring me fire.'

She trembled. What was the fire for? A deep presentiment caused her to want to say no. In tears, she obeyed him. She brought him a stick of burning firewood.

'Don't do it, husband.'

The blind man held the log like a sword. Then, he set fire to the boat. Salima screamed, as she walked round the flames, as if it were inside her that they were burning. That madness of his was an invitation to disaster. Which was why she shook his ragged shirt, so that he would listen to her decision to leave, to take the children away with her to wherever that might be. And so the woman left, without even allowing her children to see their old father in his bewitched state, as he unblessed their lives.

The fisherman was left on his own, the stretch of sand seemed even more vast. In his pitiful design he allowed his night to fall, his fumbling fingers savouring the ashes. Touching the remains gave him a feeling of greatness. At least he had the power to undo, to destroy what was forbidden him.

The days went by without Maneca noticing. One night, however, Salima's presentiment was confirmed: that fire had flown too high and disturbed the spirits. For in the top of the coconut palms, the wind began to howl. Mazembe became agitated, even the ground shivered. Suddenly, the sky was torn apart and fat hailstones fell all over the beach. The fisherman ran through the emptiness in search of shelter. The hail punished him relentlessly. Maneca knew of no explanation. He had never met such phenomena. The earth has risen to meet the sky, he thought. Turned upside down, the world was letting its contents fall. With an orphan's anguish, the fisherman dropped to his knees, his arms wrapped around his head. He wouldn't even have heard himself if he hadn't noticed himself calling for Salima, amid his own sobs and the earth's lamentations.

That was when he felt a soft hand touching his shoulders. He lifted his face: someone was soothing his fever. At first, he resisted. Then he abandoned himself to it, turning childward towards a mother's embrace. He called out:

'Salima?'

Silence. Who was that silhouette so full of tenderness? For sure it was Salima, her woman's body, so slender and firm. But this one's hands were like those of someone older, wrinkled by manifold sadnesses.

She brought him to a shelter, perhaps his old hut. There was a different silence about this place though, another fragrance. Out there, the winds were growing tired. The storm was dying down. Now, the hands were bathing his face, cooling his salt.

'You, I don't know who you are ...'

A comb tidied his hair. In the lull, Maneca was almost falling asleep. With a movement of his shoulder, he helped her to dress him in a shirt, freshly ironed clothes.

'Whoever you are, I beg one thing of you: never use your voice. I don't want ever to hear your words.'

That woman's identity was bound to be lost in the silence. No matter whether those were Salima's hands, or the hut his own: in his ignorance he would acquiesce. For the rest, he was learning to take heed of women's cleverness in taming men, converting them into children, souls with insufficient confidence.

Maneca thus began to recapture time. He allowed himself to be succoured by the solace of that unknown woman. She respected his request and never uttered so much as a sigh.

Every afternoon he would go out into the bush. He was carrying out some secret task, his sole devotion. Until one afternoon, he appeared before his voiceless companion and said:

'Take these oars. Down there, on the beach, you'll see a boat which I have made for you to go out fishing.'

And he went on: she should go out, impose her command on the boat. Nor should she worry about him. He would stay on the shore, and content himself with the jetsam washed up by the sea.

'Just take it that I'm looking for those eyes of mine that I lost.'

From then on, each and every morning without fail, the blind fisherman could be seen wandering along the beach, stirring up the foam which the sea spells out on the sand. And with such liquid steps, he appeared to be seeking the wholeness of his face among the many generations of waves.

WOMAN OF ME

'The man is the axe, the woman is the hoe.'
Mozambican proverb.

That night, the hours ran all round me, like sleepless clockhands. All I wanted was to forget me. Lying there like that, the only thing I seemed to lack was death. Not the definitive one that takes us away with it. The other: the season-death, the winter subverted by guerrilla blossoms.

The December heat made me disappear, aware only of the ice melting in my glass. The cube of ice was like me, both of us were transitory, converting ourselves into the previous substance out of which we had been formed.

In this while, she came in. She was a woman whose soft eyes cast a moist film upon the room. She wandered around, as if she did not believe in her own presence. Her fingers travelled over the furniture in distracted affection. Who knows, perhaps she was walking in her slumber, maybe that reality held more in the way of fiction for her? I wanted to warn her that she was mistaken, that that was not her correct address. But her silence alerted me to the fact that a destiny was being fulfilled right there, at the meeting point of fateful providences. Then she sat down on my bed, arranging herself tidily. Without looking at me, she began to cry.

I didn't even guide myself: my caresses were already uncoiling on her breast. She lay back, emulating the earth in a state of gestation. Her body opened itself to me. If we had gone further in the moments that followed, we would have reached the realm of concrete fact. But in the course of my advances, I shuddered. Hidden voices held me back: no, I couldn't give in.

But this unknown woman was provoking me with the descent of her cleavage. Her bust peeped out at me, corrupting my intentions. Ancient legends were giving me their warning: a woman will come who will light up the moon. If you resist, you will merit the name of the warrior people from whom you stem. Not that I could decipher the legend-like message very well. But what was certain was that there, in that very room, I was being put to the test, to see how much my powers were worth.

But thanks to the intruder's arts, I was disappearing, intermittent, from existence. I was unfulfilling myself. And when I appealed to myself to return to reason, I could not even get as far as that austere judge, my brain. All because of the woman's voice: it recalled the gentle murmur of a spring, the seduction of a return to times beyond, when there was no before. She sought to turn me into a child, to lead me back to a primitive quiescence. Bird-like, she nested in my breast. Was she seeking in me a mirror for the soft moonlight? I abandoned myself, without dignity. The dark circles of her eyes, round without end, aroused me like two sobs, it was as if they were part of my body, yet gazed longingly at me.

She told her story, the episodes of her life. Variants of truth, they fed me the sweet taste of deceit. I wanted the infinite, just like children who always ask: and then?

But the stranger noticed an absence in herself. She had to

go. She promised she would return straightaway. Presently, at the latest. From the doorway, she blew me a kiss, like a wife of many a year. She went out and blended with the shadows.

I don't know how long she took. Perhaps a night or two. Or a few scarce moments. I just don't know. For I fell asleep, anxious to extinguish myself. Waking up pained me, I cursed the morning. I understood the cause of such tribulation: waking up is not merely a passage from sleep to vigil. It's more than that, it's a gradual process of ageing, each arousal adding to the fatigue of all humanity. And I concluded: life, the whole of it, is one extended birth.

Then I remembered the previous dream, conscious of the truth that she revealed herself only in a state of delirium. After all: the dead, the living, and those awaiting their birth, make up one large canvas. The frontier between their territories can be summed up as fragile, moving. In dreams, we are all enclosed in the same space, there where time yields to total absence. Our dreams are no more than visits to these other past and future lives, conversations with the unborn and the deceased, in the language of unreason which we all speak.

The yet-to-be-born, those who are waiting for a body, are the ones we should fear most. For we know almost nothing of them. From the dead, we still go on getting messages, we take kindly to their familiar shadows. But what we are never aware of is when our soul is made up of these other, transvisible spirits. These are the pre-born, and they don't forgive us for inhabiting the light side of existence. They couple together the most perverse expectations, their powers pull downwards. They seek to make us return, insisting on keeping us in their company.

What are they envious of, these yet-to-comers? Is it that they have no name, that they do not breathe clear light? Or, like me, do they fear someone may be travelling through their lives before them? Are they scared that such anticipation will make them less possible, as if they might be worn out by some prior incumbent?

Well I, at that moment, envied both categories: the dead, because they seemed to resemble the perfection of deserts; the unborn, because they had an entire future at their disposal.

Seated on my creased sheets, I would look at the newly risen light of day, full of its restless particles of luminous dust. The sound of traffic reached me through the window, the city self-satisfied with its bustling disorders. I felt a yearning, not for supernatural beliefs, but for the other, infranatural ones, our suppressed and silent animal convictions. It wasn't human nostalgia that afflicted me. For the longing of men is always for the present, it is born of a love that fails to fulfil its duties on time. My sadness was of another type: it came from having touched that woman. I felt burdened by the expense of remorse. What misdemeanours had I committed if desire had sprouted from my fingertips alone?

I got up, looking for some sign of negligence. But the room left me unprotected, orphaned. For when things are looked at clearly, we spend our lives travelling from the uterus to our house, each house being but another edition of the womb. Like a bird that is forever weaving a nest, its nest, for its future births rather than for its offspring. This woman reminded me, after all, that the house offered me no welcome.

I glanced through the window, I saw the woman arriving. A suspicion, a certainty, came to my thought that she was no more than one of these yet-to-come creatures, dispatched in order to withdraw me from the kingdom of the living. Her temptation was as follows: to take me away into exile from the world, to migrate me to another existence. In exchange, I would feed her with bodily caresses, which only the living manage to possess.

I needed to think quickly: she enjoyed the advantage of not

needing to consult reason. I had to find, in a trice, a possible escape. It came to me through intuition: somewhere there must exist the murderers of the dead, the defenders of the unborn. What I needed to do was to summon one such killer to extinguish not the life of that woman, but rather my suspicion of her. The question was: where would I find such a killer, how to provoke his immediate apparition? For it was urgent, she was coming, her steps were already climbing the stairs.

What to do, if I had no time left? Kill her myself, in body and in blood? That would only be of any use if we were both dreaming, something which I didn't seem to be. She had been sent expressly to fetch me, to take me there where everything is still futurely possible.

She came in, I shivered. This time, the intruder seemed even more beautiful to me, ever more like a goddess, demanding the total devotion of a believer. My deliverance arrived, a plank brought by a wave.

I said to her:

'I can imagine you still tiny, as you were in the yesterday of before. Do you remember?'

Startled, she became anxious. For a moment or two, her chest failed her, and she stood with bated breath. The unborn have no memory, their first cry is yet to blossom. Her fear inspired my cunning, I prepared myself while I watched her walk up to the mirror. The stranger contemplated herself as she got undressed, smiling in the petal of each gesture.

You just pretend, you don't even see yourself, I told her, by now more in control of myself. She abandoned her self-attentions and came over to the bed and touched me. She called my name gently. She passed her fingers over my lips.

'You don't understand.'

She smiled, hurt. My fragile artfulness had caused her offence. Nevertheless, I forgave myself. Her serene smile had returned.

'Calm yourself, I haven't come to fetch you.'

What had she come there to do in that case? For the more she took possession of herself, the more concerned I became. The emissary went on:

'Don't you understand? I have come to find a place in you.'

She explained her reasons: only she harboured the eternal gestation of springs. Without me being her, I was incomplete, formed only in the arrogance of halves. In her, I had found not a woman to be mine, but the woman of me, the one who, from now on, would light me in each phase of the moon.

'Let me be born in you.'

I closed my eyes, slowly dousing myself. And so, lying there calmly, I listened to the sound of my steps as they became more distant. They weren't advancing in solitary march, but rather next to others of a female glide, as if they were hours that ran through me like sleepless clockhands that night.

THE LEGEND OF THE FOREIGNER'S BRIDE

Here is my secret: I have already died. But it is not this which causes me sadness. What ails me is that only some believe me: the dead.

It was a place that lay beyond all journeys, only ever visited waterishly by the wind. In that solitary spot, time had long since grown old, the grandfather of bygone days.

One time, however, a stranger passed that way. He was a man with neither face nor story. If he arrived there once, he stayed even longer. Everybody feared this forbidding intruder, this unaccredited ambassador to their privacy. Truly, his eyes revealed no soul, peering from their sockets like those of a blind man.

When the afternoons began to wilt, he would approach the village in search of something only he knew about. The villagers asked themselves:

'But this man: where has he come from, whose name is his?'

No one knew. He had appeared without notice. He had arrived in February, that much they remembered. The month was already moistened, its waters planted. The stranger had a dog with him, and their steps joined in unison. Man and animal bedabbled abundantly. They crossed the muddy earth, but the further they went, the less they got away. When they disappeared beyond the trees, the rain stopped in a sudden faint. Everybody understood, everybody got worried.

The stranger had built his shelter at a distance that was hard to reach. Gradually, he became a topic of conversation. And at night, under the explosion of stars, the talk never varied: the man and his dog. A conversation of shadows, to keep silence at a distance and no more. Everyone proffered their version of events, laying the blame on the intruder. They invented things, everybody knew. But all listened credulously.

Some claimed to have caught the foreigner asleep.

'We saw him as he snoozed.'

Others requested details, as if fear were a fire always in need of more wood.

'What did we see? We saw his tongue leave his mouth and walk around by itself, far from his body.'

Those listening never doubted. They could already picture the selfsame tongue roaming about, slimy and spittlish. Did it talk? Did it lick or kiss? Nobody could say for sure. Amid the sounds of night, however, they saw the work of the wandering tongue in everything.

And what about the dog? During his owner's absence, the hound never left the ground. It would only get up when his master came up to him. For anyone else, no matter what the bulk, its teeth were ever ready, professionally effective. But it didn't bark: it gave off a hoot, like the talk of an owl! It didn't resemble a voice at all, oh no. Its words were all identical, whimpering twins, the dog barked hootingly and hooted barkingly. And so dog and master would both go off, sniffing out the mornings. What were they looking for? Was it something, or someone?

Nor was it easy to find out: everybody dispersed in fear, every time man and animal approached. Most times it was because of the dog: from its lips there foamed a green slobber of unworldly evil. They had seen it bite a kid goat. The poor creature didn't dally in this world. First, its horns crumbled away. They didn't actually fall off in two solid wholes. No. They were deconsumed, shed like liquid. Then, the goat's hue turned cold, and its hairs began to blow away, feathers of ash on the wind. Hairless, with less constitution than a cloud, the ruminant retreated inside its body. In the end, it was empty, turned to dust, the husk of an animal.

All agreed: the dog could fly. That explained the hooting. The animal took the shape of an owl in the tree tops, its dripping saliva burned leaves and branches. The spittle scalded holes in the ground, producing bluish smoke.

The days were subtracted from life's expense account. The place continued its lonely, deserted existence. It was then that the strange disappearances started. The village folk, one after the other, melted into thin air. It was as if they were being hurled into a bottomless pit. Fear took up many a while, time to which only souls have a right. At night, within the comfort of the fire, murmurs mingled. The elders hauled out ancient curses: we are the Amafengu, the famished people destined to seek work to live, poor who beg from the poor. This stranger is a reminder of the times of our persecution.

'Who knows, maybe he is Amangwane?'

They were talking of a Zulu warrior, the author of much bloodshed and many a massacre. The past: was he buried deep enough? Silhouettes were distorted in brush-strokes of light. Until, by one of the fires, the hunter Chimaliro got up. He had a stern face, with heavy lines. Even before he spoke, he administered a great hush.

'I'm going to deal that shadow his death.'

It was as if someone had shouted snake: the circle scattered, the cascade of voices ceased. Chimaliro, with haughty chest, promised he would bring them the owner's head and the skin of the dog.

The hunter set off, a drop in the landscape. The whole village gathered to ensure his luck, the drums were beaten while he lost himself in the vastness of the bush. The days passed by swiftly, and there was no sign of the hunter. Voices accompanied the lull of time:

'Has Chimaliro come back yet?'

Nothing, he hadn't returned. Murima, the hunter's wife, was already shutting herself away in a widow's hollow. One morning, Murima finally left her house. There was something strange though: she was carrying a *capulana* tied to her back. Inside the cloth, you could glimpse the roundness of a new-born babe. The village began to wonder: what child could she be taking with her? If she had no children, whose was it that Murima was humping? Their looks lengthened, eager for an explanation. Around the fires, the night was filled with rumour.

'That creature she's got on her back, that's no baby. It's her own husband, Chimaliro.'

Some doubted it at, first. The hunter that tiny size? Yes, it had happened as a punishment. Who told us we should stand up to the intruder? The way it happened was a story no one saw but everyone knew. As the hunter and his prey studied each other, Chimaliro noticed that his hands were shrinking. His legs and arms began to disappear inside his clothes as if he were a tortoise. He felt a heat rising within him. Inside him, his bones were burning, melting. Chirnaliro was getting shorter, bedwindled. He tried to run away but failed. The ground now seemed huge, the forest without end. He wandered about aimlessly until his wife found him in his miniature state. She then wiped away his snot and brought him home.

The spell cast on Chimaliro had left hope breathless. Many set off into the bush, trying to escape their despair. The memory of olden times, of persecutions suffered, renewed itself in all of them. Then old Nyalombe summoned everyone together. The survivors gathered to hear his word.

'There's no war we can win against this enemy.'

They should learn from Chimaliro's lesson, which showed that courage without cunning is mere audaciousness. This enemy is going to drain us away, we are on a return journey back to the past. And he prophesied: the longest night would come, so everlasting that living creatures would forget the colour of morning. The darkness would endure so long that the cockerels would go mad and the stars would fall down exhausted. The crowd could already imagine such a night without end. In the trees, the birds could be seen, clustered together, awaiting the adjourned morning. Such that they risked forgetting their day-time warbling. The flowers refused to show their petals, biding their time.

Those present nestled together, fear was the only master. But, with sudden serenity, old Nyalombe stretched out his arm:

'Only she can save us.'

He was pointing at the lovely Jauharia. All looks converged on the girl. The old man advanced among the seated crowd and beckoned Jauharia to rise.

'You will go to this foreigner and offer him all the love in your power.'

Astonishment was laden with discontent, heartfelt censure. Was the girl, after all, not Nyambi's wife to be? Was their commitment not sealed with the bride price? The villagers raised a murmur of protest against old Nyalombe. No, their salvation could not be bought at such a price: Nyambi and Jauharia's betrothal was special, they were almost the only young couple left. The others had gone away, out into life. No one had heard any more of them, as if they had been swallowed up by the world's great emptiness. In those two young lovers lay the tribe's last seed. Offer Jauharia up to the monster's appetite? It would be better to finish it all and vanish without trace.

'*And what is your wish?*'

Nyalombe was probing the winsome young girl. But she was unfurling copious tears and only the slightest shrug of the shoulder emerged from her demeanour. Her sweetheart wrapped her in his arms and took her away from there.

Everyone understood Nyambi's pain. And they remembered how, as an adolescent, the young man had hesitated. For he had delayed too long in applying his affection. It was as if his heart were yawning: his desire did not even seem to be in bud. The elders got worried: it must be witchcraft, a curse weighing upon the boy. They carried out a ceremony to cleanse him of his ill luck. They took Nyambi to the centre of the village, and placed an elderly rooster on top of his head. The cockerel spent the whole night balancing itself on its round perch. At daybreak, they went to look: the cockerel's claws had dug into the boy's flesh and blood was running down his chest. They drove the creature away and helped Nyambi away from there.

'*Now, your ill-luck is over. You'll have as many women as a cockerel can have.*'

These were the words of old Nyalombe. But as far as the young fellow was concerned, he didn't want many. His one desire was Jauharia, the girl with the eyes that soothed the world. Next to her, the rest were nothing.

His parents, however, warned him: that girl is too pretty, her ways are those of other folk. He should choose one without appearance. Nyambi refused, loyal to his passion. His mother enlisted him in conversation, in the most solemn search for reasons:

'*That woman's behaviour belongs to another race.*'

'*She's not black like us ...*'

'That's only on the outside. She's got another race inside her.'

Such complete beauty made her a separate, remote species. If he remained stubborn, he would excite the anger of the spirits, they who safeguarded the peace of the village.

The boy stood firm. After a few months, the rules of courtship were being observed, while the young couple became one. Nyambi's family resigned itself: after all, at the time, the boy had no choice. Jauharia was the last lone female available to a suitor.

The girl was blending into womanhood, her breasts were giving her blouse an outline. Nyambi was losing his self-awareness in the heat of his passion:

'Today, I shall live for many years!'

The two lovers were like two rivers flowing in one current. But they were fulfilling the destiny of all rivers, that slowly disappear inside their own waters. For Jauharia harboured a deep sadness, as if hungering for another life. Might she have eyes for another, one who had already passed into nothingness? Was she yearning for a time that never was? Doubts that never reached another mouth, another ear.

Now Nyambi asked himself: how could he lose his sweetheart, surrender her to the arms of a mischief maker? Never. If the old man preferred, he would take up arms and face the intruder man to man.

'No, you mustn't go.'

'But, Nyalomhe, I can't let her go.'

The old man proverbalised: man is like a duck that suffers the hardness of things in its very beak. The boy would tread the path of disaster, with neither fruit nor advantage. This adversary didn't fight with the usual weapons. Only the beauty of love would take him by surprise.

'But if she doesn't come back, the village will die.'

'In this world, all villages will die.'

The old man added: it wasn't the village that merited salvation. It was the folk, the human folk, those creatures who fill villages, the families of villages.

'Now go, Nyambi. And trust Jauharia to be strong and capable of bending this foreigner.'

The boy withdrew, vexed of heart and heavy of foot.

Then he made for Jauharia's house. Darkness was already smoothing the contours of the world, the girl was at the back of the hut, seated in a pool of twilight. The boy came out of the darkness and placed his arm round Jauharia's shoulders, but she did not stir:

'It's no good, Nyambi. I'm going, I'm going to meet him.'

'But Jauharia, you know ...'

She bade him be quiet with a wave of her hand. She wanted to listen to the village, to take leave of its sounds. He let his arms fall, resigned. And when, upon their parting, he looked at the girl, her face seemed to have changed, to have become that of a foreigner too.

Her sweetheart was the last person to see her. In truth, there was no further light cast on the matter. Even though the eyes of the village became more refined. In the darkness, visions dissolved. Nor did ears peep into the comers of tranquillity. And on the basis of such paltry, doubtful detail, people to this day discuss the outcome of Jauharia's tale.

Some claim they heard the dog hooting and, later, the girl's groans, as her flesh was torn apart by the beast's fangs. Others relate that they heard drums: it was she who was dancing barefoot, upon a never before seen, moon-bathed piece of ground. As she danced, her body turned into sweat, and perspiring, she expired. And when she was almost all water, the foreigner cupped his hands and gathered her up as if, deep in the desert, she were the traveller's last drink. Others still claim for sure, that they saw the stranger heading towards the woods. Except that this time, he wasn't leading just one dog.

Two animals rubbed against his legs, dribbling slaver.

In the end, everyone conformed to her absence: the girl had run away unexplained. The boy had turned to waiting, guardian of his solitude. Next to the fence of thorns which surrounded the village, he sat for time upon end. Are tears, in their transparent descent, supposed to return life to life? Nyambi's were the raw material of vengeance. Old Nyalombe gave him the counsel of his teaching:

'Vengeance is a skill of the weak.'

'It's betrayal which pulls vengeance in its wake, Nyalombe. You should be against betrayal if you want to avoid vengeance.'

Betrayal was the name of such indifference, nobody caring any longer about Jauharia's fate. For she had offered herself, generously, in order to save the others. What gratitude did she merit now?

Ever since the beautiful Jauharia had left, the disappearances, the mysterious killings, had ceased. Fear had almost taken its leave of the village. But the villagers still did not dare enter their fields, which were now overflowing with unsolicited verdure. Only the wind did a hoe's work, turning the sands. Nyambi made up his mind: he would rescue his beloved, kill the usurper and his dog. In this way, he would give continuation to his life, right there at the confluence of time and dream. He set off, carrying a shaky knife, with a quarrelsome blade. He trudged through the dense forest for days, among lianas that rose like hawsers, keeping the clouds at their moorings.

At last, he came across the scene of his expectations. The stranger next to a deep crack in the ground, pulling a long rope to the end of which was attached a bucket. Nyambi did not recognise the place. He threw himself at the stranger, stabbing him countless times. Then, with a strength that even surprised him, he lifted up the body and cast it into the abyss. The intruder fell into the deep waters and immediately a heavy rumbling echoed, as if thunderclaps were being born from the earth's belly. The walls of the hole shook, separated from the body of the ground, and hurtled into the chasm. Minutes later, there was no sign of the fissure. Then Nyambi heard the voices of the vanished villagers, returning from their many recesses. They greeted Nyambi and his act of courage. The youth received their thanks with dispatch: he wanted news of his sweetheart, her state, her whereabouts. The others avoided answering, they solemnly hung their heads. Dead, Jauharia? Nyambi ran, perturbed, through the bush, looking for signs of his beloved. He wandered, lost, for many a day and many a lamentation. Defeated, he returned to the stranger's grave.

When he caught sight of the place, he seemed to hear the sound of sobbing, the trickling of sadness. Nyambi reached the spot: it was Jauharia who was weeping, next to the crack. When the girl noticed the boy's presence, she bent double, all spine from beginning to end.

'I was already in love with that man, Nyambi.'

He walked round the girl, intrigued. A growl alerted him. At the girl's feet, the dog unclenched its ferocity. Jauharia laid her hand on the beast, stroked it, bidding it to be quiet.

She spoke serenely: the man he had dealt death to was a creature of great kindness. He had travelled the land and learned of vastness. In the world, he had seen how time, in its hurry, destroys the family of man.

So, he had given himself a mission: to seek out a distant place, an earthly island, and protect its solitude, fighting the arrival of time. This was the stranger's task and she had understood how much love such a responsibility cost, how much tenderness lay concealed in his dishumanity.

'We are on the frontier here, Nyambi. Now choose: are you returning to the village, or are you going out into the world?'

Nyambi shook his head, as if he were shaking his soul. He stood there with a beggar's expression, believing she might still be able to pull herself out of the bewitchment into which she had fallen. But Jauharia had grown silent, merely caressing the animal. And so, he set out on the journey back to his folk. There, in the distance, the lights of the little houses were being lit. Without any further dream to dwell on, the village invented itself, ignored by the centuries, there beyond the remotest road.

THE FLAGPOLES OF BEYONDWARDS

All we want is a new world: with everything new and nothing of the world.

Rain is a gaoler, imprisoning people. Constante Bene and his children, they were prisoners of the rain, shut up inside their hut. Never before had such water been seen: the landscape had been dripping for seventeen days. Scarcely taught to swim, the water hurt the earth. Fat raindrops, pregnant with sky, pattered closely on the tin roofs. On the side of the hill, only the trees persisted, without ever interrupting each other.

Seated in a corner of the old hut, Constante Bene measured the length of time. Ever since the beginning he had been a guard on the estate of Tavares, the white man. He dwelt among the orange trees, in a place which had all but fled the earth. Up there, on the mountain top, the ground behaved itself, good and proper.

'Here only the oranges have got a thirst.'

The thirst of birds, Constante might have been more right in saying. But he simplified life. To his two children, Chiquinha and João Respectivo, he taught the countless arts of tranquillity. The children received cares from him, orphans though they were. They alone looked after household matters.

Chiquinha, her body developed, exceeded her years. Her breasts already protested at the tightness of her blouse. Her father viewed her growth with pain. The more she grew into herself, the sharper Constante's sadness as he recalled his dead spouse.

His son, João Respectivo, remained small, foreign to time. All were puzzled by his name. Respectivo? But that name had happened, independent of any desire for it. He had taken the infant boy to the town in order to register him. He presented himself at the government office with civilised intent:

'I wish to register this child.'

And the clerk, his competence sluggish:

'Have you brought the respective individual with you?'

'No sir. I've only brought my son.'

'That's what I mean: your respective son.'

Constante Bene thought another name was being added to the child. And that's how the little boy, born from his mother's death, came to be called by that name. In the course of time, he made his entrance into the world led by only one hand, in the unequal half of his orphan's condition.

The guard gazed at the lofty parts of the world, the earth's shoulders, as unwavering as the centuries. As he did so, he thought: the world is large, fuller than fullness itself. Man believes he's huge, almost touching the heavens. But if he reaches places, it's only because he's living in a borrowed size, his height is a debt owed to altitude.

Why don't folk live within their means, just as they are? Why do they thrust themselves forward in the arrogance of conquest? Constante Bene feared the dangers of desire. That's why he forbade his children to look beyond the mountain.

'Never, not ever.'

The prohibition didn't need repeating. Many a tale was told about the other side of the mountain. It was said whites had never set foot over there. Who knows, maybe the earth there still preserved its indigenous hue, the aroma of times past? And, what's more, could it not be that such places were disposed to the exclusive pursuit of happiness?

That place: Bene called it Beyondwards. Many a time, during nightly fatigue, its secret calling encircled the hut. The guard allowed his dreams to wander, so much so that he could no longer trust himself to tell their story. One morning, in the early hours, he took his courage in his own hands and set off in the direction of the heights. He scaled the rocks and reached the summit. He felt remorse, for he was disobeying his own command. He excused himself:

'Today is today.'

Then, he glanced in the direction of the forbidden side. A mist cushioned the moon, spread as pure as the light that envelops a woman's nakedness. It was so misty that the earth was able to free rain from its duty. He let himself sit there for some time. Until an owl issued him its warning. Such beauty was like fire: from afar it couldn't be seen, but once near, it burned. And he returned to the hut.

Now, on the seventeenth day of the rains, Bene sensed the afternoon sighing. The light was already weary in its climb when the leaves saw the sign. The old man's pipe paused in mid puff, the moment strayed.

That was when they saw the mulatto. He was an arrival from afar, from the outer lands. He walked wrapped inside his face, under the teeming rain. He carried a haversack on his back. He passed the hut, unaware of the curiosity of its three occupants. João Respectivo went and peeped down the path. He saw the mulatto scaling the heights, disappearing among the rocks further up.

What man was that, and where had he come from? Even without speaking, the three asked themselves. Love woes, guessed Chiquinha. A leopard hunter, João suspected.

'*That man is not a person to be trusted,*' the father pronounced.

The youngsters defended the intruder, pleading his innocence. They needed someone to happen upon them, a fright in that feverless world. But Bene repeated:

'*That man is a runaway. If he wasn't a runaway, he'd stop here and receive our welcome.*'

Then, he tendered his threat: it was up to him to find out this new arrival's story. After all, that was his job. His children begged him, the half-caste didn't merit such immediate suspicion.

'*Well, I don't place any confidence in him. He's a mulatto. You don't know the ways of such folk.*'

'*But the man passed by, he didn't even step inside our field.*'

The father reflected: in fact, young João was right. The stranger seemed to be making for the high ground, there where men write no tracks.

'*You're right, son. But he must stay away from here.*'

After the rains, the youngsters went out looking for the foreigner. They peered everywhere, among the stones on the mountain top. They came across him on the topmost height, at the mouth of a cave. They watched what he did: the mulatto had found himself a place to live. His hunger seemed to be for inhabiting the soil, deep among its lush green smells. He lived close to the ground, creeping around like an animal. Only a fire and a blanket eased his fatigue. João and Chiquinha watched from afar, lacking the courage to reveal themselves.

At home, their father chastised them for their spying:

'*Don't go there too often. I've always warned you: a fire is lit by blowing it.*'

But deep down, Constante enjoyed hearing news. He asked about the things they had seen. The children replied with loose words, pieces of a torn picture. Then their father insisted: they shouldn't go there too much, he might be a dangerous madman. Above all, he was a mulatto. And he explained himself: a half-caste is neither a yes nor a no. He's a maybe. White, when it suits him. Black, when it's to his advantage. And then again, how can one forget the shame they bear from their mother? Chiquinha broke in: surely they were not all like that. There must be as many good ones as there are bad.

'It's you people who know nothing. Don't go there, and that's all there is to it.'

For a while, his children obeyed him. But the girl. More than just sometimes, she began to climb the heights once more, pretending to look for firewood. Her old father, noticing her delays, suspected disobedience. But he said nothing, awaiting whatever fate might bring.

One night, when the spirit lamp was all but out, Chiquinha was caught coming in. Her father:

'Where have you been?'

'I was there, Father. I can't deny it.'

Constante Bene chewed over her offence, pondered her punishment. But that daughter of mine has already got her late mother's body, he reflected. And he relented.

'You know, Chiquinha, it's the bee itself that refuses its honey. Do you understand what I'm saying?'

She nodded. There then followed a slow wait. Bene blew out the flame, ushering in the dark. Now invisible, the two saw each other more clearly. Then, the father asked:

'Did he say anything?'

'Yes, he did.'

'At last? And what did this half-caste say?'

Chiquinha sat there as if she had heard nothing. Her father waiting on the corner of his curiosity. But the old man, out of respect due to him, couldn't be kept waiting for an answer.

'Listen, daughter: didn't you hear what I asked you?'

'It's that I can't even remember what the man said.'

Her father fell silent. He rocked his chair, helping himself to get up. He was closing the windows when, once again, he asked:

'*Did you manage to find out whether there are other places out there in the world?*'

'*It would seem that there are.*'

The old man hunched his shoulders in disbelief. He took a turn round the room, stumbling into noises. His daughter asked why he didn't light the lamp.

'*For me, night has already fallen.*'

Chiquinha adjusted her *capulana* round her shoulders. Then, she sat down and remained still, as if existing were her sole function. They fell asleep. But they did so with their souls bared, which is an invitation to bad dreams.

In his nightmare, the guard felt he was about to breathe his last. This is what he saw: the mulatto was a soldier and was advancing through the orchard, in his guerrilla uniform. But, what a fright: he was touching the oranges and they lit up in round balls of flame. The orange grove looked like a plantation of spirit lamps. Over the rustling of the leaves, singing could be heard:

Iripo, iripo
Ngondo iripo[1].

Suddenly, lo and behold: Tavares. Furious, his musket in his hands. What was he firing at? At the ground, at the trees, at the mountain. The white man shouted at him:

'*You there, Constante, what sort of a guard are you? Pick those oranges before everything burns.*'

---

[1] Song dating from the war of independence, heralding the approach of guerilla forces.

Constante hesitated. But the gun barrel turned towards his chest caused his obedience to return. Tree by tree, he went reaping ardour until his fingers became ten flames. The old man woke up howling. His hands were burning. His daughter bathed his arms in generous waters. Relieved, he sat down in his chair, and prepared his pipe.

'No, Father. Don't play with fire again, let me light it.'

'My daughter, let me request of you one more order: never again climb the mountain.'

Chiquinha promised, but with false conviction. For, ever since that day, her tardiness had continued. Her father said nothing: he alone suffered the pains of premonition.

One day, in expected surprise, Chiquinha presented herself, a picture of health, hands crossed on her belly.

'I'm with child, Father.'

Constante Bene felt his soul fall at his feet. Chiquinha, still so much a daughter, how could she become a mother so soon? What justice was that, dear God, how could a little orphan girl be the mother of a child without due father? It was vital that the faceless progenitor should be found.

'Was it him?'

'I swear, Father. It wasn't.'

'Then who is the owner of this pregnancy?'

'I can't say.'

'Look, daughter: you'd better talk. Who mounted you?'

'Father, leave me alone.'

The girl sat down, the better to weep. Constante thought about beating her, tearing the truth out of her. But from Chiquinha's body, there emerged the growing memory of his late spouse and his arm fell limp, vanquished. The old man returned to his room, lit his pipe and smoked the entire landscape through the window.

The months passed by in a wide detour. Chiquinha's belly

swelled, full and moon shaped. In June, she gave birth, helped by the old women of the neighbourhood. Constante wasn't at home at the time. He had gone out to do the rounds of his field. When he returned to the hut, the midwives were already preparing the meal. At first he was aware of the smoke-borne smell. Then the cry of a baby. He smiled, remembering the saying: wherever you see smoke, you'll find men; wherever babies cry, you'll find women. Now the sayings were getting mixed up. He paused in the doorway, his heart leaping. A cry in that place! It could only be one thing! His urge was to know how Chiquinha was, he felt like rushing in. But there was a deal of pride hindering him from becoming a grandfather.

'*That baby was born with too much presence,*' he confessed inside his voice. He went in.

Attentive to every noise and shadow. The women fell silent, tense. More than the others, Chiquinha sat stock still with the bundle of life in her arms.

The father settled himself in a far corner. João Respectivo was the first to utter a word:

'*Father, have you seen the birth? A fat little boy child.*'

Chiquinha's eyes yearned for her father's reply. Her gesture was almost one of repentance at showing the child but then she corrected herself. The women began to file out. Now there wasn't much space left in the place.

Days went by, full of time, and still Constante could not accept his grandfather's status. Many a time, the girl lingered by her father, in longing expectation of his blessing. Under her breath, she sang stealthy lullabies, the same ones she had learnt from him. She sang more to lull her father than the child. But Constante avoided her, bedimming himself before his daughter's looks.

One night, when everyone was asleep, a trembling light crossed the room. It halted by Chiquinha's bed and stayed there, flickering like a beacon. Touched by the light, Chica awoke and saw her father, candle in hand. Constante excused himself:

'That child of yours was crying. I came to see.'

Chiquinha smiled: he was lying. If the baby had cried, she would have heard it before anyone else. Later, João confirmed the truth: the old man crossed the darkness every night in order to peep at the cradle. Chica couldn't contain herself. She hugged her little son in blissful happiness.

On the following morning, with the sun already high, the guard was having his breakfast. He was chewing last night's leftovers, sucking his teeth with his tongue.

'Listen there Chica: isn't that son of yours ever so light?'

'Babies are like that Father. They only grow darker later. Don't you remember João?'

'That's in the beginning, before their race gets to them. But this one here: so many days have passed, and it's time he got his colour.'

Chiquinha shrugged her shoulders, at a loss. She peeled a sweet potato and blew on her overhot fingers. At last, her son was a grandson. From now on, she wouldn't be alone in securing the little boy's life.

And so a new feeling was born in the hut. Even Bene seemed younger, warbling and weaving songs. Chiquinha rewarded her father with meals that lingered longer on his palate. Little João yielded himself to childhood fantasies, running along paths known only to the animals.

Constante did not require his presence, respecting the child's ways. Previously, he used to play with the boss's son. The children, on the curved pinnacle of their laughter, ignored the frontier of their races. Bene was pleased, seeing his little Respectivo receiving borrowed cares.

'At least he gets fed there.'

Since the mulatto's arrival, however, the boy had turned to loftier whereabouts.

Once, concerned at his son's lateness, Bene went out onto the mountain, in the direction of the wilderness João had ventured into. Next to the well, he called his son. But it was Laura, the woodcutter's wife, who came out of the bushes. She carried a can of water on her head, as if she felt no weight at all. In the lull of her shoulders, the odd drop of water was spilt, wetting her back, her arms, her breasts.

'Constante, you're a guard. You should look after your life.'

'And why should that be, just because I'm a widower?'

Bene thought Laura was trying to untie his widowhood. He looked at the woman with many eyes, imagining her body beneath her *capulana*. He tried some sweet talk, but she diverted his words:

'Do you know they're all talking about your daughter, and how she caught her child?'

She repeated the gossip to him: she'd been seen, nobody could say by whom, up there on the high ground. And then the unmentionable: a man had forced her, had tumbled on top of her. Constante mumbled curses, his voice grew cold:

'Was this man black?'

'No, they say he wasn't.'

'I know who the rogue is. In fact, I've always known.'

Without taking his leave, he started back home. He didn't go into the house. From a box in the yard he took a cutlass. He drew it along his fingers, its sharpness his thought.

Then, unhurried, he climbed the mountain. Up on the summit, he searched for the mulatto. He found him, bent over the fire, giving new strength to its heat. Constante didn't hide his intention, his arm hanging beside him, in full view.

'I've come to kill you.'

The stranger showed no fear. Only his eyes, those of a cornered animal, sought an escape. With tightened throat:

'Was it your boss who sent you?'

Constante ignored the question. For sure, the other wanted to distract him. He hesitated, unsure. Not an avenger by profession, he requested help for his hatred. He prayed within himself: my God, I don't even know how to kill! Just for a second, I beseech You, give this hand of mine certainty.

'Why do you hate me so much?'

Once again, the other was diverting him away from his intentions; the guard queried:

'Tell me: do you come from over there, from Beyondwards?'

'From where?'

'From over there, the other side of the mountain?'

'Yes, I do.'

'And has the new flag been raised there yet?'

The intruder smiled, almost in slow pity. Flag? Was that what interested him, to know about a piece of cloth and its colours?

'You answer like that because you're a mulatto. And mulattos don't have a flag.'

The other laughed scornfully. That laugh, thought Bene, was a sign from God. The cutlass glinted in the air and, hey presto, stabbed the stranger. Bellowing, he fell on top of him. He clung to him, a stubborn liana. The two danced around, trampling the fire. But Bene didn't even feel his feet ablaze. Another blow and the intruder lay twisted on the ground, like a pangolin.

The guard crouched next to his victim and with his hands, checked to see if he was dead. He felt the blood, sticky to his touch. It was as if viscous fingers were pointing their blame at him. He sat down on the ground, tired. Where did such exhaustion come from? From killing? No. That deep despondency came from his feet, scorched by the fire. Only now did he feel the sores.

He tried to get up: he failed. His steps could barely touch the ground. He stared at the lights down there in the valley. It was a trackless distance away, an impossible return.

He dragged himself over to the mulatto's backpack. He took out the water flask and drank. Then he emptied the rucksack: papers fell in the firelight. He picked up loose sheets and slowly deciphered the letters. Beautiful dreams lay written there, promises of a more bounteous time. Schools, hospitals, houses: everything in abundance, enough for everybody. His pulse raced, mutinously. He shook the rucksack again. It must be there, screwed up in a corner, he'd find it.

At that moment, like a silver wave, the flag fell out of the sack. It looked huge, greater than the universe, Bene was dazzled, he had never believed that he might one day have such a vision.

Meanwhile, he recalled the present pains: the flagpole at the administration block. There, his memory fell to its knees, the policeman's truncheon, 'don't kick up dust, you shit, don't soil the flag'. And he, dragging his feet, carrying his children, without raising his step. The boss, on the pavement, feigned concern with other attentions. Can a man lose so much of his soul in such a way?

But now, this new flag didn't seem to be subject to any dust, as if it were made of the very earth. The colours of the cloth peopled his dream.

He was woken by his son, Respectivo. He looked around him, searching for the mulatto's body. Not a thing, there was no body.

'Did you bury him, João?'

'No Father. He ran away.'

'Ran away? How could he if I killed him?'

'He was only wounded, Father.'

A man of doubts, the guard shook his head. He had made sure of the other man's death. Could it be the work of witchcraft?

'He was certainly alive. I helped him down the mountain myself.'

Furious, the guard hit the little boy. How could he? Help a fellow who had abused the respect of Chiquinha, of himself, of the whole family?'

'It wasn't him, Father.'

'It wasn't? Then who gave your sister her pregnancy?'

'It was the boss, the white man.'

Constante didn't even allow himself to listen. The mulatto had taken a grip on those children's heads, had become their only faith.

'That son-of-a-bitch half-caste is from the secret police. I found a soldier's pack there in the cave. Do you think it was ever his? He's from the secret police, the PIDE, and he abused your sister, and stole a guerilla's backpack.'

'It was the boss.'

'Look, João, don't say that again.'

'It was, Father. I saw him.'

'Do you swear?'

The boy asserted himself, with tears of conviction. Bene scarcely breathed. The size of that truth was beyond his grasp. His feet hurt him more, the blood asleep on his wounds. By now, flies were buzzing around, tainting the prestige of that sacred liquid. With his fingers, he crumbled a lump of sand. The earth submitted to him, reduced to flour. Such obedience between his fingers gradually brought him back to the serene breathing of one who has come to his decision.

'Don't cry any more, son. Look what I took from the sack.'

And he held out the flag. João blinked, lame in his understanding. A flag, was it for a flag that the old man was rejoicing?

'Wrap the flag with the greatest care inside the sack. Help your father, pick up the backpack and let's go.'

João offered him his shoulders. The old man jumped up

on them, as if a child. He joked: *'We've swapped: I'm the son, you're the father.'*

And they both laughed. Secretly, the old man was astonished by the boy's strength: he didn't even pause to regain his breath.

'All right, son: enough is enough. Uncouple your body. I want to climb down from you.'

They were near the house. They sat down in the shade of a large mango tree.

João turned his tongue loose, announcing futures:

'This conversation is dangerous, my son.'

But little João was gathering courage, repeating the mulatto's teachings. That land belonged to its sons alone, tired of bleeding wealth for foreigners.

'Tavares ...'

'Leave the boss out of this.'

'Father, you can't forever be a guard, guarding this land and pretending it wasn't stolen from us by the settlers.'

Father's temper was beginning to rise. The kid should keep quiet, he was talking through other people's mouths. The old man ordered them to get moving again. João tried to help his father, but he refused it:

'I don't need you. Otherwise you might get a bit too big for your boots.'

They limped down the path. Now, Constante supported himself with a stick, mumbling a procession of complaints. At least a stick doesn't have ideas or vanities. It carries me along, that's all. As for men ... Well, I prefer things, I have no axe to grind with them.

By the stream, after refreshing himself, he changed his tone: *'Listen, João, I always have this doubt in me: now I'm a white man's servant. What will become of me after!'*

'After, there will be freedom, Father.'

'Nonsense, son. After, we'll be servants to those soldiers. You don't know about life, my boy. These gunfire folk, come the end

of the war, they won't be able to get used to doing anything else. Their hoe is a musket.'

The boy looked away, denying such circumstances. So why were you waiting for the new flag, Father? Why did you devote yourself to dreaming of the other side, the Beyondwards?

'It's just a dream that I enjoy.'

Respectivo gave up arguing. All his adolescence was opposed to was that such a clear sun should be condemned to such a summary sunset.

'Don't deceive yourself, son: tomorrow will be the same day.'

They drew near the house and heard voices. They pricked up their ears: it was the white man who was shouting inside the hut. Constante, forgetting his limp, went in. The boss was embarrassed, and lost his bridle. But soon he calmed down, puffing out his shoulders, stretching his skin:

'What's that you've got on your feet? Your paws are covered in blood.'

The old guard didn't answer. He shuffled up to the boss. Only then did he notice that he was taller: the white lacked heels. Taking his time, he lit his pipe. Tavares received the smoke of his affront:

'Don't you want to tell me how you did that? Well then, I'll tell you what that is: a black man's trickery. But you can be sure, you're not getting so much as a day off! I want to see you doing the rounds of the estate this very day.'

Impassive, Bene seemed not to hear. The boss came closer, as if to tell him a secret. There was big game in the neighbourhood, a terrorist. The administrator had alerted the farmers regarding a mulatto, a dangerous, careless fugitive.

'Keep those eyes of yours open, Bene. Fungula masso ...'

'Don't talk like that ... Boss.'

'Did you hear that?! And pray why not, Your Excellency?'

'Because it's not even your dialect.'

Tavares laughed, preferring scorn. He took his leave. Before closing the door, however, he turned to Chiquinha:

'We'll leave it at that then, do you hear?'

And he was gone. Not a single word coloured that space. Constante consulted the window, and received the silent messages of the landscape. It was as if the pipe were smoking him. After a long silence, the guard called his son.

'You know where the mulatto is. Go and tell him I want to speak to him. I need him here.'

'But the night's so late,' Chiquinha shivered. He caressed the girl's hair, mindful of her concern.

'You go with João. Give the mulatto my message, then climb the mountain, and wait for me among the stones.'

'Are we going beyondwards?'

Chiquinha opened her eyes wide with excitement. Her father smiled indulgently:

'Go, accompany your brother. And cover my grandson with this blanket. Wait there for me, I shall come.'

The children behaved obediently. They filled a basket with provisions.

'You, João: leave the half-caste's backpack with me.'

The two children left, hurrying through the long grass. They avoided the mists which, according to legend, make your legs shrink. An owl hooted, inculpating times to come. In the dark, the world lost its angles and edges. Chiquinha followed where her brother's hand led her. Young Respectivo seemed to her, at that moment, to have been promoted in his years. He had already carried out his father's order, taking the *mestizo* his message.

They reached the rocks, and sat down. Chiquinha hugged her baby with a mother's composure. She spoke:

'You two don't like Tavares, I know. But, in himself, he's a man of good heart.'

Respectivo did not understand. The white had stained her,

heaped abuses on her. What else did he deserve if not the fetters of vengeance?

'Be quiet, João. You don't even know how it happened.'

Chiquinha got up, outlined in the moonlight. In her brother's eyes, she appeared like the moon through a cloud. Chiquinha lowered her voice:

'Tavares doesn't even deserve punishment. It was I who provoked him.'

Her brother didn't want to hear any more. She wanted to explain, he wouldn't let her. The mountain awoke, startled at their double shouting. Chiquinha's rage imposed itself:

'I wanted to give him a father. Someone to get us out of this misery.'

That was when they heard the fearful crackle of flames. They looked down at the valley, it seemed like a fire suspended in mid air, flying flames which did not need the earth in order to happen. Only later did they understand: the entire orchard was ablaze.

Then, on the red-stained horizon, brother and sister saw a flag being raised over the administration block. Blossom of the plantation of fire, the cloth fled its own image. Thinking it was caused by the smoke, the children wiped their eyes. But the flag asserted itself, a star's portent, showing that it is the sun's destiny never to be beheld.

THE LETTER

The old woman bent her legs as if she were bending the centuries. The ground was her illness, as she allowed herself to fall ever nearer to it. She supported herself on dust, who knows, to accustom herself to the grave, on the surface of the world?

'Read me the letter.'

She handed me the paper, screwed up and folded in filth a thousand times over. It was a letter from her son, Ezequiel. He had long since departed, dressed in his uniform, and his head shaved to a zero. The letter, he had sent many a well-worn year ago. It was always the same, I knew it by heart, every single comma.

'Again, Mother Cacilda?'

'Yes, once again.'

I took the paper and placed it under my gaze, I pretended to caress the shape of the letters. They were hardly visible, so blurred with sweat were they. They had slept under Cacilda's kerchief ever since the war had started. Those letters smell of gunpowder, they twist around my heart. That was what the old woman was in the habit of saying. Now, with the passing of time, the bit of paper was the only proof of her Ezequiel. It was as if her son only complied with existence through that ever more faded handwriting.

The first few times, I actually read it, faithfully conveying the little soldier's original version. The letters were uneven, like school children breaking out of line. There were more mistakes than words gathered there. The filling was no bigger than the shape. For in that writing, there wasn't a line of tenderness. Had the soldier learnt war, while unlearning love? In Ezequiel, had the son not died in order for the trooper to be born?

In my first readings of it, my heart tightened so much as I invented dedications to that mother. As I read, I would glance at the aged woman's face, trying to detect a wrinkle of sadness. Nothing. The old woman was unmoved, as if she yearned for death. Her eyes did not speak of pain at all.

I tried to comfort her, to excuse the child who had failed to survive in uniform. Don't be sad, Mother Cacilda. And as for the way they carried that child off to become a soldier! Without a shirt, without a case, without news. Thrown into the back of a truck as if he were a parcel without an address on it.

'Try and understand, Mother Cacilda.'

But she was already asleep, lying in some ancient shadow. Or was she feigning sleep, leaning on the veranda of her soul? The old woman was pretending. Like a river which disguises itself as a lake when it reaches the weir. Then she would return to her eyelids and hurry me along.

'Go on. Why did you stop?'

There wasn't anything left to read. Just the greasy scrawl of a kissless farewell. Can a letter from a loving son end like this: 'unity, labour, vigilance'?

But the old woman persisted, pounding away at her daydream. Keep reading, for everyone knows that letters are the same as stars: though few, they are infinite. I must be patient with her, a poor mother without any schooling. It was at that point that I began to stretch the ink, softening the original words. I invented. At each reading, a new letter emerged from the old missive. And Ezequiel, in the meanderings of my imagination, gained the countless skills of a son's state, a man with the talent for remaining a little boy. Cacilda listened in a lull, as if my voice contained the waves of a long buried sea. She would set sail on a visit to her son, everything happening within the charity of a lie. It is said that by indulging in madness we cure ourselves of our insanity.

Until, one day, they brought me news. Ezequiel had lost his existence once and for all. He had met his end in some unknown bush, a victim of bandits. His mother suspected nothing. I asked: they didn't know her whereabouts. I was charged with giving her the sombre news. I waited. That afternoon, however, Cacilda didn't come to my house. I got scared: had she guessed Ezequiel's fate? Who knows the powers of a mother when exercising her yearnings?

I decided to pay her a visit. When I left, there were still some stains of sunset in the sky. Cacilda was cooking some miserable grains, a bird's dinner.

'Sit down, my son, have something to eat, poverty is easily shared.'

I lingered, composing my courage. How could I kindle her mourning? We ate. Rather: we pretended to eat. Imagine it's a meal, my son. Imagine. Like the way I live, imagining.

'And now, speak: why did you come to my house?'

I stared at the ground, the world was fleeing through its bottom. She broke the silence.

'Have you come to read me, my son?'

I nodded. I took the old piece of paper but delayed starting. I wanted to be sure of my tones, so as not to allow my voice to tremble. Finally, I set off across the writing, in the opposite direction of truth. I brought her news of her son, his trail of heroic deeds. He, the bravest, the most generous, the most exceptional of sons.

As always, the mother listened in careful silence. Sometimes, in the colour of a paragraph, she would smile: always the same, that son of mine. I congratulated myself, once my mission of pretence had been accomplished. I took my leave, almost in relief. It was then, in my last glance, that I saw her: the old mother was throwing the letter into the fire. As I turned, she modified her gesture. The paper took an instant to be chewed up by the flames. In that split second, I noticed the tear fall on the mat. She was pretending to wave the smoke away from her face, and affected to put the letter under her headscarf. Once again, I took my leave, kidding myself that my farewell was the same as all the other ones I had bidden her.

THE SEATED SHADOW

The sun walked barefoot over the plain, dragging its daytime feet across the landscape. My eyes coughed a lot of dust, and crouching under their eyelids, glimpsed the bony ground.

The sight of it caused pain: that earthen skeleton was, when all is said and done, the skeleton of us all. And that sand which spread lingeringly into the distance was our dying soul.

I was on my way to visit old Brakes, for I wanted to hear his counsel regarding the ways of the world. Brakes had been a level-crossing keeper. For years, his command had been enough to bring trains to a standstill. He would raise his flag and the metal would spark as the brakes were applied. Hence his name.

Later, time misted his eyes. They told him: take your pension and go. He went back to his birthplace, there where the whistle of trains had never been heard. But the old man, in his near deafness, fancied he could hear the metallic sighs of locomotives between the long silences.

'Does the line reach near here now? One day, my strength will return. I shall go and find the whereabouts of the little train.'

In the old man's mind, time abounded. That was why I liked to go back and see him. Because of this, I had abandoned my city dweller's duties and hit the trail. I followed the earth paths, those which are born of the conversation between the ground and a traveller's feet. Along the sandy tracks, my legs returned to school, twins learning the ways of distance.

When I got there, Brakes came out onto the veranda of his eyes and looked at me in surprise:

'Have you walked all this way just to see me?'

He greeted me with words of warning: a country that no longer travels no longer dreams. I gave him the cigarettes that I had wrapped in a plastic bag. The old man looked hard at the bag as if it were worth more than its contents.

'Is the plastic a present too?'

And he laughed, showing his unfurnished mouth. He corrected his laugh with the back of his hand.

'All I need teeth for is to laugh. Even if I had all of them, I wouldn't have any work to give them any more. What do I swallow nowadays? Saliva, that's all.'

And he explained himself: the shame of his laugh. Merriment should be bitten and rolled around the mouth. Merriment needs the letter L. To laugh without teeth is like drinking beer without foam. This time, it was my turn to smile.

'I'm telling you,' he said, *'what competence has a toothless smile got?'*

Such was the way we spent our leisure: slowly digressing. No longer did the subject appear than it was lost. But Brakes, in the middle of it all, asked me:

'Are they still attacking the trains?'

I remained silent in the face of the evidence: that was a subject which wore its sadness on its sleeve. I answered: sometimes. He shook his head, chasing away his anguish.

'The war is hungry: it swallows whole families.'

The old man had retreated inside himself, surrounded by his own words. Watching him in such a pained disposition, I pondered upon how we are becoming unaccustomed to innocent deaths, so many crimes are there. For the fear of his loss came to me as a requiem foretold. But I wasn't afraid that the old man's life might stumble into illness or spiral into age.

I was merely scared that they might take him by surprise and kill him.

I asked him if he still slept in the bush.

'*Not any more. I sleep here, the bush is a place for goats.*'

I reminded him of how exposed that little house of his was. He didn't answer. I couldn't make out whether he hadn't heard, or whether the wrapping had stolen his attention. He rummaged in the bag and took out the packets of cigarettes.

'*Take them, I don't need them now. The plastic can stay, nothing else.*'

His refusal surprised me. But I didn't press him, hazarding a guess at the hidden reasons he was using.

'*Something is about to happen: it's a long time since I heard the train over in that direction. Such a long time.*'

I bade the old man farewell, sensing that I would never again refresh my soul in that seated shadow.

THE RISE OF JOÃO BATE-CERTO

João Bate-Certo. People say: his obsession was the city. He wanted to go there, capture its visions. He wanted to witness for himself the reports of those who journey through distant dusts. In the end, does the smell of the fruit recall the blossom's fragrance?

More than anything, he wanted to see the buildings. To admire the concrete scaling heights, floor upon floor, storeys without end. For there where he lived, everything was earth-bound, a neighbour of the sand. Bate-Certo wagered: if there was a ground floor, then surely there must be a sky floor.

So one morning, the lad left, let's say he just went. Everyone knew: he was going to satisfy his visions. João was dissatisfied with himself, wearing the expression of one who has few friends, so much did he want to see the world. Therefore, they all hoped his wished-for journey would fulfil his dream.

He was back after only a few days. And he made no further exertions of any description. Sitting there, he began to live slowly, as if in a reverie. What was he up to? He was contemplating the topmost heights he could see, he was courting the sky and its neighbourhood. If he had left dream filled, he returned dream emptied.

'Staying is the illness my son has caught.'

His mother shook her sadness. Poor boy, she thought.

The difference between a man and a woman is that, in men, the illness is always worse. But the old woman thought she understood: her boy had never climbed a flight of steps, never savoured a height. One doubt, from time to time, made her tremble: could it be that he had it in him to detach himself from there, to migrate from that wilderness? Nor did she ever direct her inquiry to him. A woman wasn't made to ask questions. No matter how strange it might seem, she misted herself over, hidden between the brackets of her shoulders.

Time flowed through the days. And Bate-Certo ever the same. His mother, however, gradually calmed down; the boy hasn't the gift of the road. He's not the type to risk life in a suitcase. And she relaxed. Her son remained a prisoner of the same ground where she spread her mat.

Later on, the story reached its conclusion: João, after all, hadn't vacated his wits. He was merely waiting for the rain to stop. The moment the sky turned blue, he got up. He went to the tool box and took out a hammer, saw, and nails. All inherited from his father, a master carpenter. They called him Old Carp. He had died, and no one knew what illness had strung him up in eternity. It would seem that his sense had worn thin, exhausted by his treading the two sides of truth.

Well, Bate-Certo honoured his inheritance that day. He began to build a ladder. At first, people assumed it was no more than a pastime. He didn't have a hand for hard work. Days of woodwork and invention followed, and the ladder grew until it rested on the top of the *mafurreira* tree. It seemed as if the act had fulfilled its intention. Wrong. For João, climbing upwards, added more and more steps. In its vertical sequence, day after day, the ladder grew so tall that no one could make out what it was leaning against up at the top.

And Bate-Certo ever up there, mountaineering. Others scoffed at him: if the lad were to spend his time at more profitable toil. Whereupon they gave vent to their surprise: at that height, didn't he risk the temptation of jumping off the precipice? What was certain was that he would fall, and come to earth in some foreign land.

'And what are you doing up there?'

Bate-Certo gave the briefest of smiles. That was the only answer. What people said was this: up there, on the top rung, he would rest and contemplate the most distant places. Others chose the ways of laughter, avoiding the duty of trying to understand. He's bound to grow tired!

By this time, many a plank of wood had lost its leaves while people waited for João to tire. But he didn't rest from his energies. And each day, he would add a few more rungs. Even stranger was what happened after that: he was no longer taking wood up with him. All he took, as he scaled the mornings, were his tools. Where did the rest of his materials come from?

The crowd gathered to watch him climb, laughter enveloping the vision as it ascended to the sky. Until it could no longer be glimpsed, lost among the clouds and the mists. He came down less and less. From time to time, he would return to the ground, but it was only to fill his pockets with sand. Then he would go up again. In the village, mouths were mustered by rumour. And whenever Bate-Certo came down, it was an excuse for a crowd. Then they began to notice that bits of cloud, the cotton of the heavens, clung to his clothes.

His mother then found herself on the receiving end of all their anxieties: let her take advantage of one of her son's ascents to hide the tool box. The old woman even obeyed. She went into the bush and hid her late husband's former tackle.

The following day, the lad woke up, and as was his custom, went outside to turn the morning over with his dreaming eyes. As he was preparing to go up, he noticed there was no box. He wasn't put out. He went on his upward way, singing with the skill of a bird. He returned at night, carrying an embroidered bag, the like of whose colours and cloth had never been seen before. The old woman was suspicious of the bag, and she peeped inside: it contained a set of gleaming, brand-new tools. Where had he got such objects? The old woman was afflicted by so many questions that she went mad, smitten by illness. The villagers thought it was some family disgrace, an ancestral curse. The old woman soon ceased being a subject of their conversations. The others weren't that interested in knowing about her. What could be heard were the requests every time he came back: bring me a radio, a yoke of oxen, a bicycle. Bring me one, João, for the sake of your father's soul, for your mother's health.

But the only things João brought were clouds, armfuls of clouds in bunches. With these, he filled his house, where his mother was suffering the pains of her unbirth. When she looked through the window, she seemed to see the whole planet in front of her. His mother gradually began to feel the weightlessness of childhood. One night, she gripped her son's arm and babbled:

'Tell me, my son: is it prettier up there than down here?'

He smiled awkwardly, lost for words. And, with fingers made more for smoothing wood, he closed his mother's weary eyes. That night, so people say, the only place it rained was inside the house of João Bate-Certo.

THE SWAPPED MEDALS

I shall now recount some episodes in the life of Zeca Tomé, a man of chance rather than destiny. He was relaxing in the lull of his innocence when the news came: he was going to be decorated for bravery. Zeca laughed: me? Yes, his very same self. Medallioned on the Day of the Race. Zeca snorted. Why was he, ever ignored, suddenly unscorned? They explained: it's the administrator who is summoning you, he needs you on the day itself, the tenth of June.

'Go and tell mister administrator that there's been a mix up. There's another Tomé here, the medal must be for him.'

The messenger declared that time was shorter than his tongue, which was why haste was called for. Whichever Tomé it was, it didn't matter for the occasion. He himself should accompany him to the city, dressed in his best manners.

And that's how Zeca Tomé was decorated, in a public homage to cannons and to the race. When he mounted the rostrum, his knees were knocking. The Portuguese major saluted and told him to puff out his chest. Zeca still managed to stutter:

'Boss, I think this medal's too high for me, someone else deserves it more ...'

The old war-lord interrupted him: now here's an example of good Portuguese modesty. And he pinned the medal on him. However, the major's hand was an elderly one, and fingers failed to live up to the intentions of the gesture. The honour, even if it belonged to another, cost Zeca's only jacket several rips.

Times pressed on, the pages of the calendar turned. Zeca Tomé lived at ease with himself, a tenant of peace and quiet. Nor did he ever suspect how much thread wound round the fingers of his tranquillity. One afternoon, when things were already withdrawing into their shadows, Zeca received an unexpected visit:

'I'm the real Tomé. I've come for my medal.'

I don't know what's happened to the medal, brother. For I had to sell it to the tailor to pay for the repair to my jacket! Bitter words were exchanged, the other started spuming threats, staining his and his whole family's name. The scene was even supplied with some facts, and Zeca received one or two bulky ones. But, for the plaintiff, it still wasn't enough. He went straight to the administrator and made his complaint about the man who had abused the sacred emblems of the Fatherland.

Zeca and the tailor were thrown into jail. Such was the ill fortune of the former, that he was put in the same cell as the other. For the tailor, in the abundance of his rage, gave him more than a few thrashings with his tape measure.

Time spun, squandering the days. Independence had by now been hoisted and the country given its own name. In his new corner, Zeca enjoyed ample honours. He had been elevated to hero of the struggle against colonialism. His years locked up, though few, were now paying him interest. Zeca received tributes: favours, positions, identity cards. He was relieved of the ordinary difficulties of being a citizen. The pedestal of that unfounded memory was enough for him.

November was distributing its first rains when the delegation arrived. It was one of those ones from socialist countries, our natural allies. Zeca Tomé was summoned.

'You, comrade Zeca, you're also on the list.'

'The list, what list?' 'The list of those to be decorated by President Jivkov.' 'Pardon me, comrades, but that man has never set eyes on me.' They explained, it was Tudor.

'What, they're going to give me some batteries?'

'No, it's because they're celebrating thirteen hundred years.'

'But I haven't even reached forty,' argued Zeca, concerned at the reigning confusion. 'Haven't you ever heard of Bulgaria, the country where they discovered yoghurts?'

'No, never. I'm sure you're looking for someone older.'

They wouldn't listen to him any more. It was an order from higher structures. On the following day, there was our man, with his tie on, taking part in an internationalist and proletarian ceremony. This time, however, he didn't get his lapel slashed.

Once again, time overflowed. Zeca was getting along even better, free of any calamities to perturb him. Then, one day, the tailor came to him with strange talk. The matter was a confused one: people being tried for corruption. I don't understand, corruption in Mozambique?

The tailor set things straight: the thing was happening a long way away, involving old Jivkov, the fellow who distributed medals to thousand-year-olds.

'You should get rid of that medal, to avoid any confusion.'

Such was the tailor's advice. Throw your decoration into the Chiveve while there's still time. Or do you intend to take a leap into immortality?

'But I've got nothing to do with that foreigner.'

'You don't understand the news, my friend. Over there, in Bulgaria, they're all ashamed of this follow Tudor, who apparently held the yoghurt monopoly. Now that they're washing their dirty linen, they'll even claim that you're involved.'

'But how, if I've never left the district?'

'It doesn't matter, haven't you ever heard of international

conflicts?'

Zeca could already taste the sourness of the cassava. What do you think I should do, tailor, my friend? They both agreed: they would give the medal to the other Tomé, the one who'd originally been the subject of the mix up. The two of them laughed, in anticipation of the joke. When they came to check the coat lapels, little old Tomé would give them such a stammering that they'd think he was speaking Bulgarian. And they'd lock him up as a result. Serve him right, who told him to get involved?

Whether or not they went ahead with their plan, one thing is certain: Zeca Tomé didn't await the outcome. By this time, he found the neighbourhood too small for him in the face of the world's tribulations. So, without anyone witnessing it, he abandoned his birthplace, before it too commemorated one thousand three hundred years of existence.

WHITES

Let me explain the incident, write a detailed report of what happened at Inhaminga, an occurrence which took place nobody knows when exactly. There was a party. The seminar, at which relevancies and eloquences had been exchanged, had just finished. The topic had been African authenticity and conclusions had outnumbered contributions. The reception, full to overflowing, was breezing along on a fair wind. People danced, drank, danced, ate. And danced again. Time passing by on a wave of merriment, without a stain, except for those caused by the spilled wine.

It happened in a trice: suddenly, a man came into the hall, barefoot, ragged, and conveniently drunk. He was a thin fellow, whose skin touched his marrow. He staggered forward, his legs and arms taking it in turns, making his way, crab-like among the guests. The revelry was interrupted and a circle opened round the intruder. What was that good-for-nothing doing there, that drooling madman, that simpleton? Was he just another miserable wretch, a whingeing beggar? Then, the newcomer addressed his audience. He spoke in loud bellows, as if he could only glimpse the others in the distance.

'This person you can see before you is called Carlito Jonas.'

But the surprises had not yet begun: amid bleatings and discomposures, there arrived on the scene a goat with a shiny black face. But this wasn't just any member of the caprine race, for he sported a neat green tie round his neck.

'Let me introduce my godson, Zequinha Buzi.'

Shock didn't allow people to implement their desire to throw the tramp out, him and his animal that wouldn't stop chewing its tie. Were the esteemed guests biting their fingernails or scratching their teeth? Before anyone could impose the discipline which circumstances demanded, the intruder issued the following declaration: ladies and gentlemen, please excuse me. You are whites and whites are owners and bosses, they give the orders. Here you have before you a poor black, resigned to his race. He interrupted himself, bidding the goat to stop gnawing its tie, to show respect, or was this glittering hall the equal of a grass hut?

Forgive me, but this creature doesn't use its brain, and the reason for that is that it too is black. That's how things are: each one dies with what he was born with, no one alters God's commandments. An example: we could cut my godson's horns off. But would he stop shouting baah? Without meaning to offend, that's my question, gentlemen.

The crowd was growing restless. Murmurings spread, the initiative of those who believed the interruption had lasted long enough, that they should forget their paternalisms. What does this fellow want? Me? I've come to fetch my son. No son of his could survive there. That confirmed the mist-bound state of the character's mind. Send him away, enough is enough! My son, I know you're there among all these whites. Come to your senses, come home.

Someone made up his mind and pulled the man's arm, with a mind to get him out of there by force of arms rather than argument. The intruder didn't resist, his body unfurled in the face of a push. He merely covered his mouth with his hand and bent as if giving a bow. A woman warned: careful, he's going to be sick! Sure enough, he threw up. The circle widened hurriedly, leaving a space for the pool of swill.

The self-styled Carlito Jonas, poor man, bemoaned his state as he contemplated his mess: you see? Is it worth a man suffering from hunger? Little goes in, but a lot comes out ... And on he went with his lamentations, his disreputations, there goes my *malapa* stew, that dish didn't even get as far as my arsehole, begging your pardon, the white man doesn't understand a black man's suffering, and he kicked the goat's hind quarters, leave your tie alone. The animal couldn't even stay on top of itself, its hooves slid this way and that. *'Do you not know the saying? It goes like this: if you throw up beer, your relatives will visit you; throw up blood, and you won't see people for dust. Do you bosses understand me?'* No one so much as coughed. Until someone resorted to some sympathy and, passing an arm round the intruder's shoulders, sugared an explanation:

'We're blacks, my brother. We are black men like you.'

The intruder's eyes flashed. Blacks? And he brought his hand up to his face, they all drew back thinking he was going to give another show of vomitability. But what came out was a laugh, a guffaw with heavily stressed aas, as if the goat were practising ventriloquy. Explain things to him in his language, suggested a voice. But the selfsame Carlito Jonas, raising his arm, knitting his brow, said with a heavy throat: you're whites in disguise, you're pretending to be my race, you're just making fools of us folks, I, who you can see in front of you, I'm not scared of anyone, I'm no milksop, I'm going to complain about you, let's go, Zequinha, let's go and denounce these goings on.

The matter had gone beyond the bounds of a reasonable solution, they were fed up with it, which was why an arm emerged in the intruder's direction, get out of here you bumpkin, and then there were kicks, blows and shoves. That shaken body's outsize coat fell off it. Man and goat were dispatched into the faceless dark of night, there where they belonged both before and after this episode.

Gradually, the merrymaking asserted itself once more, the music filled the background, partners came together again. The party was perking up, but there was just one small problem: those remains of the drunkard's dinner, a pox on him and his horned creature.

The scene was one of harmony and laughter when, from among the crowd, a man of mark came and knelt, cloth at the ready, and prepared to clean the vomit. Immediately, comments and protestations from all sides, leave it, there are servants for that sort of thing, aren't there?

But from his kneeling position, the volunteer cleaner hissed: leave me alone. Then, he picked up the intruder's coat, the chewed remains of the tie and left, joining the tail end of night.

THE STAIN

He was on his way to where there was space to spare. His journey took him through cold and mist. Suddenly, amid the blinding light of the mist, he saw some clothes. One of those military jackets. Camouflage, I believe they call them. He stopped, suspicious. The jacket lay quietly by the side of the road. Green among greens, it was almost indistinguishable. He looked around him: just the peace of the bush, a world in itself. He walked past the camouflage, doubling his pace, as if he had not seen it. His eyes were those of one rounding a corner, it might be a trap. Finally, he stopped, and listened carefully. Then, he turned and walked back like a crab in reverse.

The jacket was caught on a thorn. He pulled it carefully, for fear of tearing it. But the material was one of consequence, made for time. Was it a soldier's? Or had a bandit left it? It could be either, but as to why it had freed itself from someone's body, that was the cause of his wrinkled brow. No one finds a loose bit of uniform like that, in the middle of the bush.

He looked at it: it was all there, and without so much as a stain. He sniffed it: all he could smell were the aromas of perspiring grass. There was no odour of thought, that jacket didn't appear to have had a man inside it before.

He was about to put his arm in one of the sleeves but hesitated. He consulted the cold in his body, felt a shiver and made up his mind, putting it on. There he was, moving his shoulders about as if he had a mirror in front of him. Dressed up like a soldier. The sleeves were too long for him. His hands were tucked in tortoise style.

He looked at himself. Now he looked like someone from the war. And he thought: might they not mix his uniform up and fire at him? Certainly, they might. Between one silence and another, gunned down, bang. He half-undressed the jacket. But he stopped in mid gesture: the surrounding cold pressed in on him. And he felt that warm half hug of the clothes, it was a force that invited him back into the jacket. And he got dressed again.

Once more, he set off on his distant way. His feet bare, sleepy, chose their own paths. The bush has measurements that only its inhabitants can decipher. From time to time, he would pause and bring fear to bear on his thoughts. Supposing he ran into bandits? The dangers of the bush he could calculate, but those of war, no.

He stopped for a moment, puzzled. He seemed to have heard a noise. He shivered, in a hurry to be out of this world. The rumble he heard filled the whole morning. It was no longer a shadow's noise, but a light exploding further ahead. Then, everything fell quiet. It was as if the bush were clinging to the ground in fear. Now, there was only a tiptoeing silence.

He stood waiting to fall, departed from himself. But death didn't arrive. Not even the pain which is death's neighbour. The man lived on, with all his blood intact. Until, as if in response to the voice of instinct, he reached a decision: he set off in the direction of the river. Why does life always seek out water, in its affliction?

When he reached the bank, he yielded to the ground. He sat down and glanced at his body. There wasn't so much as a mark, a scratch. He undressed in order to check his condition completely. When he was stark naked, he verified himself unharmed, with neither wound nor graze. He was surprised. So what was the reason for that noise which had shaken the air and its surroundings? Or could it be that he had invented what he had heard, through excess of fear? That's what had happened, for sure. The bullet had flown in an imagined thought.

He spread out the jacket in order to lie down on it. He needed to rest, to take up residence within himself once more. But as he lay back, he saw a small red stain on the camouflage. Small, tiny almost, it looked like a drop of blood. He brought the jacket up to his eyes, the better to make up his mind. It was freshly spilled blood, still damp with life. Startled, he examined his body again. He looked, he felt: nothing, nothing at all. Then where had that blood come from? And, yet again, he carefully measured the red mark on the jacket. The stain was growing, it was spreading, as if fed from a ruptured pipe. At first, it was a tiny speck of blood. Then the drop began to unravel, in rapid growth. Now, it covered the whole of the back of the jacket.

Alarmed, he held the garment up. Heavy drops fell, scarring the sand with lines. He got up to wash the uniform in the river. But then he felt weak, almost drained. He fell to his knees and, as if he were praying, he compared himself with the jacket. His body was whole, joined together, without so much as a crack. But the garment was soaked, even the sleeves were bleeding.

He began to lose consciousness. He fell to the ground face down. The last thing that struck him was how his breath and the earth's were one and the same.

Some days later, they found him, solid and at one with the ground. People wondered: how had he died if his body was intact, without sign of a blow? And in their disbelief, they saw a soldier's jacket lying beside him. And they touched it, and noticed that it was new and very clean. And that the camouflage was unstained, as if newly born, without having yet given a man's body its rank.

THE SECRET LOVE OF DEOLINDA

I met the non-practising Marxist. Put him in inverted commas, if you like. Out of respect for Marxism, I shall call him a Marxianist. Here he is then, the man. A scribble on his face, as if he had taken a dose of sodium bicarbonate. And it was all because of me, and my newspaper column. He who writes a story looks for glory, and he was aware of that. Nevertheless, I should have been more direct, have written with a sharper pen.

The world, he suggested, is a very serious matter, and cannot tolerate ambivalences. And he judged: one must be more biting. I explained myself, I who have not been trained to use my teeth on people. But he was a militant, aggressive, aggro-excessive. Wasn't I capable of targeting the class enemy any more, the internal bourgeoisie? Or did I consider the class struggle a decadent issue while it was still in an acute phase? Now isn't a decadent person someone with ten teeth? I asked. But he was growing ever more nervous and wasn't in the mood for jokes. The Marxianist made his pronouncements in block capitals. Capitalism here, imperialism there, southern Africa and so on. His ideas, in large format, embraced ample futures. While I merely suggested, he issued now complaints, now judgements. I was within an ace of being surprised: can anyone be equipped with such certainty? It was as if the fellow had read the entire story of Mozambique, while our eyes were skipping over the pages, in the style of Mussagy Papá, our enterprising and illustrious contortionist. The history of any country is no more than a text of juggled paragraphs. Only the future will put them in any order, retouching their account. And what was more, the Marxianist explained everything on a material basis. I ask you: should one conclude that the mere sight of seeing someone eat a sandwich is enough to give a man a filled feeling?

But that particular individual didn't want an answer, he wasn't seeking a dialogue. What he felt a need for was to export his anguish. He was the thief of a fellow's peace and quiet, that's what he was. So there he was, a solitary creature, with his eyes brimming with pages. He had contemplated life without a taste for human company. And now, this poor defender of the poor needed some certainty on which to lean. He knew nothing of the soul of his nation, he was a depatriate, an autogamous being. Politics had given him a veil, instead of a bridge to cross distances over. He had ceased listening to Mozambique and its many protagonists.

For fourteen years, that man didn't speak: he merely made speeches. The only theatre of his existence was the rally. He didn't linger in the street, amid the ebb and flow of passers-by. He didn't pass the time of day with his neighbours. The people, as far as he was concerned, began and ended with the houseboy. The rest were the masses. Exactly that, blurred and bemisted. He doesn't even know the concrete facts about his fellow creature, his name, his history. That poor old Marxianist, without the warmth of a hand to shake.

And so I began to measure this man's solitude. Such aloneness would even be the envy of islands. In order to distract him from sadness, I gave him a little story, one of those tiny ones that fit in the hollow of your hand. At first, he refused. A story? And he put an end to the matter: I only respond to History. Such conceit, such naivety. There are a lot like him.

For example: a friend of mine from Beira who boasts of his skills in the lobby, is convinced they are talking about him every time the 'Beira Corridor' is mentioned. Some people never learn.

What he hoped was that I would let myself go, vociferate, expending a great deal of saliva and few ideas. But after much vacillation, he listened to the following story.

■

It was the tale of Deolinda, and her devotion to Karl Marx. As far as I am aware, nobody ever arrived at Marxism by the route she took. If I'm wrong, see how this compares.

Deolinda, whose scales were tipped by sufficient years, was sent to work. Her family needed her to exercise her daughterly function, by bringing in modest but precious income. Deolinda got a job in a factory, and even enjoyed the noise of the siren as she clocked in and out. It was the work that was boring. Are fingers for shelling cashews, or is it the other way round?

One day, she returned home with a label on her lapel. It was one of those propaganda badges, with the face of an ever photogenic Karl Marx, as if unburdened by the years. As for her father, he pointed at the little medal:

'Who's that white man, then?'

Deolinda raised a shoulder, ignorance making the other one shrink. I was given this photo in the factory. She didn't even manage to finish. A slap. Two. Two and a half, for the last one already had a trace of regret in it.

'Is he some foreign aid worker?'

And her father, starved of an explanation, began to picture all manner of possibilities. He must be one of those foreigners, those who started off as internationalists, and then became aid workers. The fellow is leading her astray, the son-of-a-bitch, just by waving dollars in front of her. The father decreed, even more uncategorically than our Marxianist: never again do I want to see this fellow's snout sniffing your bra.

Whether it was because of the matter of the tit or the tantrum, the girl put the badge away in her bedside box. Every night, before she fell asleep, she would kiss the thinker's fleecy beard. Such clandestine devotion would have entered the annals of proletarian doctrine had Deolinda not thrown herself into the arms of a real grey beard one fine day. What was more, the incident occurred in the middle of Lenin Avenue. It was later discovered that the victim of the kiss was a foreign businessman, getting ready to invest his capital in Mozambique. As far as is known, the entrepreneur didn't complain. What he did was to invest in some provisional business deals by buying the wilful Deolinda a wardrobe.

Now let's get to the end of the story, because the typewriter keys are beginning to make my fingers sore. My respondent blinked and re-blinked in as many seconds. Was that all there was to the tale? I didn't go back and change it. The corn only leaves the pestle when it has turned to flour. And so, among the scattered gristle he sighed and looked disappointed. But then, and this made my day, I caught a glimpse of a smile. Was my friend beginning to see my point? Or maybe his hopes, so similar to our own, still possessed surplus parts, like the endless components our country produces, manufactured with loving care by our national soul.

FISHERMAN ON DEPARTURE, HERO ON ARRIVAL

I was travelling between the mainland and the island. Over the waves, my memories wandered free in waterish circles. The waves nipped our sides gently, besprinkling the passengers with foamish spray.

Every time I take to a boat, I am visited by questions which don't belong to earthbound doubts: is a wave a piece of surplus sea water? Or is it that the sea doesn't know its place? And the creatures of the water, do they shed tears? And if so, how does a fish's sadness drain away?

I smiled at such questions, made to pass the time of the journey. I took a deep breath as I gazed at the wide expanse of blue. That was my meal of peace and quiet. If only I could be granted the favour of being able to taste such languor.

That was when we heard the alarm raised. At a distance that was hard to read, a boat drifted, gull-like, without direction. In it, a man was waving a red cloth, asking for help. He was a fisherman, for sure. His craft danced and bobbed: the sea was angrily kicking it with waves. We cruised closer. The helmsman of our boat reduced throttle and shouted:

'Are you in trouble, friend?'

The fisherman replied:

'The wind isn't working.'

Someone on deck laughed, and he, believing he hadn't explained properly, corrected himself:

'It's the wind that isn't providing much today.'

The boats touched and remained entangled in a brief courtship. I was standing nearest to where his boat was alongside ours. I held out my arm to help him cross to our boat. He accepted with some reservation. He didn't expect such deference, he was a man used to his own company. Too much consideration would have been a cause for mistrust as far as he was concerned. I wasn't offended by his near refusal. After a whole life as a fisherman, without the benefit of a favour, who would believe a fish might surrender to him?

The man tied his little boat to our rail. His canoe had hitched a ride, following in our liquid steps.

The fisherman sat down beside me. From his pocket, he took out the most elderly cigarette that I've ever seen in my life. He lit it and put the lighted end in his mouth. He smoked it back to front, swallowing the smoke as if it were a candle. He sat there looking, maybe at nothing, the horizon floating in his pupils. One could see he was a man of lengthy patience. But his body, which was muscle from end to end, was tense. Softly, I asked him for a piece of his story. And so he told it to me.

He was a refugee from the war. The bandits burned down his house at Machangulo and he crossed over to the island with his family. But in the panic, he had left all his things on the mainland. Afflicted by hunger, the family decided he should risk the journey and try and get hold of some food which they had left on their *machamba*. Maybe there were still some animals left, who knows, could it be that the bandits had spared them?

But during the crossing, a wind had blown up and the little boat had been carried along by the currents. He had left two days ago, and only now was he returning. And what was worse: he was going back without any provisions, without anything at all.

'I'm just carrying more hunger, from these last few days when I haven't eaten.'

His bitterness was bigger than himself. How to explain to his family that the fault was the wind's alone? With his stomach gnawing like that, they wouldn't believe his story. The fisherman was vanquished by the shame of his failed mission.

When we reached our journey's end, there was a small crowd waiting. Most of them were women, wrapped in their *capulanas,* biding their time, as always, with their time-honoured patience. The fisherman pointed excitedly:

'Look, that's my family there.'

He said it with despair, as if he were being awaited by hyenas. *'I'm all mixed up, for good and certain. It would have been better if I'd died out there.'*

He disembarked slowly. I tried to guess his folks' sentiments. But when I drew near, I realised those woman were crying. No sooner did the fisherman step on to the beach than arms hugged one another in the welcome of return. He had come back, he had survived. One of the elders, more sober in the emotion of their meeting, spoke with resonance.

'We heard you went there and the bandits attacked you. It was because of this that you couldn't bring the things. Isn't that so?'

The fisherman, surprised, hesitated to answer. His eyes seemed to stammer deep in his face. He glanced at me as if he were seeking help. I, without putting my voice to use, nodded in confirmation. A feeling of relief came over the fisherman and he addressed his family:

'I'll tell you everything shortly. Let's go.'

And he left, in the company of his loved ones. With a gesture sketched for only me to see, he bade me a farewell which was almost a thank you. And so I became the accomplice of that hero of an invented battle.

A GENTLE VOICE OF DUST

I'm going to tell you about Gentipó, one of those men who never leave their shadow. Gentipó doesn't tread the highway: the narrowest footpath is a busy avenue for him. To visit me at home, he picks the least shod ground, earth as bare as his feet.

He came from there, a place not even worthy of a name. For if no one ever extracted a journey from it, either there or back, why should it have a signpost? Forget the anonymous spot, abandon his ever incomplete provenance to the mists. What did he do there, in the place from which he ebbed? His job was to be there, to help the mornings in. Mountains concern themselves with height, trees slave over their verdure. Well, this man produced nothingness, yet out of the palm of his hand there flowed a continent. Within him was the mouth of the land. His gesture exuded vast green spaces but he himself, Gentipó, didn't feature in any roll of honour. Nor did he proclaim himself master of his natural extensions.

'If I gain life, I lose time.'

In the end, his crops regaled him with very little. The sky needed fertiliser, a task for the most powerful sorcery. Hunger offered him the chance to leave life. He refused. Then the war came. The war alone baffled his understanding. Was there any good reason for turning those fields into cinder heaps? Or is a nation something to be trampled on with such scant respect?

The shots, he told me. They may go in different directions, but their intention is always the same. Well, shots pushed his existence along, forcing him to sever his own roots. Today, his title was a stark one: displaced person. Gentipó shook his head, chasing away his thoughts.

'Our home is smaller than we think.'

For him, a man of the country, the entire city was foreign. His soul lacked a passport to cross into urbanhood. Gentipó lived as if time were a Saturday, in the unruffled indecision between getting up and staying in bed.

One night, he dropped anchor in the middle of my evening, newly arrived from his wanderings, those wanderings in which all he seemed to tread was moonlight. We swapped news, his life displaying no sign of a story. Even a dead man contains more news, Gentipó roused himself by way of a joke. At last, after our long stroll had taken us nowhere in particular, he announced the reason for his visit. That the candle, placed there in order to shed some light on our exchange of fate, wasn't fit for a house with so much structure. If it were where I live, that would be a different matter.

There had been another power cut, yet more lines circumcised. But while the bandits persisted with their sabotage, he, Gentipó, had worked out a solution. They always cut it in the same place, isn't that so? Well, take a sorcerer there. Yes, that was it, get a medicine man to go there, bless it, scatter prayers around the selfsame spot. Gentipó repeated his conviction, the candle yawned, tired of contradicting the night's vocation.

I strained my eyes, smiling, and returned the visitor's reasons to him. That's not possible, my friend, the matter is not one for a sorcerer's skills. Gentipó was insistent: it wasn't a question of asking him to stop the whole war. Only that little piece of it. My displaced friend had pondered the matter, weighed the arguments. How could I justify such a scant smile? For his ambitions exceeded his hope: he wanted to return home, to the minuteness of his native land. I'm tired, was his murmur. His voice rested on the darkness like a fine dust. Up above, the sky was atwinkle with stars.

I made myself speak with heart: you'll go home, Gentipó, it's not long to go now. I didn't even notice whether he was smiling or sleeping. The candle had gone out, all that remained was the memory of another light above our silhouettes.

GLOSSARY

Capulana	A dress worn by women, akin to a sarong
Machamba	Small plot of land for cultivation
Fado	A type of popular song from Portugal
Mapira	A variety of local corn
Marimba	A type of xylophone
Chimandjemandje	A particular type of musical rhythm
Chikaka	A poor white
Marrabenta	A Mozambican dance
PIDE	The political police during the Salazar dictatorship